THE ACCOUNTS OF AMARI

REDEMPTION

DEVIN DELGROSSO

DEDICATION

To Jesus for grace and mercy

For my wife, Morgan, whose opinion I trust more than my own.
This story only exists because you dared me to write.

For Emma, Parker, and Lincoln who bring more joy to life
than any story that could be written. I'm so thankful that
God loaned you to me.

I'm yours forever.

THE FOSTERIAN WAR
25 YEARS BEFORE THE ARRIVAL OF THE PHAYLADIN

The midday sun was bearing down upon the two armies as they stood in their formations, staring each other down from across the battlefield. Both sides had already been crippled by the constant fighting between the neighboring areas. The stakes were high as each side was fighting for possession of a land filled with riches that lay on the outskirts of the desert. For centuries, the kingdoms of Fosteria and Vasteen had lived peacefully next to each other, but the threat of famine and the lust for power had driven the emperor of Vasteen to begin this war. At day's end, this would prove to be the final stage in the battle over Fosteria. It was kill or be killed.

The people of Vasteen were originally nomadic travelers who had been exiled into the desert. They were pushed out of the areas that they had lived in because they were different than the world around them. The Vasteen people cared not for riches and extravagant lifestyles. The people were simple and without any form of a moral code. They were rude and loud and carried long into the night with their drunkenness and frivolity. Some men had multiple wives that gave way to large families and they were overpopulating the area. This was unacceptable to the high class society people of Fosteria. To them, these nomads were infecting their way of life and they began to remove the Vasteens from their land. Most nomads were nowhere near dangerous, but people feared them because of their differences and because of what they were becoming. As more and more people were pushed to the desert, the natural tendency was to form a nation.

The desert did not provide much shelter or resources, but the Vasteens managed to survive. They banded together and each person helped look after another. They settled just outside of Fosteria on the banks of the Sotallian River that opened up into the Alton Sea. It was far enough away that the Fosterian people didn't have to deal with them any longer. However, the river was used as a main source of trade within the desert, and the desert had managed to harden the hearts of the Vasteens. The lack of morality gave way to evil and they soon became fierce warriors, priding themselves in their ability to hunt with their bare hands. They lived off the animals from the land and the river, and nature always seemed to provide until recently. A famine had begun in the desert and it was driving them mad.

As the people began to starve, they immediately began to look to the north. Fosteria had always loomed over them. Their land was vastly different from that of Vasteen. The land was rich in vegetation and overgrown with resources. Out of pity, the Fosterians had opened a trade route with the Vasteens, but had recently closed it off because the main road had grown violent. When the resources ran out, the people of Vasteen began to use any means necessary to acquire what they needed and that included violence. With a lack of meat to be found, rumors circled about a growing trend of cannibalism amongst the Vasteens. Travelers on the road would just disappear and never be found. This caused many traders to never attempt to come to Fosteria for fear of their lives.

The government of Fosteria had tried to take action to stop the violence but for every Vasteen that they stopped, five more seemed to appear. The more the Vasteens became oppressed the more they fought back. Soon, the ruler of Vasteen became as bloodthirsty as his people and the two nations were on the brink of war. His name was Neroni.

Neroni had inherited the position of chief from his father. His family had originally brought the people together and formed the nation. They built it up from the ground and were tolerated by the people. They ruled with an iron fist and their laws were enforced in every circumstance by death. However, under the economic strain of the famine, the people were even turning on him. If Neroni was going to stay in power, he would need to act fast. Fosteria had everything that he needed, but, more importantly, it had everything that he wanted.

As the tension between the two nations rose, the threat of war became imminent. In a drastic move, the Fosterians blocked the river to the north of the Vasteens in order to force them to come to terms. One day, the ruler of Fosteria sent an envoy to Neroni in order to discuss how to improve relations between them. When they arrived, they delivered an ultimatum to the chief. Their message demanded that Neroni step up security along the main road or their water would be cut off forever. Their demands had backed Neroni into a corner and he reacted as any wild animal would. Neroni drew his sword and killed the members of the envoy. To further his insanity, he had their heads delivered back to Fosteria with his declaration of war.

The Vasteens were well prepared for the fight. Their lifestyle as hunters coupled with their desire to survive, had created in them fierceness as warriors. The people of Fosteria were mainly simple farmers who prided themselves in their families. The threat of war scared them but they knew they would have to fight. Too proud to give up their homes, they built up their armies by adding to their security forces. Any able man was required to defend their home. If Fosteria was going to survive, they would have to fight, but their morale was fading fast. The people were warned to not leave the protection of Fosteria, but many tried their best to escape the looming battle. Neroni's army began to hunt them down and kill them off. He left their bodies in a pile on the main road as a sign of what was to come and, still, this was not enough to satisfy Neroni's blood lust.

Within the confines of his makeshift, desert palace, Neroni began a ritual to summon a great evil. The shadows began to stir and darkness began to grow as Destroyers appeared in the room before him. Neroni offered up his soul in exchange for a power that would far exceed his enemies. Using a perversion of the powers that the Amari had created them with, the Destroyers began to possess the emptiness that lived inside of Neroni, for only a heart surrendered to evil could be overtaken through this act of possession. Neroni's body began to writhe and contort as the Destroyers entered into his body and began to take control. Neroni's body welcomed the surge of power that he felt within, his strength would be doubled by this move, however, his will and his soul were no longer his own. The Destroyers could have their way with Neroni, or allow him to maintain some form of free will, but, Neroni was now dead to himself.

Today was the day that Neroni had planned to attack. His army consisted of almost everyone in Vasteen: men, women, and even some children. Neroni's determination to win this battle came in second to his lust for power. They would win at all costs, or they would die. Failure was not an option and only death would satisfy their desires. He was ready to lead his people to victory.

The army marched their way to the border and was met across the battlefield by the men of Fosteria. The Fosterian army did themselves no favors by positioning themselves up on the hill. As the Vasteens marched in, the men of Fosteria witnessed a massive army moving toward them, their faces had been painted in a tribal fashion and their screams were haunting in every way. The Fosterians knew that they were severely outnumbered and outmatched. Panic began to set in their hearts as the Vasteens began their march on the city. Knowing that there was no way to survive this onslaught, the king of Fosteria ordered the evacuation of the area. He had little hope for a victory today.

The two armies wasted no time. Neroni led the charge forward and his people began to overtake the Fosterians. It really wasn't much of a fight. The warriors of Vasteen were extremely effective in their hunt. Their savagery led to the slaughter of the Fosterian army. Once they broke through the front lines, they turned their attention to the remaining citizens. The Fosterians gave it their best but, after a day or two of fighting, they fell to the power of Neroni and his new strength. It became a tragedy of epic proportions and many unspeakable evils occurred that day.

The Vasteens moved into their new locale and began to ransack the area. Each man was allowed to claim a new home for his family and whatever they could carry. Any remaining Fosterians were either killed, enslaved, or they escaped from the onslaught. The battle was over and the famine that had overtaken the desert was soon forgotten.

Neroni made his way to the palace, but found its lack of size to be quite offensive. He vowed to himself that he would build a much bigger one for himself soon. As he stared down his new throne room, some men entered the room from behind him. It was just a small group of men from his army, but they were bringing him an excellent prize.

In the middle of the group, a man, woman, and child were being carried in, kicking and fighting to be free. They separated the man from his family and threw him to the ground at Neroni's feet. He tried to back out of the room but the soldiers pushed him closer and he tripped and fell before the ruthless dictator. The man was the king of Fosteria.

Neroni brought his foot up and dropped it onto the king's neck. The king desperately tried to free himself but Neroni drew his sword and pointed the tip of the blade directly between the king's eyes. Neroni had a look in his eyes that brought fear to all those who opposed him. He stared down at the fallen king and dropped his sword to the ground. With evil in his eyes, he pounced on top of the petrified man and began to carry out his sentence of death. The king's wife screamed as she covered the face of their young son to hide him from his father's death. When Neroni was satisfied with the death of the king, he turned his wrath toward the king's wife as well. However, in a moment of weakness, he allowed the young boy to live. Neroni would claim him as his son and keep him as a constant reminder of his victory there that day. The boy was too young to ever know the difference.

What happened in the throne room that day has not been passed down over the years. It is rumored that what Neroni did to the king was so awful that no one in the room could bear to watch. The screams of the king had echoed throughout the area, but, even wilder, was the laughter of Neroni. The torture that he performed had brought him intense pleasure. Neroni had officially become mentally unstable.

It did not take long for the kingdom of Fosteria to see the same fate as that of the desert. The people ravished whatever supplies they could find. Neroni declared himself to be the new emperor and horded most of the supplies for his own delight. The lush vegetation that was growing there was never taken care of and soon dissipated. A few years of Emperor Neroni had brought Fosteria to ruin. As the vegetation died, the desert took over.

The winds blowing in from the west dragged the sand from the desert inward. What was once a land vast of resources was now empty. The people under Neroni's rule feared him and what he would do to those who opposed him. Those who worked for him remained loyal to him but only because Neroni had the resources. Once again, famine and sickness took over the area. Those once fierce warriors were beginning to waste away to nothing. With their strength gone, they had no choice but to do what the emperor told them to do.

Emperor Neroni sent his army out to conquer the lands around their failing kingdom. Their armies moved in and took the people as slaves and destroyed their homes. The emperor decided to call this new area the Desert Kingdom and claimed all of it for himself. The Destroyers that had possessed him never released their hold on Neroni, and Neroni never wanted them to let go. He began to force people to become slaves to help further his power. His goal was to make for himself a palace that would make the richest of kings jealous. With the food being rationed, and the heat growing intensely, the people had no choice. Work as slaves for the emperor, or face certain death. The divide between the wealthy and the poor grew to an extreme.

The present day Desert Kingdom looked nothing like what it used to be. The inhabitants in the city were quick to oppress all those that they considered slaves, however, the power they believed they had was nothing more than an illusion. The once great warriors had lost their will to fight, Neroni had lost his sanity, and the people had lost their hope. If no one intervened soon, the kingdom would die away along with all the people living there.

1. BALAK

The journey to Bodain had taken much longer than they would've expected. The cold snow was beginning to take a toll on Balak and his family. After Balak's rescue of his family outside of Seaport, they headed north using the Great Divide as their guide. However, the closer they moved toward the mountains, the colder the wind and air became. As they rounded the northern bend, his mother Jael started showing signs of sickness. With much urgency needed, Balak decided to improvise on their situation.

After finding shelter for his family inside of an abandoned house, Balak made his way out to a nearby camp. When the last man retired for the night, Balak moved in and stole a horse to carry his mother. When his family awoke in the morning, Balak simply told them that he had found the horse running loose in the forest. Jael viewed the horse as a gift from the Amari, but Jeremiah, Balak's father, still held contempt for Balak in his heart and was unwilling to accept Balak's reasoning. However, he realized that the horse was needed no matter where it came from, and they continued on through the morning.

For the first time in a very long time, Balak felt as though he was close to home. It had been years since he was able to have his family around and his mind raced with the feeling of familiarity. He hoped that this was a sign of his old life beginning to fade away. As they walked, his left hand moved to cover the Seal of Ozgul that was located on his right arm. It was a chilling reminder of the life that he had chosen. Balak knew that as long as the symbol of Ozgul remained on his flesh, he would always be reminded of the crimes that he had committed. Hatred for Ozgul now fueled his heart and a desire for revenge was beginning to overtake him, but all of that was a distant second to getting his family safely to Bodain. This was his second chance at doing things right in their eyes, and he wasn't about to mess things up again.

His thoughts were interrupted by the touch of a hand around his arm. He turned his head to see Nadia moving in to hold his arm. She looked at him and smiled. Balak was caught off guard by the gesture, but seeing his sister smile at him was a relief and it stole his mind away from the thoughts of revenge and hate. Balak's mood was lightened and a smile began to appear on his face as he looked at his sister.

"What is that?" Nadia asked. "Is that a smile I see on my brother's face?"

Balak quickly turned away as he was beginning to blush. Nadia continued.

"My word!" she exclaimed as she leaned forward to get a good look at his face as they walked. "I think the big, brave Balak is actually beginning to blush. Now, how is that possible, I wonder?"

Balak looked back at her, still smiling, and gently bumped into her, causing her to stumble just slightly. Caught off guard, Nadia let go of Balak's arm and hit him on the shoulder.

"Hey, wait a minute!" Balak said.

"Don't shove me!" Nadia replied.

She was enjoying this interaction with her brother, and she continued to playfully hit him. They went back and forth for a short while. Balak acted as though all of his strength was no match for Nadia's attack, and he grabbed his arm as though he was in pain. She eventually stopped hitting him, and they continued to walk side by side. Jeremiah was walking Jael's horse not far behind the two siblings. He felt Jael's hand on his shoulder and looked up to see her smiling down at him. He could tell by the look in her eyes that she was pleased with what she was seeing. They had their family back together. What more could a mother want?

"You know, Balak," Nadia began, "it's so nice to have you back with us. We have been praying for this day for a long time."

The expression on Balak's face went blank as his mind returned to the thoughts of his former life.

Nadia continued, "What troubles you now?"

Balak hesitated for a moment and then said, "What I am thinking about, you do not want to know nor could you understand."

"You can't keep all this inside, Balak. Your past sins will turn you against yourself."

"But they are my sins, and I will deal with them accordingly," replied Balak.

"All I am saying, dear brother, is that you no longer have to go through this alone. We are here for you – the Amari is here for you."

Balak welcomed the sentiment, but he knew that they were in more danger now than they were before and the Amari would do nothing to intervene. He turned his face away from Nadia.

Sensing that Balak was dissatisfied with her comments, she said, "So tell me, what happens next?"

"Bodain should be just outside this forest," Balak replied. "We will go there and find food and shelter, and get our mother to a doctor."

"But what of money?" asked Nadia. "How will we pay for all of this?"

With sarcasm in his voice, Balak replied, "Why don't you ask your beloved Amari for help with that? We will see if he even cares for our lives. However, do not be surprised if he turns his back on you just for being with me."

The two were interrupted by the sound of their father's voice.

"Come on, you stupid horse! We don't have time for this!" yelled Jeremiah.

Balak turned to make his way back to his parents.

"What's wrong?" asked Balak.

"I have no idea," replied Jael. "The horse just stopped in the path and won't go any further."

Balak moved forward and grabbed the horse's reigns along with his father. Together, they tried to pull the horse but the horse wouldn't move. The horse kept fighting until at last they let go of the reigns.

Jeremiah turned to Balak and said, "Let's get your mother down before the horse loses its mind altogether."

Balak moved to the side and helped his mother down. As soon as she was clear of the horse, the horse turned and ran away.

Balak shouted for it to stop, but the horse showed no sign of stopping. If they didn't get the horse back, Jael might never make it to Bodain. Balak took off after the horse. He realized he would never be able to catch it, but he was hoping that the horse had just become spooked and would soon stop. Balak watched in surprise as the horse ran only a short distance and began to prance around in a circle. Startled, Balak slowed his run and moved cautiously toward the horse. It pranced in place and, as Balak moved closer, the animal lowered its head to the ground and started flipping the snow with its nose. Balak looked down to see what the horse had found and noticed a body lying under a thick covering of the snow. He quickly moved to see if the body was alive. He uncovered it for the most part, but clearly the man had been dead for a while. Balak could hear his family moving in from behind.

"Watch your eyes," Balak said. "There's a dead man over here."

His family stopped in their approach and curiously peered toward the body.

"Are you sure he is dead?" Jeremiah asked.

"Father, I have seen enough dead people to know what one looks like. This man has been dead for awhile."

"How strange for the horse to run off like that," said Jael.

The family stood there as Balak ruffled through the man's clothes. As he was uncovering the man's hands, he noticed a purple bag no larger than his hand. Balak dusted the snow off of the top and opened the bag up. He could not believe what he was seeing. He put his hand to his forehead, looked up at the horse, and began to slightly laugh. The horse raised its head in pride over what it had just done.

"Balak, what is it?" Nadia asked.

Balak placed his hand into the bag and pulled out a handful of gold coins. His family quickly rushed to his side to get a closer look.

"How much is in there?" Nadia asked.

Balak responded, "Enough to get Mother some medicine and help provide for us for some time to come. We will also be able to afford a place to stay temporarily once inside Bodain."

"But we can't take the money," objected Jael. "Can we?"

"Mother," Balak said, "the man is dead. He certainly has no use for it any longer. Of course we can take it."

"I have to agree with Balak," said Jeremiah. "We certainly need the money."

Balak emptied the coins from his hand back into the bag and scooped it up. He moved to stand up, but the hand of the dead man caught his attention. On one of his ring fingers was a very large ring. Balak bent down to examine it. All he could tell was that this man must be of great notoriety, or a thief. Either way, the gold ring would bring them some extra money along the way. He grabbed the ring, half frozen to the man's finger, and removed it. He placed it on his own finger and turned to go. The horse was now willing to move, and they began to make their way back to the path.

Nadia moved quickly to Balak's side and said, "What was that you were saying about the Amari turning his back on us?"

Balak looked at the smirk on his sister's face and replied, "It could've been a coincidence."

She ran slightly ahead of him and turned to face him.

"My dear brother, you will come to understand that when the Amari is involved there is no such thing as a coincidence."

Balak was silent, but smiled as he watched his sister dance and sing through the snow. Perhaps it wasn't a coincidence after all, but it would take more than that to convince Balak that the Amari cared at all for him. Balak could see the edge of the forest and, in the distance, he could see the thick walls of Bodain. It wouldn't be long now. They made their way across the long, open field and headed for the gates, but they weren't the only ones. Balak was surprised to see the fields filled with people making their way toward Bodain. Apparently, Abaylin's war had given many people the idea to flee to Bodain, and that would mean that Bodain was going to become more crowded as the days moved forward.

Balak wondered where Abaylin's army was right now. If they followed the original plan, then Todere should already be overrun. Hopefully, he would find some answers once inside of Bodain.

After crossing through the large, snow covered field that surrounded Bodain, Balak and his family had to wait in the long line to enter. As Balak stood there, he suddenly became very nervous. The name of Balak was notorious throughout the region. He could be in a lot of trouble if he was recognized and that was not the situation he wanted to put his family in at this moment. All that mattered was getting his mother to a physician and soon. Balak covered his head to hide his face from the crowd and looked toward the main gate. As they moved closer, he could see that they were checking for weapons at the door. For once, Balak was happy that he was unarmed.

They were next in line to enter the kingdom. Balak took a deep breath and moved forward with his family. They placed their only belongings they had on the ground to be searched. The guards moved forward and were oblivious to Balak's appearance. They rummaged through their bags and checked under their warm, winter coats for any weapons. Balak was surprised at their lack of thoroughness. The guards cleared them to enter, and the family reclaimed their belongings. However, their approach to the gates was abruptly stopped.

From inside the gate, a guard yelled, "Stop them! Move them back!"

The other guards quickly stepped forward while drawing their swords and moved toward Balak's family. Balak began to tense up and became ready for the fight. He would get his family inside one way or another.

As the guards neared, Balak stood his ground and said, "Let us in! We've done nothing wrong!"

"Just move back," replied the guard. His voice was not friendly at all.

"I must get my mother inside!" shouted Balak. "She is sick and needs medical attention."

The guards didn't seem to care and began to push Balak's family back into the crowd. Balak started shoving back. One of the guards had enough, and placed the tip of his sword in front of Balak's face.

"Sir! You will calm down, or be arrested!" the guard insisted.

Balak relaxed as the tip of the sword was too close for comfort. He felt the hands of his family pull him back.

A voice rang out from a tower above, "Clear the Road!"

Balak looked to his left to see a group of riders coming up the front pass. The guards moved the last of the people out of the way, and everyone watched as the group of around thirty soldiers came storming into Bodain.

From the crowd, someone shouted, "Why do they get special treatment?"

One of the guards answered, "Because, you idiot! Those were some of Bodain's finest soldiers! Now get back in line! You're lucky I was told to let you all in!"

The guard who had held the sword to Balak's chest looked at him and said, "Come on, now. Get your stuff and get inside."

Balak released the breath that he was holding, relieved that it was not his past that was keeping them from Bodain. The family quickly gathered their belongings and moved into the gates. None of them had ever seen the inside of Bodain before. They had no idea where to go to find anything. Balak wanted answers quickly, and he grabbed the arm of a man passing by.

"Hey!" the man shouted. "What's your problem?"

"Where can I find a physician?" asked Balak.

"Is that all you want?" the man replied. "All you had to do was ask! You didn't have to attack me with that death grip you've got on my arm."

Balak released the man's arm and the man continued.

"It's right up the road. Just turn right at the first intersection and you will see the line coming out the door."

The man turned to go. He was clearly annoyed with the whole situation.

Balak's father spoke up and said, "Balak, you're going to have to take on a new way of doing things if you really want to blend in around here. How about trying to use a little compassion? Maybe you shouldn't be so quick to jump, if you know what I mean."

Balak knew his father was right and he nodded his head in agreement. He grabbed the reigns of his mother's horse and they began to make their way up the road.

The man who gave them directions was correct; the line for the physician was long. The family took their place in the line and Balak helped his mother down from the horse. Balak tied the horse to a nearby post and joined his family.

As they stood there, Balak could see that his mother was growing more tired. Her face was becoming very pale, and she was using all the strength that she could just to stand up straight. Jeremiah was doing his best to help his beloved wife, but even he was beginning to strain under the pressure. Without warning, Jael collapsed in his arms.

2. THE NEW FACE OF EVIL

The Valley of Shadows had been decimated by the attack of the Guardians. The fight left many dead and their bodies were lying amongst the rubble from buildings and tents. Not everyone lost their life during the attack, but the ones who survived had no intentions of staying. There was no word from the battlefield and the Shadow Walkers had all been killed. There was nothing keeping them in the valley so most of them left once they realized that this was their best chance at freedom. The impossible had occurred; the valley had been destroyed.

The air in the valley was cold and damp, and the victory over evil had done nothing to help with the fog. Within the silence, a lone sound began to resonate through the trees. The fog began to swirl as a large being began to move into the heart of the valley. The sound of wings flapping could be heard echoing off the distant hills. The dark figure moved quickly toward the collapsed entrance of the Temple of Ozgul and, without hesitation, it flew directly through the rubble as though it wasn't even there.

The inside of the temple was well preserved except for a few minor scars from the battle. The throne room of Abaylin was intact but the throne itself had been toppled to the ground. There was no light but none was needed. The dark figure did not need the light as he proceeded to make his way into the underground city. This time he used the door. He pulled his wings in tight, rose up on the wind, and then dove to the bottom. The sound of each flap echoed off the stone walls without a hindrance. Many of the torches here were still burning with fire and the way down was clear. He dodged the remaining rope bridges with ease and, as he approached the floor, he slowed his descent and landed on the stones. The battle for the prophecy had taken place here. Ozgul had returned to the scene of his defeat.

The wings on his back were no longer needed. They folded tightly into place and disappeared from view. Destroyers, like Persuaders, could hold two different forms; the spiritual and the physical. In their spiritual form, they were completely hidden from the sight of mankind and only visible to each other. Their spiritual bodies were giant in size, standing a few feet taller than the common man. Each being had its own distinct look and build, and Ozgul's form had been distorted over time by the evil in his soul. Ozgul didn't just want to be like the Amari. He wanted to destroy everything the Amari loved.

Upon choosing to reveal themselves and take on their physical form, they could appear as any common man, or reveal themselves as they were created; wings and everything. Once the change occurred, their material bodies would remain in that form until it began to waste away, however, they could change between the two as they willed. This was all a part of the Amari's original design. These beings were created to help the world, not to rule it. But all of that changed for the rebellious Destroyers.

Ozgul remained in his spiritual body and walked across the floor toward the back wall. He was reeling from the recent defeat of his army. It wasn't so much that they lost the battle and were destroyed, but they had failed in their mission. Ozgul was strong but the Amari had given him this faulty existence that limited his powers and forced him to rely on the weakness of human beings to achieve his purpose.

It was never difficult. Humans had many weaknesses. Tempt them in the right direction and they would do whatever he wanted them to do. Most people chose evil on their own. It was in their nature. If they were greedy, he tempted them with money and wealth. If they struggled with pride, he introduced them to power and esteem. The power of sin is so intense because it comes so naturally. Humanity had long thought that it was in control of its own desires but it had been fooled. Everyone is controlled by something. Everyone has their god. Ozgul desired to be god over humanity. In a complete perversion of power, if he couldn't persuade someone to pursue their evil desires, he, and the other

Destroyers, could possess their souls. The only way this could work was if the soul being possessed didn't already belong to the Amari. They could be persuaded and tempted, but they could never be possessed.

Ozgul knew that he could never be the Amari. The Amari was self-existent and never ending. He had to live with the fact that he was nothing more than a created being, but, in the end, he never desired to be the Amari. He only wanted the power and the devotion. Fortunately, for Ozgul, the army that he sent out to find the Phayladin was not his only plan. And this one would have to be better.

Ozgul was finished with the Valley of Shadows. The place was essentially destroyed and worthless to him now. It would take years to rebuild this barren place, but Ozgul didn't have years. He needed results now and there was something that he had left in the valley that he needed. As Ozgul established himself on Eret, he took every opportunity he could to model his existence after the Amari. For years, he had kept a dark secret from everyone. Only a handful of the Shadow Walkers had knowledge of this plan and they were all dead.

Ozgul approached the back wall and walked directly through the stone as if it wasn't there. On the other side of the wall was an empty hallway lit by a single torch. At the end of the hall, there was a chamber that had been locked up for years. The doorway to the chamber was small, but it opened up into a larger cavern. The inside of the large cavern was well lit. In one corner, there was a makeshift bed that was covered in layers of hay with blankets on top. Directly across from the bed, there was a large weapon rack that held swords and various other weapons of all shapes and sizes. Some more deadly than others. There was nothing more in the room than a small chest for clothing and a few lanterns lying around. Ozgul walked across the floor of the cavern and stood before the chamber's treasure as a repetitive noise echoed against the walls.

Standing in front of the back wall of the cavern was a beast of a man. The man was completely unaware of Ozgul's presence. His attention was directed at the wall in front of him. The sound within the room was coming from his fists as he punched the wall repeatedly. He had been doing this for some time as holes had appeared within the rocks a few inches deep. This creature was unlike anything else, only this was no creature made from the fiery pits of hell, dreamt up by some Destroyer's mind. This unfortunate soul was born as a human. Someone's child, abandoned long ago because of deformities on his body, had been taken by Ozgul and stored away. His face was severely distorted and gave him the look of a demon. The Amari had the Phayladin as his champion, and, now, Ozgul had one too. His name was Shod.

It was what he was being trained for – to bring destruction to Eret. Ozgul began this experiment long ago to create for himself a warrior; a mindless beast that knew no good. Shod never had the opportunity to choose what was right. The only thing that brought innocence to the world was the presence of the Amari's spirit living in the souls of those who wanted him. However, Shod had grown up alone and with no knowledge of the Amari, and no one to teach him. He was the perfect weapon, an empty shell of humanity that knew only one father - evil.

Ozgul transformed into a physical form and moved closer to his creation. His transformation did not startle Shod who stopped hitting the wall once Ozgul's presence was felt. In his physical form, Ozgul was smaller than Shod who was tall and thick. Shod turned around and moved closer to Ozgul and fell to his knees with his head bowed.

The Shadow Walkers had beaten Shod into submission by treating him like an animal. They deprived him of any love and replaced it with loyalty and devotion for only Ozgul. For 20 years, they kept him locked up, never allowing him to go beyond the lower floor of the underground city. They had taken their time to educate the boy as he became a man, teaching him the ways of war and hate. They fed him well and trained him to be a warrior. His mind was sharp as well and functioned perfectly. His deformities in his face had left him unable to communicate except for in deep groans and mutterings. Those sounds alone would drive fear into his enemy. Ozgul's goal was not to reduce Shod to nothing, but to make him strong and skilled. The training Shod received was of the best quality, and had made him stronger than most humans, if not all. He was the perfect soldier and his only obedience was to Ozgul.

Ozgul bent down to one knee and pulled Shod's face up from the ground. He looked into those dark, inset eyes and smiled a hideous smile at Shod. The young man smiled back with a twisted and sinister smile. It was time for him to be unleashed into the world. Ozgul explained to Shod what his duty entailed and told him to prepare for the journey ahead. Shod scrambled to his feet, once again, revealing his size. He didn't waste any time getting out of the chamber.

After collecting a few of his favorite weapons, including a large broad sword with jagged edges, he looked toward Ozgul and roared in readiness. Ozgul had one last thing to do before allowing Shod to go free. Using his power, he placed his hands on Shod's bare chest and, in an instant, the smell of burning flesh entered into the cavern as the seal of Ozgul was burned into the skin of Shod. Shod showed no signs of pain as the flesh began to melt away. Ozgul's wings fanned out in delight behind him as he marked his prized possession. Once the seal was in place, Ozgul opened the door to the chamber. For the first time, Shod was allowed entrance into the world where he belonged, but his mission was to destroy it. He moved his way out of the underground city and into the throne room of Abaylin. The main entrance was blocked but there was a tunnel leading out the back that was still intact. Ozgul flew close behind as Shod ran down the tunnel. They stopped at the exit.

Shod looked back at Ozgul as if he was seeking his approval. Ozgul nodded his head and Shod cautiously inched his way into the light. As he stepped forward and became immersed by the sun, he was blinded by the intense light. This was something he had never experienced before. Shod was being born into the world. Standing before him, stretching across the valley, was an army of Destroyers as far as the eye could see. They were there awaiting Ozgul's arrival as this was the next step in Ozgul's great plan.

Ozgul walked up beside Shod, grabbed Shod's left arm, and raised it high in the air. The army of Destroyers cheered and squealed with joy at the sight of their human champion.

The Destroyers began to celebrate at their leader's charge. They spread their wings and lifted their voices in celebration. It was a sick and deafening sound that radiated out of their mouths. Ozgul waved his arm into the air and, one by one, the Destroyers leapt from the ground and flew into the air. As they did, their bodies transformed from the physical as they became spiritual once again. Their final destination would be the people of Eret.

Ozgul was growing tired of his physical form as it began to waste away. He nodded toward Shod and Shod pounded on his chest violently as he let out a deafening roar. He was free. He looked back one more time at Ozgul and then he took off running for his destination. The journey would be long, but Shod did not know how to quit. From above the cave entrance, a swarm of Destroyers flew off after Shod. They were charged with following and aiding him on his quest. The beginning was here in the valley, and the end was at the gate to Bodain.

Ozgul watched as Shod disappeared into the remaining fog. The new plan was in motion but there were other pieces to it that needed to be put in play. He spread his wings wide and bent at the knees. In one motion, he sprang into the air and disappeared into his spiritual form. He had other matters to attend to.

Eret was unaware as to what was about to happen to them. In Bodain, a dark band of clouds began to roll in from the west. Thunder sounded and lighting began to fill the sky as rain began to fall on the cold night. The darkness was moving in as thousands of Destroyers began searching for their targets. They remained in spiritual form as they flew through the streets of Bodain. They were searching for hearts that were already evil and for souls that didn't belong to the Amari. Once they found their victim, they joined their souls with their own, flying directly into the bodies of the unknowing. The humans collapsed to the ground and clutched at their chests at the moment of possession. The pain lasted only moments and the victims were none the wiser. The Destroyers would inhabit these bodies and begin to control their lives, their thoughts, and their actions. When the time was right, they would use these unfortunate souls to wreak havoc upon the kingdom of Bodain and steal all that the Phayladin loved. This battle was no longer being fought by mankind alone. The battlefield would forever be changed but that didn't mean that Ozgul had resigned the need for an army.

3. KING HEZRA

Lillian pleaded, "Ethan, please don't go! Help me!"

He looked back at her as she made her way down the steps toward King Hezra's lifeless body and then looked back at Morgan.

"I have to bring Morgan back!" he shouted.

Ethan watched as Morgan disappeared down the road. He desperately wanted to chase down his brother and bring him back home. Ethan knew that Morgan's world would soon become chaos, if it hadn't already become that. However, there was a problem that required more of his immediate attention, and he knew that Morgan's role was not yet finished, but his redemption would be difficult. Ethan's thoughts were interrupted by the sound of Lillian's voice.

Lillian pleaded, "Ethan! Please don't go! You have to help me! If you leave me, I will be alone, and I cannot face this alone! I need you to stay! Please, stay with me!"

Ethan whispered a few words of prayer for Morgan and then made his way back to King Hezra. Lillian was already tending to the king.

"This can't be happening!" Lillian cried through her tears. "Ethan, he is no longer breathing. This can't be happening!"

Ethan knelt down beside Lillian and wrapped his arms around her thin frame. Instinctively, she turned to bury her face in his chest and sobbed intensely. Over the past few months, Lillian had grown extremely close to King Hezra and his death was not one that she could tolerate. Ethan used this time to comfort her as he looked around the room. Servants and guards were slowly appearing from within the palace and a crowd was beginning to gather. Cries of disbelief echoed throughout the main hall.

Lillian looked into Ethan's eyes and said, "You are the son of the Amari. You must be able to do something."

Ethan looked back at her with no response. He could see the desperation in her eyes, and he could hear it in her voice. Within his heart, he felt a deep sense of peace about what to do next. It was time to bring the Amari glory.

Ethan released her from his arms and grabbed her by the shoulders. He looked her in the eyes and said, "Do you really believe what you have just asked of me?"

"I believe this cannot be his end," Lillian replied through her tears.

"Lillian, as the Phayladin, do you have faith that I can help in this situation?"

Lillian thought for just a moment and then whispered, "With all of my heart."

That was all that Ethan needed to hear.

He looked to a few of the palace guards and said, "Help me move him to the king's quarters."

"But sir," responded one of the guards, "we shouldn't move his body."

"Just do as I ask of you," said Ethan.

The guards quickly moved to lift King Hezra's body. Lillian instructed two of the guards to go retrieve the king's physician, Dr. Forthen. The two immediately ran to find him.

The men carried Hezra up to his quarters and laid him gently on the bed. Lillian was close behind them, and the crowd was following her. The news was spreading through the palace and the hallway was beginning to fill up with concerned people.

Ethan looked at the guards and asked for them to leave and to make sure no one came near the door. The guards quickly exited.

"Lillian, I need you to step outside as well," said Ethan.

Lillian objected, "I need to be in here with him!"

"Do you trust me?" asked Ethan adamantly.

"Of course, I do," replied Lillian.

"Then, this will be done so that you will know that I am the one that the Amari has sent. But for now, I need you to trust me and to tell no one of what is about to occur. I'm doing this for you and you alone."

Lillian wanted to stay, but there was something about the look in his eyes that brought her a sense of peace. She turned to leave the room.

"Please, close the door behind you. I'll retrieve you when it is finished," Ethan said.

Lillian did not look back, but pulled the door shut behind her. She knew that she had to trust Ethan. Once in the hallway, she looked at the faces of the people that had gathered and became overwhelmed by the sorrow in their eyes. She could not stand to look at them and turned her head away as she choked back the tears.

"Princess! Princess Lillian!"

Lillian turned her head to see her best friend and servant running down the palace hall. She was holding the bottom of her dress up off the floor as she ran to where Lillian was standing. The look of concern in her eyes said everything about the moment.

"Princess Lillian, are the rumors true? Is King Hezra dead?"

Lillian held out her arms as Emma approached. As soon as Emma touched Lillian's hands, she squeezed them tightly and, immediately, Lillian began to sob as the two embraced each other.

Emma saw an extreme amount of despair in Lillian's eyes and said through her own tears, "No, no, it can't be! He can't be dead. Is he dead, Princess?"

Lillian used the back of her hand to wipe some of the tears from her face and attempted to speak. She pulled back from Emma and said, "Yes...and no. I . . . don't know what he is in this moment. Oh Emma, it was terrible!"

Lillian let go of Emma and began to pace the hall. The guards had pushed everyone back and it was just the two of them in the immediate area. It took all of her energy just to replay the events in her mind.

"I don't know exactly what has happened," began Lillian. "First, Morgan begins to accuse me of essentially falling love with Ethan and slaps me in the face. I've never seen him so mad. Then, King Hezra steps into defend me and my honor and...it all happened so fast. Somehow, they became entangled with each other and all I could do was watch them tumble down the stairs. Emma, I have never been so scared in all of my life."

Lillian couldn't hold back the tears as she continued speaking.

"Now, Ethan is in there alone with the king, who, by all signs is dead."

"But Princess," responded Emma, "that is terrific news. If anyone can save the king in this moment, it is the Phayladin. I'm sure he will be fine now."

Lillian tried to compose herself as she wiped the tears from her eyes again. She quickly nodded her head in agreement and said, "You're right, Emma. Everything should be fine. Will you please take this moment to pray with me?"

Emma nodded her head and moved closer to Lillian.

Inside the room, Ethan moved King Hezra's body to the middle of the bed. He took the king's arms and crossed them over his chest. He leaned over the bed and pushed the king's hair back from his face.

"This is for all you have done for me," Ethan said, "and it still isn't enough to ever repay you."

Ethan placed his hands on both sides of King Hezra's head and offered a prayer to the Amari. After only a few seconds, he released his grip and moved toward the king's feet. He took a deep breath and exhaled it over Hezra's body. He started from the feet and moved up toward the king's face. When the breath was over, he stood up straight and grabbed hold of King Hezra's hands and continued to pray. As he finished the prayer, he opened his eyes and looked at the king. While Ethan watched, the king's chest swelled up with air and the king began to breathe. Life had returned to the king through the hands of the Phayladin.

Ethan smiled and said, "Perfect."

He turned and walked toward the door. Lillian heard the latch on the door begin to move and her body tensed.

As Ethan appeared, he looked at her and said, "Do not worry. He is merely sleeping. Your faith has made him well."

Lillian realized she wasn't breathing and exhaled quickly. Tears of joy began to fill her eyes and she immediately threw her arms around Ethan's neck in an embrace. Emma smiled as the guard standing by the door turned to the crowd and yelled, "The king lives!" The hallway erupted with cheers and excitement. Feeling the love of the people forced even Ethan to smile with joy.

As Lillian released him and ran into the room, Ethan turned to the crowd and said, "The king will be fine, but he remains unconscious. Go back to what you were doing and we will keep you updated on his condition. Your prayers will be welcomed."

With that, he moved into the room to join Lillian and Emma at the bedside. He walked to the other side and directly faced them.

Lillian looked up and said, "Thank you, Ethan. You have no idea how much this means to me."

"Don't thank me," replied Ethan, "it was your faith in the Amari that made him well."

She smiled back at him and asked, "But why is he not awake?"

"All of our lives are a part of one big, master plan," replied Ethan. "It's not yet his time to be awake. The Amari's will is perfect and all will occur when it is time. I placed his sword next to him. A king should never be without his sword, especially when he is in this state."

"But what about food and water? How will he survive if he is unconscious like this?" asked Emma.

"You do not have to worry about any of that. The Amari will keep him safe and it will be just a matter of time. He has been through a lot already. For now, Lillian, I think you should be getting ready."

"What do you mean by that?" asked Lillian.

They were immediately interrupted by the door opening to the room. A small, older man entered the room first and was quickly followed by others. The man's name was, Lorcene, and he was the king's top advisor and head of the senate in Bodain. His entourage consisted of a few of the king's advisors.

He looked at Ethan and bypassed Princess Lillian and asked, "What has happened here? The rumors are beginning to spread throughout the kingdom and Prince Morgan was seen fleeing from the palace. Now, please tell me what is wrong the king?"

"Lorcene, the king has had an accident," Ethan said.

"Clearly, I can see that," fired back Lorcene. "Where is Prince Morgan? Why was he seen leaving on his horse?"

"Unfortunately, Prince Morgan was a part of that accident. The two tripped on the stairs in the main hall. When they reached the bottom, Morgan saw what happened to his father and he fled. He doesn't know that King Hezra is alive and probably believes it is his entire fault."

"Why didn't anyone go after him, and where is his doctor?" asked Lorcene.

Lillian spoke, "I have already—"

Lorcene abruptly lifted his hand toward Lillian and said, "I was not speaking with you, my dear. Please do not interrupt our conversation."

Lillian was taken back by Lorcene's tone and withdrew from the conversation. Her face showed defeat and she looked toward the ground. Ethan looked at her and saw the hurt in her eyes.

"Ethan, are you going to answer my question or not?" continued Lorcene.

"Everything is taken care of Lorcene. Princess Lillian has sent for Dr. Forthen and he should arrive shortly. You should be thanking her, however. If it wasn't for her faith, I am sure that King Hezra would not be in as good a condition as he is now."

Princess Lillian's face changed only a little, but she continued to look down at the ground.

"I know where Prince Morgan has gone and I will go after him here in the next few days," Ethan said.

One of Lorcene's advisors said, "But Ethan, with the king unconscious and Morgan not within the kingdom you are the acting king. If you leave, then we have no one."

Ethan replied, "Not exactly. In my absence, I plan on leaving the princess to oversee the affairs of the kingdom."

Lillian's head turned immediately to Ethan who was slightly grinning at her reaction.

"What?" asked Lillian.

"You can't possibly be serious!" shouted Lorcene. "She hasn't been here but for more than a few weeks! What does she know about running a kingdom that she is not even a citizen of? This is ridiculous."

"Lorcene, as acting king you are required to do what I ask. Is it not stated in Bodainian law that, in his absence, the king can appoint whomever he pleases to sit in his place?"

Lorcene fumbled over his words as he replied, "I suppose it does, but it is a ridiculous law and she cannot be expected—"

"She can be expected to perform her duty as the princess until such time as Prince Morgan and I return. There is no room for debate. I have made my decision. Let us meet together sometime in the next few days to make these arrangements true."

Lorcene's eyes fumed in the direction of Ethan. In Lorcene's opinion, Ethan should not even be able to take the place as king. Being adopted into a family was not the same as being born from that bloodline and Lorcene was not happy with the situation as it was.

"Very well, Your Highness," he said with great reluctance.

The sarcasm could be heard by everyone, but Lorcene turned to go. As he approached the door to the king's room, he looked back at them and said, "But when this kingdom collapses due to your incompetence in this matter, the Senate will move to take control of your authority. Please, have someone inform me of the king's condition after the physician has arrived."

Ethan nodded toward Lorcene, and Lorcene departed from the room.

As soon as he was gone, Lillian said, "What could you possibly be thinking, Ethan? I am not ready to run the kingdom. I have only been here for a short while and haven't the first clue about where to begin."

Ethan tried to calm Lillian down and said, "Lillian, the kingdom can practically run itself. All you have to do is assume the role of King Hezra while he is unable to do so himself. You needn't worry and I promise it will all be fine."

"I'm sure it will be all right," chimed in Emma.

"But why not let Lorcene and the Senate handle these things?" asked Lillian.

"Do you know what would happen if the royal family was ever disposed of here in Bodain?" Ethan asked.

"I suppose that the Senate would take control like in most kingdoms."

"You're close," responded Ethan, "as head of the Senate, Lorcene would be crowned as the king. In our laws, the head of the Senate is voted on by the people for just such a reason. Behind the royal family, his seat is the most powerful. When the people vote for the head of the Senate, they are basically saying that this is who they want to see become king if anything should happen to the royal family."

"You are telling me, then, that Lorcene is next in line to the throne," said Lillian.

"Exactly," Ethan replied. "All of that would be okay except for one problem. Lorcene is not a nice man. The king has been very cautious of him lately. If Lorcene had his way, he would be the king and not Hezra."

Lillian was shocked at what she was hearing.

"Perhaps today is the closest that Lorcene has ever come to acquiring his dream," continued Ethan.

Lillian was beginning to comprehend the situation better now and said, "You are worried that Lorcene would try to take control of the kingdom while you are away, aren't you?"

"I *know* that he would definitely try to do just that, and that is why you are here."

The weight of those words fell quickly upon Lillian's ears.

Ethan continued, "You have to look at your life and the world around you from the perspective of the Amari. There is a time and a purpose for everything and nothing happens merely by chance. Your coming to this kingdom, King Hezra's accident, and Morgan's departure are all a part of one gigantic story, and we are the main characters. Your actions in the next few months will not decide the fate of this kingdom, but it will determine the path we travel to get there. Ozgul and his Destroyers are present in every situation; their hands help craft the evil that humans commit. In fact, there is already a darkness that has moved inside of the walls of this kingdom. You must be on your guard. The days ahead will be difficult but remember whom you serve and everything will turn out just fine. This is what you were created for. Besides, if the Amari fights on your side, then who could possibly stand against you?"

Lillian turned away from Ethan and tried to clear her head. She took a few deep breaths and said, "When will you leave to find Morgan?"

"Not for a few days," replied Ethan.

"What do you mean? You can't possibly let him go for a few days. What if something happens to him, or worse, what if he does something to bring himself harm? Do you even know where he is?"

"You have to trust in me, Lillian. When Morgan and I were children, we always said that if we ever ran away, we would head straight into the Desert Lands. It is a few days away from here, but I know Morgan, and that's where he is headed."

"Do you promise me that he will be okay?" asked Lillian.

"If it is in the Amari's will, then he will be alright, but I have to prepare for my time in the desert. There is a task that waits for me there. You, on the other hand, need to prepare yourself for the days ahead. It won't be easy. Evil loves to strike when we are at our weakest."

"I'm not looking forward to this at all," replied Lillian, "but I believe in you. Somehow, I have a feeling it will all be as it should in the end."

"Please remember Lillian, we are judged by what we do in this life. Every decision we make – whether for good or for evil, in public or in private – it all affects the world around us. Guard your heart and your mind and, in the end, you will succeed."

"Ethan, I must admit, I am worried about my life. If Lorcene is as evil as you say, doesn't that mean that I could be in danger while you are gone?"

"You will have the palace guards at your disposal, and I will be asking Master Tomar to stay and help protect you. You're going to be fine. Remember, whatever happens, you are going to be fine."

Lillian was only slightly reassured by Ethan's last comments, but something in his eyes left her with a feeling of timidity and fear. However, even at that moment, she knew that she could trust him. She inhaled deeply as she gathered up her wits and turned her attention back to the king.

Lorcene stormed down the hallway toward the palace exit, his advisors were close in tow. The exchange with Ethan had only infuriated him. This was as close as he had ever been to becoming the ruler of Bodain and two teenagers were all that stood in his way.

They continued out the palace doors and made their way down the front steps. At the bottom, he turned to his advisors and stopped them in stride.

"Somebody please tell me what just happened in there? That was not how it was supposed to go. I was told that the king was dead," said Lorcene.

"That is the information that we were given at the time," one of the advisors responded. "Apparently, we were misinformed."

"Apparently," hissed Lorcene, "apparently! Obviously something went wrong! Mark my words; I will not let that boy stand in my way of glory."

"Keep your voice down, Lorcene. Do you want to be accused of treason against the throne? You will do us no good if you are thrown into prison."

Lorcene fumed for a moment, but allowed himself to relax. He looked toward his companions and said, "Well? What do we do now?"

Silence was among them as they all looked for a plausible answer.

"With the king in his current condition, we will have to move fast. Ethan told us that he will be leaving to find Prince Morgan, so our best chance will be to wait until he is gone and then make our move."

"With Ethan gone, the princess will be vulnerable and alone."

"This is true," replied Lorcene. "Maybe we will just let these things unfold a little more before we act too rashly. Perhaps she will be the means of her own undoing."

The advisors were in agreement with the plan; except for one minor detail.

"After the princess is gone, what will we do about the king? He isn't dead."

There was silence amongst the men.

4. BODAIN AT LAST

"Jael!" shouted Jeremiah. "Somebody help me!"

The people standing in line turned to look at the commotion as Nadia and Balak rushed to help their father. Nadia quickly checked to see if her mother was breathing.

"She's still breathing!" Nadia said.

Balak rushed to pick his mother up in his arms and carried her to the door to the clinic. A rather large and plump man stepped in their way. His hand was bandaged poorly by just a mere rag.

"Where do you think you are going?" asked the man. "Get back in line like everyone else."

Balak looked the man in the eyes and said, "Stay out of my way, or when I am done I will come back out and take care of your hand by removing it myself!"

Balak dipped his shoulder down and pushed the retreating man backward, and entered the physician's office.

"Quickly, we need some help!" Jeremiah shouted.

One of the physician's assistants rushed to their side.

"Tell me what is wrong with her," she said.

"We don't know," Jeremiah replied. "She was growing very tired and collapsed while we stood in line."

The physician entered the room and said, "Quickly, lay her down over here."

Balak laid his mother down on the table and the physician went to work.

"This woman is extremely cold," the physician said. "Grab me some blankets from that shelf over there."

The assistant quickly moved for the blankets but Nadia had already beaten her to them. Together, they covered up Jael from head to toe.

Jeremiah was seated at the head of the table and asked, "Is she going to be okay?"

The physician replied, "As long as the temperature of her body continues to climb she should be fine, but we will have to watch over her for the next couple of hours. Let's put her in my quarters. I have a fire already burning in there."

Balak and Jeremiah picked up Jael and moved her into the back room and placed her near the fire.

"There's nothing else that can be done for her now," the physician said. "You are more than welcome to stay with her until she begins to recover. We should know something within the next few hours. She's in the Amari's hands now. I'll be back to check on her."

The room was silent as Jeremiah sat next to his bride. His hand slowly caressed the side of her face. Gently he whispered words too quiet to be heard by anyone but her. Balak could see tears beginning to show in his father's eyes. Jeremiah was not the kind of man that ever cried. He turned his face away from his two children.

"Balak," Jeremiah said through the sniffles, "perhaps you could locate us a place to stay?"

"But Father—"

"Please, Balak," Jeremiah interrupted, "there's nothing else you can do here now."

Balak wanted to argue with his father, but when he saw the look in Jeremiah's eyes, he knew he should keep to himself.

"Very well," said Balak. "I'll be back to check in on her. Hopefully, I will find us a place to stay soon."

Nadia reached out and squeezed Balak's hand. She smiled as he turned to go. He made his way out the front door and turned to the fat man with the bloody hand.

The man cowered away from Balak and said, "Please don't hurt me, sir!"

Balak looked at the man and replied, "I'm not going to hurt you. Tell me where I can find a place to stay for the night."

"There's an inn just up the road here," the man replied. "Go back toward the gate and turn right. That will take you to a large village square. The inn will be on your left."

Balak nodded toward the man and turned to go. He moved quickly up the road. On his way, he decided he would stop at the local tavern and get something to drink. He kept an eye out for a place he could stop at, but something else caught his attention first.

A young boy was running down the street jumping and yelling something at the top of his lungs. Apparently, he was saying something important because everyone on the street stopped and cheered each time after the boy spoke. Balak was not close enough to hear what it was just yet, but he swore he heard the word Abaylin. He moved closer to the boy.

"The armies of Abaylin are dead!" shouted the boy. "The armies of Abaylin are dead! The Phayladin is alive!"

Balak couldn't believe what he was hearing and he grabbed the young boy's arm as he passed by.

"What are you talking about, boy?" Balak asked. "Where did you hear this?"

The boy replied, "The news is starting to spread all over the town. Lord Abaylin and his entire army were destroyed at Todere. Rumor has it; the Phayladin showed up and blew them all up! Even more, the Phayladin could be with the prince who just returned to the kingdom a few minutes ago."

"Who told you all this?" asked Balak.

"I heard while cleaning floors in the tavern, just under the inn."

Balak let the boy go, and quickly made his way to the inn. He entered the doors to the tavern and stopped to look around. A few people were celebrating, but most of the people in there were sitting with no one but themselves. Balak made his way to the bar and sat down.

"What can I get you to drink?" the innkeeper asked. "Today's a day of celebration!"

"What do you mean by that?" asked Balak.

"Haven't you heard the news?"

Balak shook his head.

"A couple a days ago, the evil Lord Abaylin and a large army of men moved to make an attack on Todere. `Parently, they were doing a fine job at it too. After somehow flooding the city with some kind of magic, everyone thought that Todere was finished. However, rumor has it that the Phayladin showed up and challenged Lord Abaylin face to face. They say that the Phayladin killed Lord Abaylin and then called down some kind of fire from the sky that killed off most of those wicked scoundrels – if not all of them. And the best part of all of this is that the Phayladin is said to be here in Bodain right now. `Parently, he returned with Prince Morgan just a little while ago. Truly exciting if you ask me!"

"That can't be true," Balak said. "The Phayladin wasn't supposed to come until the end of the year."

The innkeeper looked at him funny and asked, "How would you know somethin' like that? Nobody knew when the Phayladin was coming."

Balak knew he had been caught and needed an excuse quick. He thought for a moment and said, "You're not the only one who hears rumors around here."

The innkeeper continued to look at Balak and then burst out in laughter at the joy of the occasion.

"A free round of drinks for everyone!" he shouted.

Balak couldn't help but smile at the jolly, large man.

"Why don't you give me something that will help wipe away my troubles?" asked Balak.

"Sorry, son," the innkeeper said, "we don't serve those kinds of drinks in here. They are bad for the soul and causes good men to behave like animals. I can offer you some warm milk, or some grape juice maybe. We's a family establishment."

The look of pride in the man's eyes caused Balak to laugh back at him. He ordered up some milk and took in all that was just told to him. *Could it really be possible that Lord Abaylin was dead?* Just the thought of that warmed his heart. *But if all of this was true, what does that mean for Ozgul?* The lord of darkness would be furious right now which meant that he wouldn't be too concerned with finding Balak. This was, perhaps, the greatest day of his life. He had his family and his freedom, and, now, all he had to do was disappear into his new world. Of course, this would be easier said then done. He drank his milk and stared at the wall in front of him only to be interrupted by the innkeeper again.

"Son, is there anything else I can get you?"

"I need to know how to rent out a room here," Balak replied.

"You'd be talking to the right person then," said the innkeeper. "How long will you be staying?"

"Indefinitely for now," replied Balak. "How big are the rooms?"

"They probably fit two people comfortably. I'm going to be honest with you; it'll cost you a good bit. You can choose to stay for a few days or to stay for the month."

Balak reached into the bag and pulled out a few of the gold coins and handed them to the bartender.

"What will that get me?" he asked.

The innkeeper looked at the coins in surprise and said, "That much will get you a couple months of living here."

"I'll need two rooms for the month then," said Balak.

"You don't see too many of these coins coming in here," replied the innkeeper.

The innkeeper inspected the gold coins and then retrieved two keys from the wall and handed them to Balak. He informed Balak on how to get to his rooms, and Balak turned to go. It was just after midday even though the darkened clouds in the sky covered the sun. Balak looked around the square and noticed a lot of people starting to clutter up the streets. Families of all sizes were huddled together against buildings, trying their best to stay warm. The rain that had been coming down off and on wasn't helping anything. Balak was feeling compassion for them now that he had become one of them. He knew the war was not his fault, but it was his direction as the general of Abaylin's army that had forced these people to leave. He stepped out into the street, and headed back to the physician's office.

He had only made it halfway down the road when he heard the sound of a horse running up behind him. He turned just in time to see that the horse had no intention of slowing down for him. Fortunately, as the horse drew near, it stopped and raised its front hooves into the air. Balak moved backward to flee the wild kicking.

"Get out of the way," the man on the horse shouted, "or I will have you removed!"

Balak didn't like the man's tone and replied, "Who are you to tell me what I should do and shouldn't do?"

The man's horse pranced frantically in a circle and the rider said, "I am Prince Morgan of Bodain! Move or I will have you thrown into shackles."

Balak realized that it would not be smart to try fighting with the prince and he graciously stepped out of the way. He watched as Prince Morgan fled toward the gate. Now he knew who Prince Morgan was. Balak shook it off and continued on.

When he arrived at the physician's office, he was pleased to find that his mother was awake and drinking some hot tea. She smiled at Balak as he entered. He informed his family about their rooms at the inn and that they could go as soon as Jael was ready. He sat down and together they waited. Balak decided to close his eyes and get some rest.

A short time had passed by and Balak was awakened by the voice of the physician talking with his father.

"Make sure she stays plenty warm for the next few days."

Jeremiah nodded his head in agreement.

"But she's free to go now. Supposing that you are one of the few people who actually have money, we should discuss payment now."

Balak said, "I can only pay you with a few gold coins. It's all we have."

"Now, now. I do not want to empty your pockets for this. One coin will be sufficient," the physician said.

Balak thought it over for a minute and said, "Then, please. I insist that you take two for the treatment and your generosity. You saved my mother's life and I wish to repay you."

Their conversation was abruptly interrupted by the sound of the front door slamming into the wall of the small building.

Everyone in the room turned their heads to see what caused the commotion.

Two guards entered the room as one of them said, "Dr. Forthen, you are requested at the palace, immediately!"

Dr. Forthen replied, "I can't leave now. Look at all the patients I have lined up outside. Unless you can give me a good reason as to why I should go, I am staying right here."

The guards looked at each other and replied, "King Hezra has been severely injured and Princess Lillian has ordered us to retrieve you."

"What do you mean severely injured? What has happened?"

The guards pulled the physician away from Balak and did a poor job at whispering. Balak leaned in to listen to what they were saying.

"The prince and the king became entangled on the stairs and fell down them. We are not certain, but King Hezra could be dead and the prince has fled the kingdom. Princess Lillian sent us out to find you before we found out his status. You must come quickly and discreetly."

The physician nodded his head and told his assistants that he would return later on today. He grabbed his bag and followed the guards out the door.

So that's where the prince was off to, thought Balak to himself.

Not bothered with the affairs of the kingdom, Balak helped his family get ready to move their mother. Balak couldn't wait to finally get some rest in a comfortable bed. In the morning, he would need to find some work but, for now, his only concern was for his family.

5. MICHAEL'S NEW ROLE

As Michael crawled through the shadows of the forest, he continued to recall all that had just occurred on the battlefield days ago. He had just been appointed general of Abaylin's army when Balak was removed from power, and was positioned next to the Shadow Walkers on the battlefield for Todere. Everything happened so fast that most of it was just a blur. He remembered giving the order to fire hundreds of arrows at that boy challenging them alone. He remembered those arrows stopping in mid-flight and then being sent back in flight to his army. It was at that point, that Michael decided he needed to run away. He wasn't certain as to what happened after that, but, when he looked back at the battlefield, he saw a gigantic flash of light and everyone in his army fell to the ground dead.

Now he was unsure of what to do. He had decided to make his way back to the Valley of Shadows, but it had not been easy. For days, he had traveled through the cold. While moving through one of the villages, he had overheard that there was a group of men who were hunting down all of those with the Seal of Ozgul branded into their skin and who swore their allegiance to Ozgul. Fortunately, his dark skin had helped him move along the shadows without being spotted.

Michael had made his way to the position of general through craftiness, deceit, and betrayal, and even he would admit that none of those things resembled courage in any way. He was determined to stay free and his cowardice would hopefully keep him alive.

Many times along the way, Michael felt this terrible chill as he moved. His fears were always his weakness, but they also kept him alive. Being paranoid of mostly everything gave him an advantage as he was always on the edge, waiting for the worst to occur. Tonight's fear was unlike the others. Everywhere he moved, he could feel eyes watching him, but there was never anyone around. More than once, he swore that he could hear something moving in the trees above him, or hiding in the forest around him. Michael may have escaped the battlefield alive, but now he was being followed by his own personal Destroyer. He had no way of knowing it, but Ozgul was more interested in finding Michael, than Michael was in getting away from him. As Michael approached a local village, he knew that if he didn't get something to eat soon he would never make it home.

He crept up behind a hut on the outskirts of the village, and scanned the surrounding area. If there was anyone around, he couldn't see them. As he came around the side of the rugged building, he saw a fire cooking what looked to be a very plump bird. Michael, being led by his stomach, didn't stop to wonder where the person was cooking the bird. He moved quickly to the fire to release the bird from its fiery perch. As he fiddled with his meal, he heard a voice behind him.

"We've been waiting for you."

Michael quickly tried to turn, but never quite made it. The last thing he remembered was the feel of something very hard making contact with the back of his head. Michael's world turned black and he fell to the ground. Finally, he would get his much needed sleep.

Michael awoke to a massive headache. He slowly raised himself to his hands and knees and paused only to rub the back of his aching head. As his eyes cleared, he found himself inside of a dark room. He scanned the walls only to find his worst fears had come true. His only escape was blocked by giant, steel bars.

"Welcome back to the living," a man's voice said.

Michael looked through the bars to see what appeared to be a guard peering back at him.

"We've been tracking you for about a day now. Why don't you tell me where you are going?" the man continued.

Michael just stared back at the guard.

"Let's try this again. My name is Tobiah. What is yours?"

After the attack on Todere, Tobiah and his men committed themselves to freeing the towns and villages that were being held by the remnants of Ozgul's army. He and his men were a long way from their home in the Desert Lands, and they were beginning to get grouchy.

"I'm not telling you anything," said Michael.

"I noticed that you had the Seal of Ozgul on your arm," Tobiah said. "Did you know that in this village, it is now illegal to be branded by that seal? If you give me some information, perhaps I can make things easier on you. Perhaps you would like the rest of your dinner?"

The very mention of food made Michael's mouth water, but Michael remained silent.

"Well, you are in luck," continued Tobiah as he waved for someone to come to the cell. "This man says he knows who you are, and he has agreed to tell us in exchange for his freedom."

As the man approached, Michael could see the Seal of Ozgul on the man's arm and grew visibly worried.

Tobiah asked the prisoner, "Is this the man you were talking about?"

The man looked at Michael and said, "Yeah, this is him. His name is Michael, and he was the general of our army."

Michael jumped to his feet and grabbed onto the bars of his cell as he yelled, "You coward! How could you betray us? May Ozgul find you and deal with you justly!"

His accuser just smiled and chuckled at the squirming general. He had just earned his reward and Michael's threats meant nothing to him. Tobiah excused the prisoner and ordered his release. A few more men appeared behind him and Tobiah moved to open the cell door. As the door opened, Michael fled to the back of his cell as the men moved into grab him. He had one man on each of his arms holding them behind his back as they pushed him to the ground.

Tobiah moved forward and said, "If you want to live, you will tell me everything I need to know!"

Just for good measure, Tobiah raised his hand and brought the back of it to Michael's face.

"You killed hundreds of people in your raids on these villages! Who knows, probably hundreds more before your attempt at world conquest! I want to know how many villages are under your control."

"Please," cried Michael, sniveling behind his tears, "I have no idea what you are talking about. That man doesn't know who I am."

"Then why do you bear the Seal of Ozgul on your arm?" asked Tobiah.

"I . . . I . . . I was forced to get it on my arm, or I would die," replied Michael.

Tobiah looked at his men as if almost believing that Michael could be telling the truth.

Michael could tell that the lies were working and said, "They took my family away from me and told me that if I didn't help, my family would be killed!"

"Then why have you been hiding all day?" asked Tobiah.

"I was afraid that they were still out there. It seems like they are everywhere, and I didn't know what I should do. And then, one of your guys hits me on the head and I wind up in here."

Tobiah didn't know what to make of Michael's story anymore, and it was getting late. He would let this one go for the night.

He looked to his men and said, "Lock him up away from everyone else." He looked to Michael and said, "I don't believe you, but I don't know what to do with you yet. If you are who that man said you were, then you should be punished to the fullest extent of the law."

He motioned for the men to take Michael away, and then he turned to go. The two men carried Michael down the hall to an empty cell. It was dark and he was alone. They threw him to the ground and closed the jail door behind him.

Michael realized that he had just survived a close one and he was glad to finally be away from Tobiah. He knew he could only keep up the lies for a little awhile. It was just a matter of time until he slipped up and sealed his fate. He immediately started looking for a way out of the jail, but, after scraping at the walls, he realized that he was there for the night.

Exhaustion was taking over Michael's body and he lay down on the stone floor. He closed his eyes and began to fall asleep. As he drifted away, he felt a presence standing beside him. In a daze, he slowly opened his eyes to see the dark face of something evil staring back at him.

Michael began to panic and moved away as fast as he could. This was not Michael's best day. The creature in front of him unfurled his wings and hissed at Michael's retreat. It leapt forward and landed on top of Michael, pinning him to the ground. It placed his face directly in front of Michael's and hissed again. The open mouth allowed some type of slime to drip from the corners. Michael tried to move his head to dodge the impact from this falling slime, but he could not move. It landed in his eye and slowly crept down his face. In an instant, the creature jumped off of Michael and flew around the small cell, jumping from wall to wall. It finally came to a stop in the corner of the room.

Michael backed himself up against the wall and pushed himself up to his feet. He found that no matter how hard he tried, he could not get far enough away from his attacker. The creature moved slowly around the room; its gaze never turning away from Michael. There was silence between the two of them. Michael could do nothing as he was paralyzed with fear. The creature crouched down and placed its hands on the floor in front of him. The wings on its back moved up and down with each breath. From deep within, the creature let out a low growl. Finally, it spoke.

"I have come for you, Michael."

Michael's whimpering grew stronger at the sound of its voice. The slow, deliberate speech of the creature was intertwined with a hiss that resembled that of a snake. It was hollow, and it was frightening.

"Who…who…are you?" stammered Michael. "What do you want with me?"

The creature continued, "My name is Sanathi. I have come to give you a new purpose. A gift from Ozgul."

"Are you a Destroyer?" asked Michael.

"There is no time for questions," replied Sanathi. "I am going to give you power like you have never known. Today I shall give you a rebirth."

"What can I do to help?

Sanathi slowly approached Michael as he said, "You are missing the point. I do not need you to do anything. I just need your body."

Sanathi screeched loud enough to awaken those within the village and charged at Michael. Michael attempted to scream as Sanathi moved quickly toward him. Sanathi's hands reached out in front of him and he buried them deep into Michael's chest. Instantly, Michael lost control of his own will as he held the arms of Sanathi standing before him. His muscles twitched as a new feeling began to overtake him; his mind was beginning to change as it became one with Sanathi's. Dark light filled his eyes as Sanathi began to change into his spiritual form as he disappeared into Michael's soul. He was possessing his body. Michael had fallen to his knees, but was no longer himself. The feeling was unlike anything else. Michael's mind still existed in its original state but he felt a power pulsing through his soul. He was essentially one with Sanathi. The fear he had before was disappearing from within.

The new evil could be felt racing through his blood. He knew his purpose. However, his first move was to get out of this cell. He walked over to the door and placed his hand over the lock. He paused momentarily as a commotion had arisen outside of the jail. He smiled as he heard the screams for help.

Outside in the village, people began to run for their lives. Destroyers were revealing themselves and were attacking the village. They circled overhead like bats within the night and would swoop down to chase the villagers. The attacks were real and at times violent. Tobiah and his men frantically tried to fight back but the Destroyers were far too fast and too powerful. As one of the men attempted to attack a Destroyer, he was quickly disarmed and thrown into the night. Fires began to burn through the village and chaos ensued. The people were helpless.

"I command you to leave!"

The voice could be heard over the commotion in the streets.

"I command you to leave these people alone!"

The Destroyers immediately screeched and disappeared into the night. The people turned to see whose voice it was that called for an end to the attack. They turned to see Michael standing in the middle of the road. The people slowly regained their composure and were drawn in by Michael's presence. Tobiah lowered his sword, shocked at Michael's presence outside of the prison. Tobiah quickly rushed to arrest Michael again and called his men to his side. Michael did not resist as they rushed in to restrain him.

"What are you doing out of your cell?" asked Tobiah.

"Relax," Michael said, "I told you earlier, I'm not a bad man. I was set free."

"Set free by whom?"

"There are some things in this world that you could not understand, Tobiah, and, today, your understanding of things is about to be challenged."

"Enough!" shouted Tobiah. "Take this man back to his cell. I have seen enough."

"*Have you!*" shouted Michael. "Have *you really seen enough?*"

Michael's voice grew thunderously loud as he continued. The Destroyer inside of him was filling Michael with a power unknown to him. The people around him stepped back as he continued his rant, sensing that something was different.

"For too long the world has listened to the lies that the Amari has spread. He claims to care for this world and his people but, tell me, what has he done to show his love for you? Are you not still suffering in this retched place? Where is the relief that he promised you long ago? Can anyone here tell me how he has changed your life at all?"

The crowd murmured amongst themselves but no one spoke up to Michael's claims.

Tobiah pointed his sword at Michael and said, "The Amari is everything to us. Without him, this world would not exist – *you*, would not exist."

"You've trusted in empty words from a maniacal dictator who has silenced all other thought, all other gods. Tonight, I will show you all that those who have been oppressed deserve to be free!"

"And what god do you propose we turn to?" shouted someone from the crowd as the people balked at Michael's statement.

By this time, the guards had released their hold on Michael and he was free to move about. He raised his hands up to quiet the crowd. He knew this would be a tough sell.

"People, I ask you to consider what I am about to say and keep an open mind. This will not be easy for you to accept. The god that I am asking you to turn to is none other than the true god of this world, Ozgul."

The crowd immediately erupted with their disapproval. Everyone took their turn yelling back insults at Michael's rant. Laughter grew within the ranks of the people, especially Tobiah.

"After all the evil that has been done in Ozgul's name, you want us to believe that we've been lied to all this time! The people in this village may not be able to tell you a time when the Amari has interacted with them but they can tell you the last time Ozgul affected their lives. The army that just raided their village and plundered their goods has affected their lives! They know well the evil that is Ozgul!"

"Exactly," shouted Michael, "that is exactly what I expect. You said it yourself; all the evil that has been committed against these poor people was all done in the *name* of Ozgul! Not by Ozgul himself! It was Lord Abaylin that brought you so much pain. He perverted Ozgul's good name. This is what the Amari wants. He wants you to feel afraid because then he has control over you! You give him your devotion because you need him. However, I am here to prove to you that Ozgul is not who you believe him to be."

The crowd was listening once again as Tobiah asked, "And how do you plan to do that? You have thousands of years to make up for the pain that Ozgul, himself, has convinced others to cause."

"It's easy," replied Michael. "Just wait and see what I can do. I have been given the power, as Ozgul's ambassador, to bring healing and peace to this world. You've been praying to an empty god who serves only himself. You have already admitted that he has done nothing for you. Let me show you what Ozgul desires for your life."

Michael turned his head to the side and pointed at a woman standing near him. She had a bandage around her head that covered her right eye. It was an injury that she received when Abaylin's army moved through just days before.

"Young lady, would you be so kind as to remove your bandage from your eye? The people need to see that I am not playing tricks with you all."

"Don't do it," said Tobiah. "Don't play his games. You will regret it."

The crowd disagreed with him. They prodded her to do what Michael asked. He was intriguing to say the least. The woman shyly looked around and slowly gave in to the growing pressure. She began to unwrap the bandage until the last strand of fabric fell from her face. The crowd gasped at her injury. Burns had enveloped that side of her face and left her blind in the one eye. She waited for Michael's response.

"My dear sister," he began, "this never should have happened to you. If I may, I would like to right that which has been made wrong."

She gave her consent as Michael stretched his hand out toward her head. She closed her eyes as he laid his hand upon her wound. Nothing magical happened that anyone could see but the woman's breath was taken away as chills were sent through her body. She reached up and took hold of his arm. After a few moments, Michael slowly released his grip. The crowd stood in amazement as the scarred skin on the side of her face was completely healed. The woman reached up and felt her face, amazed at the lack of scarring that remained. She opened her eyes and was amazed to be seeing clearly again. Michael's lies were beginning to work. The power that Sanathi's possession had given him was starting to make believers out of all those who were present.

Michael stepped back and said, "This is just the beginning of what I can do for the people of Eret. Bring me your sick and your hurting and I will bring them healing. Tobiah, what do you have to say now?"

Tobiah was speechless. In his mind, he questioned this man and his abilities. None of it seemed to make any sense, but his heart was being compelled to believe. He was pushed out of the way as people rushed toward Michael. Tobiah watched as Michael did everything that he had promised. Those who were wounded were miraculously healed and the people were now starting to rejoice. Tobiah had seen enough.

"People listen!" he shouted. "A few miracles should not be enough to prove that this man is good. Just minutes before, he was the ex-leader of Ozgul's army, and now he is some kind of savior?

We don't need another savior! We already have the Phayladin! Does anyone else see something wrong here?"

"What Phayladin?" someone shouted from the crowd. "How do we know that you haven't been lying to us all this time? Maybe this man is right? Maybe the Amari has been lying to us all this time! Besides, even if he isn't some redeemer, look at the good he has done."

"This man is no criminal," shouted another. "He is a god!"

The people cheered at the comment, and Tobiah's voice was silenced by the roar. *Perhaps they were right*, thought Tobiah. Why would someone so evil be doing so much good? It just didn't make sense.

Ozgul's plan to steal as many hearts away from the Amari as possible was beginning to work. Michael's new ability was impressive.

6. LILLIAN'S EMPOWERMENT

It had been days since King Hezra's unfortunate accident on the palace steps. His condition had not changed, and, according to Ethan, they would have to wait to see what would happen with his life. There was nothing anyone could do but wait, and that was driving Lillian absolutely crazy.

For days, she had been dreading the moment when Ethan would leave and she would be in charge. There had been many sleepless hours throughout those days, and she had spent most of her time pacing back and forth in her room. Even Emma was kept at bay while Lillian tried to collect her thoughts. Perhaps even more frightening to her was the fact that today they would be meeting with members of the senate to discuss the upcoming future. Lorcene wanted to meet with Ethan and her to settle the matter of who would reign from the throne in Ethan's absence. In her mind, she longed to see her mother's face again. She missed the people of her kingdom so much right now. She just wanted a friendly face to reassure her that everything would be okay.

As she walked to the meeting room, Lillian tried to remember the last person that ever hated her and she was drawing a blank. But every time she looked into Lorcene's eyes she could sense his absolute detest for her. She had done nothing to deserve it, but Lorcene had chosen to give it freely. She dreaded ruling over him and could tell that Ethan's upcoming absence would be extremely difficult to bear if she had to also work at keeping Lorcene at arm's length. He was like an attack dog waiting for the right chance to strike. Her fear of making a mistake before him almost crippled her at times. As she entered the room where they would meet, she was surprised to find that she was the last one to join them.

"Well then, it's about time she showed up. Now maybe we can get started," said Lorcene.

Lorcene made it a point to not talk directly to her. He never felt that she deserved more than that. However, Ethan immediately tried to put a stop to it.

"Lorcene, I would expect more civility to come from the one in charge of the Senate. If we cannot get along, how can the kingdom expect to survive under our watch?"

Lorcene shot Ethan a glance of contempt and said, "Let's just get this over with shall we? Let it first be known that myself, and many members of the Senate, disagree with your desire to leave the princess in charge of the kingdom in your absence. We believe it would be reckless to leave someone of her inexperience to rule from the most powerful throne in the land."

"Your concerns are noted, Lorcene, but I have made my decision. Prince Morgan is in need of help, and I need to go after him. Lillian is in line to inherit the position of queen and I suggest that we begin trusting her now."

"Why do you have to be the one to retrieve the prince?" interrupted Lorcene. "Just tell us where he is and we will send the palace guards to find him. This will solve all of our problems and we won't have to worry about her youthfulness destroying this kingdom."

Lillian was growing more and more uncomfortable as the conversation carried on. They kept referring to her as if she wasn't even there and it was starting to bother her

"It does not matter who is left in charge as long as we are all in agreement that we should work together," replied Ethan.

"Are you forgetting the fact that there is a war brewing even as we speak? If the reports of Todere are true, then we need to be worried about protecting our citizens from war. What can she possibly know of war?"

Lorcene was beginning to raise his voice, and Lillian was quickly becoming annoyed.

"Prince Ethan, with all due respect, this should be a decision left to those of us with experience in this matter! Leaving the kingdom to this child will lead to disaster. Even her own father couldn't keep his people safe from harm!"

Lillian had enough and said, "You can say all you want about my inexperience and youthfulness, but you will mind what you say about my father. He is a great man and a great king. He loves his people more that you could ever know and would be willing to lay down his life to save them. From where I sit, I can tell that he is twice the man that you are."

Lorcene stared her down as she spoke. Ethan, in the seat next to her, looked down at the ground but was smiling coyly as the princess continued.

"You may talk badly about me all you want, but I have always been taught to never let anyone look down on me because I am young but rather be an example before them. It has been far too long since this kingdom has had a queen to turn to in time of need, but I have willingly accepted that this is my future. If Ethan desires that I run this kingdom in his absence, then I will do my best to see that the needs of the people are being met to the fullest extent. I will not back down from this fight and you will learn to give me the respect that I deserve. Not as an experienced leader, nor as a woman, but as a human being. I will accept nothing less."

The men in the room sat in silence at the end of Lillian's speech and Ethan was the first to speak.

"This meeting was held as a courtesy to you all and the Senate. I have already made my decision and expect that you will help her fulfill her role as queen in my absence. I should only be away for a short time anyways. You have my word. All will be fine. Besides, with the level of expertise that comes from the men in this room, you should be able to provide an excellent supporting cast to her role."

Lorcene shot up from his chair and shouted, "Never in my life have I been treated with such disrespect! Blessed be the Amari and all of his wisdom for he alone knows the damage that would have come if King Hezra had died this very day."

Lorcene's advisors began to cheer him on in agreement. Lillian tried to speak but their interruptions were loud and obnoxious and her voice was not heard. Lillian looked to Ethan for help but his eyes were staring at the wall in front of him. She couldn't help but feel a sense of helplessness. Her heart began to race and her breathing became quick and shallow.

Lorcene shouted, "I understand that this meeting is pointless! Why would you waste our time by bringing us here? Why don't you take your childish games somewhere else where your stupidity cannot affect our lives! This meeting is done!"

Lorcene motioned for his advisors to stand and follow his lead.

However, Lillian jumped up from her chair in a fury of boldness and slammed her hand down upon the table.

"Senator Lorcene! You have gone too far this time! Sit down in your chairs or I will have you all arrested under the charge of treason! Then you can all sit together in a dirty, old cell and discuss what you would do to run the kingdom, all the while, being fed water and bread three times a day until I see fit to let you live a normal life!"

Silence overtook the room. Lorcene was taken back and looked around. He turned toward Ethan and said, "She can't do that."

Lillian looked at Ethan and asked, "Can I do that?"

Ethan shrugged his shoulders and said, "I suppose—"

"Of course I can do that!" shouted Lillian. "Until further notice, I am the ruler of this kingdom, and you, Senator, would do well to remember that. I haven't destroyed a kingdom yet, and I have no desire to start with this one."

Ethan began to speak, "This is the first kingdom that you—"

"You do not want to finish that sentence."

The tone of her voice could not be missed. Lillian was finally ready to accept her role and no one was standing in her way. The men in the room sat down and waited for her to address them.

Lillian took a deep breath and said, "I will decide when this meeting has ended and I have decided that time is now. I will call on you when I need you again. Until then, may the Amari watch over you all."

Lillian turned and left the room. The Senator and his advisors sat in complete shock, trying to figure out what had just happened.

Ethan slid his chair back and said, "Thank you, gentlemen. We will be in touch."

He walked out of the room and hurried after Lillian. He approached her from behind and, as he drew near, she turned and addressed him.

"The nerve of those men!" she shouted. "How dare they treat me like a child? I mean, I know I'm not old but why can I not be treated with respect? They should be willing to help me in this position and not fight with me. I didn't ask for this! I didn't desire for this to happen! In fact, this is all your fault! Why didn't you stand up for me in there?"

"My fault?" asked Ethan.

"Well, I don't mean that it is your fault. I mean, you're not the one who started this all. If it wasn't for Morgan losing his mind I'd . . . oh, dear," Lillian paused. "I almost forgot. What about Morgan? I wonder if he's okay."

Tears began to form in her eyes as all that had happened over the past few days finally began to overtake her. She turned her face away and began to cry as Ethan moved in and wrapped his arms around her. She clung to him and the tears ran down her face.

"We only knew each other for a short time, but I miss him terribly. I do not want to be here in Bodain if he is not with me."

Ethan held her tighter as she continued.

"My people in Todere are suffering right now and I am so far away. My father is always caught up in ruling the kingdom that he probably doesn't even know that my mother is dying inside at the loss of life. And here I am, with absolutely no clue about what I am getting myself into. I haven't been in this position for more than a few days and already those who know what is about to happen have contempt in their hearts for me. How will I make my way in the coming days? What if tomorrow is worse than today? I am so scared."

She buried her head into Ethan's chest and let her emotions go. She didn't know what else to do.

Ethan grabbed her by the shoulders and pulled her away. He looked into her eyes and said, "Please, do not worry about tomorrow. You have enough to worry about today. But I promise you, you will survive this. I will do everything I can to return Morgan to your side, but you must trust me."

"What is taking so long?" asked Lillian. "Why haven't you gone after him yet?"

The desperation in her voice reached to the bottom of Ethan's heart. Sometimes, waiting to fulfill the Amari's purpose was more difficult than the actual process of fulfilling it. Her suffering brought tears to his eyes as well.

"I can only promise you that I will do my best to bring Morgan home. In the end, his redemption lies in his hands alone. We can only hope that his love for both of us will triumph over his pride. Please, be strong. Hold tight to hope. The Amari has brought you this far and he will not abandon you. Believe me. In fact, I must go into the city and meet someone there about my trip. I must begin to set some things in motion before I leave. You are going to be fine."

"How can you say that?" Lillian asked with frustration in her voice. "I don't know what it is like to be the Phayladin, but I do not have your strength. You tell me how everything will be fine but you aren't me. You don't have to feel so helpless and so fragile."

"Lillian, please—"

"No, Ethan, I need to get this off my chest and you are the only one that I have here besides Emma. So please just let me speak my mind."

Her tears just increased as her speech became more rapid.

"I am alone and I am scared, and if this is the Amari's purpose, then I'm not so sure I want this! How can you say that everything will be all right? What do you know that I don't? Please, just tell me so I can finally relax!"

Lillian turned away from Ethan and faced the wall. She buried her face into her hands and then tried to wipe the tears away. Ethan stood there in silence, allowed her to have a moment for herself, and then quietly spoke.

"Lillian, I know how you must feel, but open your eyes and look around you. You are not alone."

"I know," responded Lillian, "but you will be gone soon. It's just not the same as knowing that –"

"No, Lillian. Open your eyes and look around you. You are not alone."

There was something in the tone of Ethan's voice that caught her attention. She lifted her head and looked at his eyes. There was something about them that drew her gaze. The puzzled look on her face gave away the fact that she was confused.

"Lillian," continued Ethan for the third time, "stop looking at me and look around. You are not alone."

Lillian disconnected her gaze from Ethan and turned her head to the side. At first glance, she saw nothing but an empty hall, but then a new reality began to catch her attention. There was a slight rippling effect and then, before her eyes, a Persuader appeared from nowhere. One by one, they began to appear before her. She couldn't believe what she was seeing. Persuaders began to fill the hall, standing side by side with each other. Their large forms towered over her and Ethan and the hall seemed as though it was illuminated by their presence. She noticed that they looked as though they were ready for battle and saw that they carried the mark of the symbol of the Amari, the Orb of Pashii. Lillian spun her head around to look in the other direction as Persuaders began to fill up the other end. A deep sense of peace flooded through her mind and Lillian's tears began to turn to absolute joy at the sight before her. The two of them were surrounded by an army of Persuaders.

Lillian smiled at Ethan and asked, "Am I dreaming? Is this real?"

"This is definitely real," responded Ethan. "You asked me to tell you what it is I knew that you didn't. I just thought it was be more amazing to show you. Words cannot describe this."

"No," Lillian softly replied, "they cannot."

"One more thing," said Ethan, "there is someone I would like you to meet. This is Sevron."

Ethan pointed to the Persuader directly to his right. The Persuader acknowledged Lillian with a respectful nod of his head, but said no words.

"Sevron has been tasked with watching over you from the moment you were born. He has been protecting you your entire life for this moment. That doesn't happen with just anyone. A Persuader's interaction with our world goes much deeper than you know or could even understand. As long as they are here, they will be fighting on your side. You . . . are not . . . alone."

The thought of having a Persuader watching her life filled Lillian with joy. She walked over to Sevron and looked at his face. He smiled down toward here. Lillian reached out and grabbed his hand. All she could say was "Thank you!"

Sevron spoke, "It has, and will continue to be my pleasure. I live to serve the Amari first and then you, Lillian."

She released his hand and turned toward Ethan. She leapt forward and wrapped her arms around his neck. She squeezed her eyes shut tightly as tears of joy began to saturate her face. Ethan embraced her tightly and gave her a moment. Lillian regained some of her composure, released her grip on Ethan, and opened her eyes again. However, the hall was once again empty, leaving the two of them alone. That did not matter to Lillian now. After being a part of that experience, Lillian was ready to face the days ahead. She would never forget the face of Sevron for as long as she lived.

Josiah and the other Guardians had made the trip back home to the Tikva Mountains. They had hastened their journey home with supernatural speed. Their presence amongst men was no longer needed. For the first time in his existence, Josiah felt what it was like to be old. From the moment he lost his eternal life, the pains in his body began to surface. He knew inside that he would not last long in this world, but saving the life of those men on the Sea of the Dead was well worth it. Josiah was looking forward to his eternity after death in the presence of the Amari.

The climb up the mountain was long and difficult. The snow and ice had already begun to form on the path. Josiah noticed that the temple looked more inviting than it ever did before. As the Guardians made their way inside, they quickly found that they were not the only ones there. Standing in the main hall was a group of Persuaders in human form. Their large, white wings were pulled in tightly behind their strong physique. They had been waiting for the

Guardians to arrive. Standing in the front, directly in the middle of them all was Kitaan.

"Josiah," began Kitaan, "it is good to see you are all in one piece, especially you. Hopefully, the journey was not too hard on your newly acquired body."

"I can't say it was easy," answered Josiah, "and I wouldn't mind lying down for a very long time."

Kitaan and Josiah embraced by grabbing the forearm of each other as a hand shake. They released their grip and Josiah said, "It is good to see you, but I must question as to why you are here?"

Kitaan looked into Josiah's eyes and said, "Always straight to the point with you."

He turned away from Josiah and paced around the floor. "I've got great news for you, for all of you. We have been sent here to tell you that your service to the Amari is finished. The prophecy has been revealed, the Phayladin has been found, and the Shadow Walkers are gone. You have served him faithfully for almost an entire millennium, and now it is time for you to depart."

The Guardians looked at each other with slight disbelief.

"I believe we are all a little confused," Josiah stated.

Kitaan turned again to face them and smiled as he said, "Your presence in this world is no longer needed. You're being called home."

After 1000 years, and the fight of their lives, the Guardians welcomed this news with great joy. They began to congratulate each other as the Persuaders looked on.

Kitaan spoke again, "The better news is that your passage from this world to the next will be incredibly easy on you. Each of you will be taken to the heavens that are awaiting you by one of the Persuaders. Painless and simple. You should be rejoicing! This is your reward for a life of faithful service. From now on, you will be in the presence of the Amari, for the rest of eternity, and believe me, there is no better place to be. That is, everyone except for you Josiah."

At Kitaan's announcement, the room instantly grew quiet. Josiah was puzzled by this news, but deep within he was not all that surprised. He took a deep breath as Kitaan continued.

"Josiah, the Amari has one more job for you to perform and it is incredibly important. He needs you to remain here until it is done. As always, the choice is yours."

Josiah looked at Kitaan and said, "What choice do I have? Who have I but the Amari? He is all I've ever known. I will do whatever it is he requires."

"Thank you Josiah," replied Kitaan. "I will tell you more in a moment, but in the meantime, let us give our warriors a proper farewell."

Around the room, the Guardians said their farewells to Josiah. The atmosphere in the room was filled with a mixture of excitement and unrest. Josiah did his best to keep his composure but he couldn't help but shed a few tears. A lifetime was spent with his friends and, in a moment, they would all be gone. To make the matter even more difficult to bear, they were receiving the opportunity to see the one they had served for all this time. The Guardians were going to be presented to the very one who had defined them. Josiah knew that his delay was only temporary but it still pained him to his very soul to see his friends go.

The rest of the Guardians made their way over to the Persuaders in the room. Each of them turned to face Josiah as they stood directly in front of a Persuader. One by one, the Persuaders spread out their wings and wrapped them over the Guardian in front of them, encircling them completely. Josiah stood before them with pride and watched as they began to disappear into the heavenly realms. It took only moments, but eventually, all that remained in the room were Josiah and Kitaan.

Kitaan spoke first and said, "I understand that this could be difficult for you, but you know that when the Amari begins to work, he will always finish what he started."

"I am ready," replied Josiah. "What is this task you speak of?"

"We are heading north to the land of the giants. There is something that you need to retrieve. I will explain as we travel," replied Kitaan, "but for now, we must move from here. This temple serves no purpose now."

"What about the Orb of Pashii?" asked Josiah.

Kitaan moved over to the orb. The color of it had changed to a dark grey and would only continue to change with each new day.

"The orb is no longer necessary to the Amari, or to Eret," replied Kitaan.

He placed both hands on the side of the stand holding the orb and pushed it over violently. As the stand crashed to the ground, the orb rolled out on to the floor and shattered completely. Pieces of glass scattered all around as the power that filled the ball disappeared into the air.

Kitaan looked back at Josiah and said, "We won't need the orb to tell us that things are only going to get worse before they even come close to getting better. Grab your things and let's get out of here."

7. FOR THE NEED OF MONEY

Balak knocked on the door to his mother's room and waited for his father to open it. Balak had searched for some more blankets to help keep his mother warm as she was being nursed back to health. He had to use part of his last gold coins to obtain them, but the sacrifice would be worth it. They were quickly running out of money and his mother was only slowly recovering. At least they had a place to sleep.

The inn's accommodations were more than adequate and exactly what his family needed. Balak shared one with his sister while his mother and father stayed in their room. Each room came equipped with a wood burning stove and only one bed. Balak and Nadia were brother and sister, but Balak had decided to sleep on the floor and give Nadia the solo bed in their room. The nights had been long but Balak had never slept well anyways. It took a few moments but Jeremiah finally opened the door and invited Balak inside.

"How is she doing?" asked Balak.

"I'm not really sure. The physician said she would recover soon. I can see some signs of life returning, but I'm still not sure."

"Here are some more blankets to help keep her warm. I don't know what we are going to do as we will soon be out of money."

"Well we have these rooms for three more weeks," replied Jeremiah. "That should be more than an adequate amount of time for one of us to find work. We must keep our hopes alive."

"Certainly there is no point in keeping hope alive if we cannot keep ourselves alive," said Balak. "I must see that something is done."

Balak turned to leave but was interrupted by the sound of his mother's voice.

"Balak, where are you going?" she asked. Her voice was broken and extremely subdued. Balak quickly rushed to his mother's side and took her by the hand.

"Mother, you should get some rest."

"Yes, Jael, he is right," chimed in Jeremiah. "You have not recovered completely yet."

"I have been resting for quite some time," replied Jael. "I just wanted to know how my family was holding up. Where are we now?"

"Jael, my dear, we are at the local inn in Bodain. Balak managed to find us two rooms to stay in while you recover."

Jeremiah moved closer to his wife and knelt down beside her bed. He ran his fingers through Jael's hair as he spoke to her.

"You really gave us quite a scare back there," he said softly. "I thought that I might lose you forever."

"You can't get rid of me that easily," she replied. "I'll be around forever."

"I hope so," said Jeremiah. "I truly hope so."

She smiled at him and closed her eyes. In moments, she was asleep again. Jeremiah was still smiling at her but tears were beginning to grow in his eyes. Balak could see that he was scared and knew that he needed to do something. Without a word, he slipped out of the room and left his father to attend to his mother. Things were getting desperate and he needed to do something to better the situation. If he no longer had the money to provide for his family, he would obtain the necessary supplies elsewhere.

Balak told his family he would return and made his way down to the tavern in the inn. The place was cluttered with people, some paying customers, some just looking for refuge from the cold. The atmosphere was light and the people were a bit rowdy for a family establishment. He made his way through the crowd and to the bar. The innkeeper from before was wiping down some dishes as Balak approached.

"Ah, good evening, sir!" said the innkeeper, grinning from ear to ear. "What can I get for ya tonight?"

Balak placed his hands on the countertop and said, "I thought you told me earlier that this was a family establishment."

"Therein lies me trick! Any good 'n respectable family should be doing well to fall asleep by now. We're just doing our part to promote family time!"

Balak grinned and shook his head at the bartender's faulty logic. He could tell by the man's composure that he had a few too many drinks in him.

"Listen," said Balak, "what do I call you?"

"Well, my mother calls me Balpa, but me father called me any other word you can think of. And if you can't think of them, there's a man in the corner who seems to know them all tonight. Do you know what Balpa means?"

Balak shook his head. "No, what does Balpa mean?"

Balpa burst out laughing, "I haven't the foggiest clue! Me mother tried so hard birthing me that by the time I entered the world, she had passed out from all the work. Although, me father says she was stone drunk at the time. Anyways, the doctor asked what me name would be and me uneducated father couldn't come up with anything, so he said the first thing that came to his head! Ha ha! He made up the name Balpa and I've been stuck with it ever since. Now it's not so much a name as it is me trademark." Balpa tightened up and became very serious as he said, "But, now, I guarantee it's a name that drives fear into the hearts of men."

That caused Balak to burst out laughing. As he calmed himself down he said, "All right, Balpa. I will do my best to remember that. I need your help now. My family is running out of gold and I need to find some work. Do you know of anything around here?"

"No, sir. I can't think of a single job opening anywhere in the kingdom. After the earthquake shook things up around here, there were plenty of jobs but they're all gone now. Too many people movin' in here. It feels like most of the world is coming here for safety. No better place to do that if you ask me. What set of skills might you have?"

That was one answer Balak wasn't willing to share. "I would say I'm pretty good with my hands."

"Aye, I can see that," said Balpa. "By the looks of your hands, I'd say you've dabbled in a little more than carpentry. Those hands have seen a fight or two. I can tell."

"That they have," Balak replied. "I suppose fighting has always been something I was good at."

Balpa stopped what he was doing and leaned in closer to Balak.

"I do know of a little something, but it's gotta stay between me and you. Understand?"

Balak nodded his head in agreement.

Balpa glanced around to make sure no one was listening in and said, "Tonight, there's a group of people getting together to participate in a friendly wager. But it involves a little violence."

"What kind of violence?" asked Balak.

"Nothing more than some good ole fashioned fist fighting," replied Balpa. "Most people only walk away with some bronze or silver coins, but the more rounds you survive, the more coins you can get. Survive all five without being knocked out and you get half of whatever's in the pot. You look like you could go a couple, and I get a finder's fee just for bringing you in."

Balak was intrigued by the offer. He knew his family wouldn't approve of obtaining gold like this, but it was the only option he had and fighting was certainly something he was good at.

"Where are these fights taking place?"

"That's my boy!" shouted Balpa. "Let me get my coat and I will take ya there meself. Wait a minute! Here I go possibly taking you to get the tar beat out of ya and I don't even know your name."

Balak hadn't thought about facing this line of questioning yet. To give his real name would invite unwanted attention to him and his family. He thought for just a moment and said, "My name is Benjamin."

"Hmmm," replied Balpa. "That really isn't much of a fighting name, but I suppose no one will care once you've got them lying flat on their back!"

Balpa laughed deep from within at his own joke and turned to go. Balak shook his head in disbelief. *So much for keeping a low profile,* he thought.

The two of them had ventured a good distance from the inn and into the slums of Bodain. Bodain was a prosperous kingdom but every great society always had a seedier side to it. These slums had become known as the Shakack, which meant the "forgotten". People came to the Shakack slums to disappear from society and that made it an ideal place to hide from the law.

In response to the poverty, King Hezra had instituted a series of helps to keep the people here going, but crime and poverty had taken its toll. In order to protect the innocent ones living here, he had soldiers increase their rounds day and night, but he couldn't watch over them himself. Unfortunately, those guards had given into corruption and didn't care about the people who lived there. The area essentially ran itself as it became a place for criminals and unfortunates. Not everyone here was evil, but those who lived here had given up hope of ever changing their status, or leaving the Shakack.

The night had grown quite chilly and the streets of the Shakack were barely lit along the way. Balpa's jolly self was walking with pride in his larger than life winter coat that just seemed to make the big man bigger. Balak kept pace with him and was a man of few words. Balpa didn't mind at all. He continued to tell story after story about things that didn't interest Balak at all. The big man's charm was finally beginning to wear off and Balak was becoming annoyed. They had to walk quite a distance to get to the Shakack slums.

As they entered the area, Balak looked around at his surroundings. The buildings that lined the streets were in shambles. The earthquake had shaken more than just the foundations of these broken down homes. The buildings that could be occupied had been boarded up, however, Balak noticed the faint glow of light coming from within these buildings. People were active throughout the streets. Even children were running around at this late hour. If the two of them had wanted to not draw attention to themselves, Balpa had made it almost impossible. Everywhere they walked, people took notice of their approach. People were yelling crude phrases at Balpa in attempts to get him to stop talking, but Balpa kept on with himself, oblivious to the cries around him.

They turned down a small alley that came to a dead end at an entrance to an old barn-like building that stood a few stories tall. In front of the main doors there stood two Bodainian guards in full uniform with their swords attached to their hips.

As they approached, Balpa looked to Balak and said, "Now, let me do all the talking. These are crooked guards but they won't hesitate to arrest ya if they don't like ya. I'm kind of a regular 'round here."

One of the two guards spoke first, "Balpa, you old, fat man. You're looking skinnier these days."

"Aha!" replied Balpa. "Thanks for noticin'! The walk here tonight had to of taken off 10 or so pounds."

Balpa reached out and shook their hands while Balak waited behind him.

The second guard took notice and said, "Who's the man hiding behind you?"

"This, my boys, is the fighter I'm sponsoring for the night. He's just an ole bloke who is a little down on his luck right now. We was hoping you could squeeze him in for a couple rounds tonight, you know, to let him prove his worth 'n what not."

"Balpa, you know we don't just take anyone off the street. Besides, this piece of street trash doesn't look like much of a threat to anyone."

Balak stood silently in front of the man. The expression on his face never changed but every muscle in his body was beginning to tense up. Balak knew that he needed to get in there for the sake of his family and no one would stand in the way.

Balpa stepped lightly between the two men and said, "Now, now, there be no need to start throwin' names around. Every man deserves his fair chance to let the snot get kicked out of 'em, and we are just asking for ours."

The guard at the door placed his hand on Balpa's shoulder and shoved him out of the way. He stepped forward until he was inches from Balak's face. There was not much of a height difference so their eyes met on the same level. The man looked Balak up and down.

"So tell me, street trash, what makes you think you can come up in here and play with the big boys? Looks like whatever dog gave birth to you should've thrown you back with the rest of the garbage."

The guard spit on the ground directly next to Balak's feet as he laughed at his own joke. Without hesitation, Balak decided to prove his worth to the man. He quickly delivered a solid punch directly into the man's stomach. As he was doubling over, Balak brought his elbow squarely into the man's face and sent him flying backward into the wall behind him. The second man jumped forward and landed a punch into the side of Balak's face. Balak's head spun to the side. He recovered quickly enough to block the next blow and then drove his upper body into the chest of the second man, knocking him back. The two charged forward again as Balpa jumped in the middle of the fight and tried to hold the two back.

A voice shouted from behind them all, "*Enough!*"

The fight was over, not by choice, but by the sheer fact that a group of men had moved in and pulled the fighters apart. Balak struggled for a moment as he forgot how good the surge of adrenaline felt. His mind had drifted away as the man he used to be had overtaken all sense of reason. He was pushed backward and, as he came to a stop, he used his sleeve to wipe the blood off of his face that was streaming from the corner of his lips. He looked around to see where the voice had come from. Standing in the doorway was a large, bald man who happened to be missing his shirt at the time. His body showed signs of scarring all over, and the expression on his face did not seem too happy at the moment.

Balpa was the next to speak as he proclaimed, "Lamen, you ole bum! Good to see you tonight! I was just getting…"

Lamen interrupted Balpa and said, "Balpa, I should have known you'd be out here somewhere. Trouble seems to find you often."

The first guard that Balak had knocked down was dusting himself off as he said, "Balpa brought this fool in here to fight tonight and he flipped on us!"

Balak stood still as Balpa argued his case for him.

"Now that's not the way it happened at all! We was just lookin' for a fair chance to get in and fight but these two donkey's offspring wanted to be stupid 'bout the whole thing!"

Lamen looked over at Balak but, as he began to speak, two Bodainian soldiers walked up to where the meeting was taking place. Everyone present instantly became tense, everyone except for Lamen.

"It's all right, boys," shouted Lamen. "We're just working through a little disagreement here."

The soldiers looked around at the crowd and then back at Lamen. One of them spoke and said, "Lamen, we aren't hanging around here all night. Get inside, get your fights done and get us our cuts or we won't be turning our eye much longer. Understand?"

"Very well, gentlemen," responded Lamen. "We will be on our way."

Lamen waved his hand in the air and motioned for everyone to enter. The crowd began to follow suit and Balpa made his way over to Balak.

"You dolt!" said Balpa. "What happened to 'let me do the talking'? You could have got us both arrested there. I got a reputation to keep with these guys and I'm taking a chance on you. I can't fight, but I'm kinda addicted to the gamblin'. Now, stop actin' like my second and third wives and leave the fighting until you are on the inside."

Balak nodded his head in agreement and didn't say a word. They followed the crowd inside. As they passed the guard, Balak could see that he had broken the man's nose with his elbow. He couldn't help but smile. The guard sneered back at him. In Balak's mind, he knew this was going to be fun.

8. A PLAN FOR BALAK

The door to the barn opened up into a large room. There were torches all around to keep the room lit and a large gathering of people were waiting for the fight to begin. Balak looked around and saw all types of people: fighters and gamblers alike. In the middle of the room, there was a square made up of wooden planks to define what Balak assumed to be the location of the fights.

Lamen had led the way into the building. He walked forward into the middle of the room and turned back around to face Balak. All eyes were on him as the doors to the barn closed behind them. In the shadows, Lamen's figure stood wide and tall. Balak could tell that Lamen would probably be able to put up quite a good fight if necessary. Balpa pulled in close beside Balak and quickly injected himself into the already thick tension.

"Now, with that all done, let's get me man signed up to go a few rounds. He may not look like much but he's got a fire inside burnin' as bright as a pot-bellied pig being lit up in flames! The sooner we start the sooner we…"

"Balpa," said Lamen.

"Yes, Lamen, what can I do for ya?"

"Stop talking."

"Absolutely, I was just thinking of doin' that meself," replied Balpa.

Lamen stepped toward Balak. The look in his eyes was one that was not very pleased. He placed himself directly in front of Balak and said, "You caused me a lot of trouble out there. What makes you think I won't just take you out and string you up somewhere?"

"You wouldn't have made it very far if you tried," replied Balak. "Besides that, I didn't like the way your man out there talked about my mother. It was disrespectful."

Lamen smiled at Balak's resolve.

"I like that. It shows you're either stupid or brave. Either one can make for a good fighter. I too have a soft spot for my mother. So which one are you: stupid or brave?"

"I'm just here to fight and take my money and leave. I think I've already proven that I can handle myself. The people here didn't come to watch the two of us bicker like children, so let's just get this started."

Random people throughout the crowd spoke up in agreement as everyone was getting anxious for the nights activities to begin. Lamen looked around and raised his hands in the air asking for their silence. He turned away from Balak and moved into the makeshift ring behind him as he addressed the crowd.

"Due to the disruption that occurred outside, things have gotten off to a bit of a slow start. However, I offer you better terms than were offered before! Tonight, we have a stranger in our midst that is looking to prove his worth both inside and outside of our ring. I say we give him an opportunity to pay us back for the trouble he has caused already."

Balak could feel all eyes on him as the crowd grew into an uproar at Lamen's discourse.

"In order to give this man a proper welcome tonight, we will allow him to take on each of our fighters, one at a time. If he manages to make it past the first round, he will fight the next fight and so on. Five rounds, one man! If he fails, we will drag whatever is left of him out to the street and leave him there to rot.

"For tonight, our challenger will take on Matthew, Sarin, Abol, and Joseph. If he makes it to the final round, I will take care of him myself."

He turned back toward Balak and said, "I hope you're ready for this because we aren't letting you go without a fight."

Balak knew he might have gotten himself in a little too deep. He had just been looking for some quick money to get by, however, he realized how much he had missed the adrenaline rush of a good fight just moments before. He had managed to triumph his fears through years of service to Abaylin and, for Balak, this was going to be a way to let out some of the aggression he had been holding back for a while. This wasn't just going to be about making money anymore. Balak was about to take out his revenge on whomever was put in front of him. Balak nodded in agreement to Lamen but said nothing more. He didn't need to. Balpa was ready to say it all.

"Not only will my pal, Benjamin, wipe the floor wit' the likes of you, but he'll also make it so that even your own mother will wish she had given you back at your birth!"

Balpa turned to Balak and quickly whispered, "I'll take the guard on the left, you get the right and then I'll use me weight to burst through the door. We still got time to flee for your life!"

Balak placed his hand on Balpa's shoulder and said, "Balpa, my friend, I'm not going anywhere."

Balpa looked at him with a peculiar face, shrugged his shoulders and said, "Well, I'll be sure to take your body back to your family when you're gone then!"

Balpa spun around and shouted, "Where do I place me bets?"

The room came alive with excitement as Balak was pushed forward into the ring. A man with a bucket moved around the room collecting up all the bets that would be placed. The crowd pushed in close as people clamored toward the edge to see the action. All around the barn, people positioned themselves to get a good view of the fight with a look of chaos in their eyes. This was what they were waiting to see.

Balak had no rituals to begin a fight. He removed the coat that he was wearing and laid it on the ground at the edge of the ring. He bent down and grabbed some dirt from the floor, rubbed it into his hands, and stood to his feet. His hand moved to roll up the sleeves of his shirt but he stopped himself quickly. He couldn't expose the Seal of Ozgul on his arm without the possibility of giving himself away. He pulled his hand away from his arms and waited for the first fighter.

The man named Matthew hopped into the ring and immediately started boxing the air. His hands moved with a speed that showed his quickness. He was not overly muscular and was shorter than Balak. He danced around the floor for a little while as he attempted to show off for the crowd. The crowd gave off mixed emotions as some cheered and others offered their discontent toward the fighter. All the bets were in and Lamen gave his approval for the fight to begin.

Balak and Matthew moved in opposite ways around the outside of the ring, making sure that they faced each other. Balak raised his hands slightly in front of him to ready himself for an attack. In his mind, he slipped into a place where there was no crowd and no noise, just the man in front of him. He waited for Matthew to make the first move.

Matthew was light on his feet as he bounced from side to side. He used his thumb to quickly brush the tip of his nose and pretended to dodge a punch or two by leaning left to right. After a few seconds of circling, Matthew launched forward in his attack. He ran straight at Balak and leapt into the air. As he glided forward through the air, he raised his right arm back to deliver his first blow. Balak was unimpressed with the theatrics and patiently waited for Matthew to strike. As the fist of Matthew came down from above, Balak blocked the blow with his left hand and, using his right hand, he landed a punch directly into the throat of Matthew. Balak stepped to the side as Matthew reached for his throat, unable to breathe. He collapsed to his knees next to Balak, trying to gasp for air as panic set into his mind. Balak decided to show no mercy to the struggling man and landed a violent punch into Matthew's back. Matthew rolled onto the ground as Balak towered above him. He knew the fight was over as did Matthew. While still attempting to breathe, he reached out and tapped the floor of the barn and conceded the fight to Balak.

The crowd erupted at the quickness of the fight. Some cheered while others cringed at their loss of money. They were finding out that most of them had bet on the wrong man. Balak rolled his shoulders around to stretch them out some more as Matthew was helped out of the ring. That was the first of five fights and the rest were not going to be so easy.

Balak fought the next rounds with the fierceness of a warrior. He was not fighting for anything but survival and he soon found that his mind and body were now as sharp as ever. Sarin was the first fighter to make him bleed. He had managed to land a series of blows to the face of Balak causing his lip to split open and allowing bruises to quickly appear on his face. Balak ended the fight with him by slipping underneath one of Sarin's punches and hitting him directly in the area of his kidneys. A stunned Sarin was helpless to respond as Balak reached around his neck, slid his body behind him, and threw him backward over his hip. Sarin collided violently with the ground face first, his body sliding along the dirt. Balak ran up behind him, placed his arm around his neck and pulled his upper body backward until it would bend no more. Sarin found himself immobilized at the strength of Balak and chose to end the fight.

Abol proved to be tougher than the other two fighters as he was both muscular and overweight. He managed to throw Balak around a few times as Abol was difficult to move. After a series of exchanges between the two fighters, Balak finally managed to dislocate Abol's knee under all that weight by stomping down on the side of Abol's leg, essentially crippling it with the one blow. The man collapsed under his own weight and the fight was over.

Balak took a moment to breathe and collect himself. This was turning out to be as hard as he had expected and his body was beginning to rebel against him. He placed his hands on his knees and watched as the blood dripped from his face and on to the ground, quickly being absorbed into the dirt. He could only imagine what his face looked like after some of the hits that he had taken. While he was resting, Balpa ran over to his side.

"All right, Benjamin, I think you've proved yourself in a good way. Whatcha say we call this thing off here? We can find another way to get ya some money. It doesn't have to be here. This just doesn't seem much worth it in the end."

It was in that moment that Balak stopped to actually think about the reason he had come here. His family would be wondering where he was and would not even come close to understanding why he had done this to begin with. Even still, he needed to make right by his mother and father and, until her health returned, they would need all the money they could get. Fighting was the only skill he had that he had mastered.

Balpa raised his hand in the air and made the decision for Balak.

"That's it! That's enough! Me boy Benjamin is done fighting for tonight. We will just be takin' our cut of the winnings and be on our way."

Lamen walked over to Balpa and said, "That was not our agreement. Five fights or this man leaves under our terms, not his own."

"Come now, Lamen. I enjoy a good tussle like the rest of ya here, but enough is enough. Just let us be on our way."

"I'm not in the mood to negotiate," replied Lamen. "This is turning out to be a very profitable night for myself and, when I win, it gets even better. Now get out of the way and let the next fight begin."

Lamen grabbed Balpa by the collar and threw him into a nearby support beam. Balpa smacked hard into the beam and tumbled to the ground as the room erupted in laughter at the sight of the fat man stumbling about. Everyone but Balak.

Balak rushed Lamen, blindsiding him successfully. The first punch landed square on Lamen's jaw and he began to pummel the side of Lamen's face with a series of punches. Lamen was caught completely off guard and could only shuffle to the side under Balak's weight. Lamen clung to Balak's shirt as he tried to scramble away. His escape was pointless as Balak would not be letting go. The wrath of Balak was being poured out in that moment and, after a series of blows, Balak finally released Lamen as Lamen stumbled to the ground. He slid across the floor as some of his people scrambled to help him to his feet.

"Touch my friend again and I will do worse," threatened Balak. "And I will not show mercy again."

Balak was surprised at the reaction in the room. Even Lamen was staring at him unpredictably. Bewilderment filled the faces in the room. Balak looked over at a recovering Balpa and even he gave him a look of shock. It took Balak a moment to catch on to the problem, but, when he did; he realized it was a big one. In Lamen's hands was a large piece of Balak's shirt, the part that had concealed the seal on his arm. At least part of Balak's identity, had been revealed.

Lamen stood to his feet and said, "I'm no religious man, but that seal on your arm is not welcomed here. It's going to be an honor to be the one who brings you down."

The Seal of Ozgul was known all throughout the world. Once the news began to spread of the victory at Todere, the seal also became the universal subject of hatred. Bodain was home to many different people, from many different lands, and the loss of life at the hands of Abaylin had reached even inside the kingdom's walls. Not everyone was devoted to the Amari. There would be those who would have joined the fight on Abaylin's side if they could, but, unfortunately for Balak, most of them were not in this room. Hatred poured from their eyes in Balak's direction. In his head, Balak just accepted the fact that this was part of the punishment that he deserved for all of the crimes that he had committed. Even if he was able to fight off Lamen, there would surely be others to follow.

Balak braced himself for the worse. From every side, people looking to fight started to close in on him. It was him against them all. The attacks started off one at a time, giving Balak the opportunity to fight back. However, it quickly turned into a mob mentality and they were doing their best to see him broken. Balak was driven to the floor as kicks came from all directions. As he braced himself the best he could against their blows, his mind drifted to the face of his sister. Balak could feel in his heart how disappointed she would be with him. He had broken yet another promise and put himself in this position. If he survived this somehow, he would make things right.

For a moment, the attacks stopped. Balak tried to raise himself to his feet when, from out of nowhere, Balak saw a wooden board swing through the air. It struck him on the side of the head with great force and splintered during the impact. The blow dazed him completely and his vision became blurred. Balak sat up and fell back onto his heels; his body was swaying from side to side. The faces in the room began to shift into haunting images as all of Balak's demons seemed to be revealing themselves to him at once. Voices began to swirl in his head and none of them made sense. They were cries of pain and agony.

Right before Balak began to slip into unconsciousness, the doors to the barn burst open. The people screamed as Bodainian guards came piling through them. With swords drawn, they pushed the crowds back toward the wall. A few people tried to fight back, including Lamen, but they were quickly subdued as they were heavily outnumbered.

Balak remained in the center of the room, hunched back on his heels. His head was beginning to clear and he watched as one of the guards came to check on him. The man pulled back Balak's eyelids and stared into his eyes. Balak tried to push him away but couldn't muster up the force. The soldier grabbed the arm with the Seal of Ozgul on it.

"This is the one we are looking for," he said. "He is the one with the seal!"

The soldier in charge ran over to verify that it was indeed the seal. He looked to the first soldier and said, "Quickly, take him outside to the prince. Take the rest of these people and hold them for questioning, and place Lamen under arrest. It's about time he paid for his crimes. Lock him up with the guards he's been bribing and take them to the dungeons immediately."

Balak was able to stand to his feet as the soldiers helped him up. They draped Balak's arms over their shoulders and began to escort him out. Through all of the chaos, Balak swore he heard them say he was being taken to the prince, but at this moment, he didn't care. He looked over at Lamen and gave a half smile at the man's misfortune. His strength was coming back a little at a time but his body felt wrecked. He had no idea why the prince would want to meet with him or how the prince even knew that he was marked with the Seal of Ozgul, but he had no choice but to go find out.

There were more guards outside the barn and all the commotion had caused the locals to stick their heads out to see what was happening. The soldiers helping Balak out set him gently down in front of Ethan. Ethan motioned for the guards to give them some privacy and knelt down before the broken man on the ground before him. Balak gave Ethan the respect that he deserved and bowed his head to Ethan.

"What do you want from me, Your Highness?" Balak asked. "I truly am nothing before you. However, if you knew what I have done, you would have let those people finish the job they started."

"I know who you are, Balak, and I know what you've done."

Those words cut deep into Balak's soul. How could he possibly know who he was? These next few moments could be the most important moments of his and his family's life here in Bodain. He lifted his face to Ethan once more.

"I'm sorry, Your Highness, but you must have me mistaken for someone else."

"I am not mistaken," said Ethan. "I know who you are. I know that you have spent most of your adult life in the Valley of Shadows as a general in Abaylin's army. I know that you have participated in the deaths of countless people. I know that you have no love for the Amari and that you believe that he has forsaken you."

Balak could not believe what he was hearing. This man knew a lot about him. He started to laugh a little through the pain.

"How could you possibly know that? Have we met before?" asked Balak.

"No, we have not, but there is something else you should know. I know that during the battle of Seaport, you fled from Abaylin and your army, and I know that you came here seeking to start your life over again. I want to help."

"Who are you?" he asked.

"I am Prince Ethan, and I am the Phayladin."

Balak froze for a moment. The man he had originally set out to kill was now standing in front of him, unafraid.

"So, it's true, then," said Balak. "The Phayladin really has come, has he?"

Ethan nodded.

"How do I know that you aren't just pretending to be him?" asked Balak.

"You're just going to have to take my word for it," replied Ethan. "I'm sure you will believe it soon enough."

"You were at the battle of Todere," said Balak.

"Yes, I was. I returned here shortly thereafter with my brother, Prince Morgan."

Balak was having a difficult time wrapping his mind around all of this.

"If you are the Phayladin as you say, then you know of the countless lives that have been taken at my hand, my commands.

How could you possibly let me live knowing all of that? It would be a crime."

Ethan looked directly into Balak's eyes and said, "Everyone deserves a chance to redeem themselves. The Amari doesn't want you to have to live your life condemned by your own guilt; I don't want to see that happen either. I want to help you become the man you were supposed to be. There is always a second chance, even after you've blown that one too."

Balak tried to stand to his feet and Ethan quickly rushed in and gave him the support he needed. Balak no longer wanted to look pathetic and wanted to face Ethan as a man.

Ethan helped to stabilize him and, before letting go, Balak leaned in close to Ethan's face and said, "The Amari wants nothing to do with me. He has long forgotten who I am."

"On the contrary," said Ethan, "he has sent me here to find you. Life is not a series of stories placed together, but there is one story and it has a lot of chapters. The book doesn't close until you are dead. In fact, that is why I came to find you. I want to help write a new chapter in your story; you've been stuck in this one for too long. I have arranged a safe place for you and your family to stay. The Sisters of the Amari have an orphanage just outside of the palace. After the earthquake we had here, they could use some help repairing the building. They are willing to provide you with housing and food in exchange for some work. What do you say?"

Balak thought long enough for his old self to come out.

"I am not in need of your charity. We will be able to take care of ourselves. It is almost impossible for me to believe that the Amari would dare help me now after he abandoned me long ago."

"He never left you," replied Ethan.

"How can you say that? Look at how my life turned out! I never wanted to join Abaylin's filthy army! I never wanted to kill anyone! But the precious Amari wrote me off as worthless and abandoned me to darkness. I am here today because of one thing - I saved myself!"

"Balak, you know as well as I do that you were running away from him long before you were forced into Abaylin's army. The Amari never let you out of his sight. There is nowhere you could go that he couldn't find you. You chose to remain there all those years, and, if you were honest, there was a part of you that found twisted joy in being who you were. Fortunately, for you, there were people praying for you from the moment you left. There is a plan for everything and you are now a part of it. I know that you aren't the same man you were then. You have something to live for now."

"I don't want anything to do with *his* plans! Just leave me alone!"

Ethan calmly continued, "You have a choice to make. You can either live in the past or accept what is right in front of you. You can be redeemed and forgiven and finally be free. All you have to do is trust in him and in me. I can see that you are not ready to let go, but when you do decide, there is a place for you with the sisters. And I have a feeling that time is coming sooner than you think."

With that, Ethan turned and walked away. Balak was confused at the gesture as Ethan climbed on his horse and called on the soldiers to leave. The soldiers took their prisoners but left Balak standing where he was. He assumed there was more that needed to be said, but the Phayladin had just walked away. Balak breathed a sigh of relief as he thought he had reached his end. He wasn't happy about it, but he couldn't get Ethan's words out of his head. Balak collected himself and took the opportunity to leave before Ethan changed his mind.

He started making his way down the street when a man stepped out from the shadows. Balak stopped walking and was pleased to see that it was only Balpa.

"Balpa, I'm sorry that I lied to you. It was unfair of me to put you in that position. I was being selfish."

"That's all right, my lad," replied Balpa. "What you did for me in there was somethin' priceless. Ain't nobody stood up for me in a long while and I 'ppreciate what you done. I'm not sure who you used to be, but I'm thankful for the man that you are today."

Balak managed to force out a smile and said, "Then perhaps you would like to help me hobble back to the inn."

"I would be pleased to," said Balpa. "But first, I need to know your real name."

"Balpa, it would be better for both of us if you didn't," replied Balak.

"Come now, it can't be all that bad."

Balak looked at the only man who had been nice to him in a long while and figured that he owed Balpa that much.

"My name is Balak."

Balpa looked at him with curiosity and said, "Balak. As in…General Balak?"

"One and the same," he replied. He waited for Balpa to respond as there was a moment of silence between them.

Balpa half smiled back, slapped Balak on the back, and began to laugh as he asked, "Are ya still in the business? I've got a brother-in-law who needs a good lesson in how to treat a woman!"

Balak couldn't help but chuckle as the two started to walk again.

"No, really," continued Balpa, "you don't have to kill the man. Maybe you could just break a few fingers, or an arm or a leg. Nothing too serious ya know, just enough to get a message across. I've got a few more options for ya but they are hardly civil, if ya know what I mean."

Balak put his arm around Balpa and smiled as he said, "Maybe I can look into that for you as soon as I can feel the left side of my face again."

The pair made their way back to the inn. As they got closer to their destination, they could smell something burning in the air. They picked the pace up a little to see what was going on around the corner but they were unprepared for what they saw. Balak's heart sank deep within his chest.

"Curse the day!" shouted Balpa. "Me inn is on fire!"

Flames jumped high into the night sky and had replaced the building that used to be there. In that moment, Balak left Balpa behind and ran as fast as he could. His only concern was to save his family and he knew he should have never left them. He approached the inn and tried to run inside, but he was quickly grabbed by some of the men and held back. He fought with them, pleading for them to let him go but he didn't have the strength to get through.

"You can't go in there! The whole place is coming down!"

"I must get to my family," shouted Balak.

"Calm down, sir! Everybody was evacuated. I'm sure they are around here somewhere."

Balak realized how foolish he had been. He hadn't even stopped to look for his family. He calmed down and scanned the growing crowd. Toward the back and huddled together under their blankets, Balak's family waited for his return. Relieved, he hurriedly made his way to them. He ran up and threw his arms around his family. They embraced each other tightly, happy that they were together.

Nadia looked up at Balak's face and asked, "Where have you been, and what happened to your face?"

Balak had forgotten about the way he must have looked. He was just glad to see his family alive and together. He ignored his sister's question for the moment and reached out to embrace his mother and father. The moment was driving him crazy. Everything that the Phayladin had said about Balak needing help was coming true. He couldn't help but laugh.

"Why are you laughing at a time like this?" asked Nadia.

As much as he didn't like it, he knew there was only one choice. It was time to find the Sisters of the Amari. Balak hadn't noticed it, but Balpa had walked up beside them and was staring at what was left of his inn.

"Balpa," said Balak, "I'm sorry for your loss."

"I suppose everything will be fine," replied Balpa. "Maybe I can take that vacation I always wanted."

Balak patted Balpa on the back, said goodbye, and helped his family collect their things. He had a lot of explaining to do but, first, he had to get his family out of the cold.

9. PRINCE MORGAN

The ride seemed like it would never end. The images in Morgan's head kept screaming at him to run further and further and he had done that quite well. It had been days since the accident and he had ridden almost continuously, stopping only when the horse refused to move any farther. The look of his dead father's face haunted him every time he closed his eyes so he refused to sleep anymore. His eyes were throbbing from the tears that he had cried.

In his head, he knew it was only an accident, a terrible misfortune of events.

Why did his father try to stop him from leaving? Why did he strike Lillian across the face? What was wrong with him?

All of these questions and more plagued him every step of the ride. He just wanted to escape and he knew he could never go back. He was a murderer and a betrayer, but, in his mind, only one question mattered.

How could Ethan betray me? This is all his fault.

Nothing had turned out how it was supposed to. He was in line to be the Phayladin and Ethan stole that right out from underneath him. Morgan swore to himself that he would never return to his home as long as Ethan was alive. There was only one place to go to disappear and he was approaching its border now.

The Desert Lands were located southeast of Bodain. There was not much to see or experience. If you searched hard enough, you would be able to find some form of life, but mostly the desert was filled with nomadic travelers, moving from one water hole to the next. The place had shown no signs of life in recent years, but it hadn't always been that way.

Even with the sun below the horizon, the heat was still highly noticeable. His horse had been running for almost a day straight and he could feel it beginning to tire. If they didn't stop for water soon, they may never find it. Morgan was not too concerned whether he lived or died but he couldn't do that to his horse. He would keep his eyes open for a source. Desperation had overtaken his will and his emotions.

He continued into the desert and noticed some vegetation was beginning to show which meant water must be nearby. As he approached, he could see the glimmer of the moon bouncing off of the water. The disheveled prince pulled alongside the water and prepared to dismount. His muscles were tired and his motions were sloppy. Instead of dismounting, Morgan fell from his horse's saddle. He fell face first toward the ground and winced as the wrist he landed on twisted under the weight of his body. The pain was a welcomed feeling compared to the emotional wreck that he was. Slowly, he collected himself and made his way to the water. His horse was already there and Morgan came alongside of him. He was instantly disgusted at the site of his reflection; repulsed by the face of a killer. For a moment, he wished himself dead, but the moment soon passed as Morgan collapsed into the water out of exhaustion. Fortunately, his horse took noticed and gently pulled his body to safety.

Time passed as Morgan rested. His body did not move, but his mind was racing. He was taken back to the dream that he had when Ethan was brought to life on Healing Hill, but this time it had changed. He was taken back home to Bodain. The skies were dark and ominous as opposed to the blue that he remembered; there was no sunlight breaking through the clouds. He was instantly transported to the throne and felt the king's crown on his head. Before him rested a body inside of a wooden coffin, but the opening was turned away from his gaze. He stood up from the throne and made his way to the coffin. As he walked around the end, his heart melted at the sight of his father – the look of death had captured his face. Then the real nightmare began.

As he stood over his father's dead body, his eyes began to tear up and he reached to touch his father's hand but, this time, the guards moved in and pulled him away. No matter how hard he tried he couldn't get by them. Desperately he reached out to his father but felt his body being dragged away.

From the side of the room, a host of people appeared dressed in black. He recognized many of the faces, including Ethan and Lillian. He struggled to draw their attention, but they moved on without him; his presence was never felt. It was his fault his father had died. Within his eyes, a bright light consumed his vision from the outside in until only the light was visible, and, then, it all went black. He felt his body being thrown into a dark cell. As he tumbled backward, hands came out of the walls and grabbed for him. No matter how hard he tried, his body could not move and his screams were never heard. The hands pinned him against the wall and he felt the coldness of steal. While his heart raced, he noticed the room becoming lit with sunlight, and, in the distance, he could hear the sound of his horse. In his dream, he felt like he was being dragged into the light. Suddenly, the dream was over and he awoke to reality again.

The sun was shining bright and he felt like he was floating through the air. He went to cover his eyes and realized that his hands had been pinned down. As his eyes focused, he saw the cage that he was now trapped in. The last part of his dream was not a dream at all. It had happened to him. He was a prisoner.

He jiggled his hands to check the pull of the chains and felt something poke him in the back.

"Settle down in there," came a voice from behind him, "we've got a long way to go and you are expendable."

Morgan looked around to see that he wasn't the only prisoner locked in a cage. There were many more shackled together walking on the outside. For a moment, Morgan was thankful to be locked in a cage.

Morgan turned slightly to the man who poked at him and asked, "Where am I?"

"You, my friend, are a guest of the great Emperor Neroni."

Morgan was surprised that he had made it that far into the Desert Lands to be this close to the emperor. He didn't know much about this portion of the desert, but he did know that the emperor had a reputation of being a crazy dictator.

"Actually," the man continued, "you are more of a prisoner than a guest, but, if you play your cards right, perhaps you'll get to work closer to the kingdom than the sewers."

"Listen," said Morgan, "why don't you just let me go? I am of no value to the emperor. Leave me here to die in the desert."

The man laughed at Morgan. "We can't leave someone as valuable as you on the desert floor. We would all be run through just for thinking about it."

Morgan was confused, "What do you mean? What makes me so valuable? In fact, where's my horse?"

"Do not worry; your horse is being taken care of. Why don't you tell me what you were doing with such an expensive horse that was decorated for a king?"

Morgan rolled his eyes. In the escape from Bodain, he had never thought once to change the appearance of his horse. It still had the symbol of Bodain imprinted on the saddle, along with various other riches strewn about. They must have figured it out on their own.

"What are you talking about? I stole the horse."

Morgan lied, not that it mattered much to him.

The man laughed at him again and said, "We will let the emperor decide what to do with you. Until then, why don't you try to relax? We are almost there."

"Why do you need me?" asked Morgan.

"If you ask me, the emperor has lost his mind, but don't tell him I told you that. He is convinced that he can build a tower to the heavens and become like a god. I think he will just be making a really tall building. But I also think we will be getting a bonus by bringing him you. His ego will be massively inflated when he finds out he has royalty working for him."

Morgan laid his head back against the wooden bars. His luck just went from bad to worse. At the very least, he would be able to disappear. Maybe this is exactly what he wanted.

"Ah, yes. There it is. The Desert Kingdom!"

As they came over the hill, Morgan could see the tower that the man spoke of. It had only been under construction for a short while, but it was already beginning to tower over the rest of the

Desert Kingdom. Morgan closed his eyes and waited for the time to pass.

Once they made it to the kingdom, the other slaves were separated from Morgan. He gazed around at the sites but, ultimately, there was nothing to see. Everywhere that he looked, he saw slave after slave pounding away at something, working without end. It appeared as though the entire kingdom was made up of slaves. The ramp to Emperor Neroni's palace was wide and demanded the attention of those that approached it. They ascended up to the top. The guards around Morgan's cage released him from his cell and shackled his hands to his feet. They marched him into the palace and straight into Neroni's throne room.

The emperor was seated on his throne. The once vicious warrior had taken to indulging himself more than he should and had grown increasingly large since becoming a king. The fat on his body had slowed him down but he was still known to have great muscular strength beneath all of the extra weight. He was dressed in a bright red and yellow outfit that stood out amongst the dark stone that lined his perch. The black color of his skin had grown darker from all of the years under the desert sun. Ten years ago, Neroni was a vicious warrior but, now, wealth and power had quieted the warrior side of him and replaced it with a frailer version. The crown on his head looked heavy as it stood nearly a foot tall. Morgan couldn't help but think that the emperor looked ridiculous and even slightly pathetic. The Destroyers' presence within Neroni had all but destroyed him.

"Why are you bothering me with this slave? I should have you all whipped and thrown away into the dungeon."

"My Liege, we have brought you a very special slave today. We found him unconscious, lying in the desert near his horse."

The emperor struggled to stand up from his throne and said, "What is so special about this one? He looks ordinary to me; a little on the scrawny side as well. You better have a good reason for interrupting my day with this."

The man waved for his men to come near. They brought forth everything that they had obtained from Morgan's horse, but of particular importance was the saddle. Morgan stared ahead with an empty look on his face.

"My Liege, we took these things from his horse and no common man would have access to these."

The men presented the items before Neroni.

"And, on top of all of this, we found the symbol of Bodain's royal family burned into the saddle."

"Oh really," squealed Neroni. "All the way from Bodain?"

He walked over in front of Morgan and began sizing him up. Morgan continued to stare straight ahead and never said a word.

"So, I am in the presence of royalty," continued Neroni. "You are too young to be the king, so that must make you his son. Is that what you are? Are you a prince?"

Morgan said nothing. His will to do anything had left him.

Neroni slapped Morgan across the face and shouted, "Answer me, slave!"

Morgan said nothing. Neroni nodded to the guards and they delivered a beating to Morgan's sides. He groaned at each blow, but still said nothing.

"Well, if you aren't a prince that makes you a thief. Cut off his hands!"

The guards pushed Morgan into the ground and pulled his hands out in front of him. Two men stepped hard onto Morgan's outstretched arms, pinning them to the ground. It was, however, unnecessary as Morgan had no intentions of fighting back. He just kept thinking to himself that this was exactly what he deserved.

The man with the sword held it high in the air in order to deliver the blow.

"*Wait!*" shouted Neroni.

Morgan winced at the sound of his voice.

"If this man is a prince, maybe Bodain would go to war to get him back. This could be fun. I am tired of living in the shadows of the great kingdom of Bodain. Let's keep him and see what happens. Maybe we'll get lucky, and they will come attack us first, or bring us lots of gold in exchange for his life. Either way, we will prove that my kingdom is better than his. In the meantime, throw him in with the other slaves. But don't let him die just yet. We may need him."

The men who brought Morgan to the emperor looked on at him puzzled. Lately, the emperor's demeanor was known to flip back and forth as though he was two people inside of one body. One of them seemed just slightly off; the other came off as rather insane.

The general of Neroni's small army interjected his opinion by saying, "Emperor Neroni, we are not capable of a war with Bodain. They have many resources, we have so little. I agree that this man is valuable but is it really worth going to war over?"

The emperor stopped and let out a loud sigh of relief. He swiveled on his heals and smiled at his general.

"What was I thinking? What could I have possibly been thinking?"

He delicately danced his way down the steps to the men. His arms were flailing out to the side as we walked, moving to the music inside of his head.

"They have soldiers. We have soldiers. They have weapons. We have weapons. They have a prince - oh, wait - maybe they don't anymore."

He danced his way in a circle and found himself behind his men.

"They have generals—"

The emperor's voice trailed off as he removed the sword from his side and dug it deeply into his general's back, viciously and more than once. The general made no sound as he fell to his knees and died.

"And now we need a new one."

The men around him gasped.

The emperor pointed at a random man and said, "Congratulations, you're the new general."

"But, Your Majesty, I have no ranking now. I couldn't possibly..."

"Perhaps, you would like a sword protruding from your corpse as well," Neroni teased.

The man quickly shook his head no.

"Very well, now, do as I say. Take this prisoner and flog him. Then send a letter to Bodain and find out who this really is. I will have a war."

They pulled Morgan back up to his knees and released his hands from the shackles. They tied two ropes, one for each hand, around each of his wrists. Two men pulled his arms wide out to his side and held him there tightly.

"This is what I deserve," thought Morgan.

That was the last thought he had before the pain was delivered. The crack of the whip echoed through his mind and his eyes watched as Emperor Neroni squealed with glee at the sight.

Morgan screamed louder with each whip and, in a moment of exhaustion, he blacked out into unconsciousness.

Lillian stood on the balcony overlooking the kingdom. The sun was coming up over the horizon but it could not be seen behind the cloudy skies. The winter wind swirled around her as snow fell gently to the ground, but she didn't mind the cold. The weather was changing constantly and without consistency as it would change from rain to snow on a regular basis. The world was so big, and she felt so small. She remembered this view from when she first arrived at the palace. Her relationship with Morgan had started off shaky, to say the least, and this is where she always came for comfort from the day. So much had happened in such a little amount of time and she occasionally found it difficult to appreciate the day. It was becoming easy to overlook the blessings in her life, but this is what her world had become. She needed some time to pray and the balcony was perfect for that.

Ethan watched from within the palace walls. He wished this upon no one, least of all, someone as fragile as Lillian. However, he knew she had an inner strength that she had not discovered yet. He did not want to interrupt her prayers, but the time had come for him to leave and he knew she would be protected.

"Lillian, I must speak to you."

Ethan watched as Lillian wiped the tears from her eyes. She stood up straight, smoothed out her dress, and took a deep breath. When she had gained her composure, she turned to face Ethan.

"Are you off to find Morgan?" she asked.

Ethan nodded his head.

"How long will you be gone?"

"I'm afraid I don't have that answer."

Lillian had nothing to say. She felt an overwhelming sense of sadness.

Ethan stepped forward and said, "I promise, we will be home again soon. Morgan is in the Desert Lands and it will take time, but, with the help of the Amari, time will seem as though it ran by quickly."

"Forgive my doubt, but how will you find him?" Lillian asked.

"The same way a bird finds its food," replied Ethan. "The same way the sun knows to rise every morning. The Amari is faithful and has not failed us yet. I will just go where he leads me and I encourage you to do the same."

Lillian merely nodded her head in agreement.

"Watch over the king," said Ethan, "and, please, remember that you have an entire army at your disposal who have sworn with their lives to protect you. You will be fine. I promise."

Again, Lillian just nodded her head. Desperation had appeared on her face and she appeared as though she was about to let her emotions go. She looked to the ground to hide her face.

"Well," she whispered, "do not worry about me. I am going to be fine. The gift you allowed me to see the other day has given me a new resolve. I'm not sure what will happen next, and I may still be a little afraid but now I know that in whatever happens, the Amari is with me. What more could I ask for? You go do what you have to do, and I will stay here and do what I must do - which is to not let this kingdom completely fall apart on my watch."

He reached out and embraced her with a hug, and, for a moment, she felt a peace that went beyond all of her understanding. She felt the breeze on the balcony blow warmer for the first time. She noticed the sun sparkling on the water below. Somewhere, in the distance or maybe closer, she could hear the laughter of children. All at once, it was as if the world had come alive and she had witnessed its birth.

She released herself from Ethan's embrace, looked at him, and said, "I don't know how you do it."

Ethan smiled and said, "I will return shortly. As I said before, keep a close eye on King Hezra and continue to pray. The world needs it now more than ever."

10. REDEMPTION BEGINS

In a drastic turn of events, the days in Bodain seemed to be getting darker and warmer. The snow on the ground was beginning to melt, leaving puddles of water flooding the street. The warm weather was made even more peculiar by the fact that there had been no break in the clouds. The winter season was still here, but this was anything from typical.

There were moments when Balak couldn't help but feel some sense of hopelessness. He explained to his family everything that had happened the night before and, to his surprise, they didn't fight with him much at all about it. As he told of the events to his father, he could almost see a sense of pride in his eyes. The fact that his father did not fight with him was Jeremiah's way of saying that he didn't approve of the action, but he appreciated Balak's desire to help his family get by. That was something that Balak could live with. He did, however, leave out one minor detail to the story. He did not tell them of his meeting with the Phayladin. He didn't want his mother to get worked up over the news, at least, that's the excuse he told himself.

After asking around, they had finally made their way to the entrance of the orphanage. Balak noticed the symbol of the Amari on the door above and, for the first time, he found himself not cringing at the sight of it. He might not be completely swayed toward the Amari, but the Phayladin was right, in his heart, Balak knew that he had never completely turned away from the Amari. There was always a part of him that wanted to return. Besides, how could he argue with the chain of events that unfolded the night before? He never believed in coincidences anyways.

Balak couldn't help but notice the palace just down the street as it was the only thing his father had talked about since they had turned the corner. Jeremiah had lived all of his life in Seaport, and this was the most magnificent thing that he had seen. The good news was that Jael was able to stand on her own, but not for too long. The warming of the weather had begun to give her some of the strength that she was missing.

As they approached the orphanage, Nadia ran up and knocked on the door. They waited patiently for an answer. The door was opened and they were greeted by a tiny, old woman.

"Welcome! We are so glad to have you here. My name is Sister Mary. Please come in."

Balak's family made their way inside the orphanage. They were instantly greeted with warm smiles from the sisters. Nadia was the first to speak.

"Thank you all, so much, for letting us stay with you. I hope it's not too much of a burden."

"Not at all," said Sister Mary. "The Phayladin said you might be coming."

Balak's family was taken aback by her words.

"Did you say the Phayladin spoke to you?" asked Jeremiah. "He's here? Are you sure?"

"Yes indeed," continued Sister Mary, "we all just found out a few days ago. As a matter of fact, the Phayladin turned out to be Bodain's very own Prince Ethan. He stopped by to tell us that you all would need a place to stay."

Balak's family was in shock. They had been waiting their entire life to hear of this news, and, now, their Redeemer had finally come. Everyone, except for Balak, began to rejoice with each other. Even Jael managed to speak.

"Praise to the Amari. We knew he would save us."

"Well, we aren't completely out of the woods yet. Times are about to get harder before they get better, but, you are right; he will save us. Won't you all come inside now? All of the snow melting is making things very soggy."

"My name is Nadia and this is my mother and father, Jeremiah and Jael, and the brooding man in the back is my brother Ba -"

Balak quickly interrupted, "Benjamin. My name is Benjamin."

Sister Mary shot him a quick look of discontent, but turned her attention to Jael.

"Please, let's get your mother into one of our beds. Most of the orphanage has damage to it from the earthquake but that's what we were hoping you could help us fix. We are simply a bunch of old and tired women who have no skills in construction. Why don't we put you right in here, Jael? This is the most comfortable bed that we have in this place. It's not the best living arrangements, but it will do for now. The Phayladin is housing all the children in the palace right now until this building is repaired, so you should have plenty of privacy."

"Thank you, again," said Jeremiah, "but we have no money to repay you."

"Nonsense, you stay as long as you want and we will provide for you. And, while we wait, perhaps I can show this young man around and talk about getting started on the repairs."

"Certainly," was all Balak said.

"Excuse me, sister," said Nadia. "You said that the Phayladin said we would be coming here. Is that true?"

"Yes, of course it is. Why else would I say it?" replied the sister.

"How could he have possibly have known that we were in need of a place to stay?"

"Didn't your brother tell you, darling?"

Nadia looked over at Balak and said, "No, he never mentioned a word."

"Well, that's odd," replied Sister Mary. "Ethan, I mean, the Phayladin, said that he was going to talk to your brother about all the arrangements."

Balak didn't know what to say or think in the moment. He looked at Nadia's face and saw, once again, a look of disappointment.

"Unfortunately, Sister Mary, my brother seems to keep a lot of secrets from his family. He especially forgets to share the important ones."

"That he does," said Jeremiah while shaking his finger at Balak. "Be careful with this one; he's got a bit of a temper at times."

Balak tried to speak but Nadia quickly turned away. He decided to let her go. Balak made sure that his family was situated and followed Sister Mary out the door. She waited until they were halfway down the hall and abruptly turned to face Balak.

"Listen to me very carefully," said Sister Mary. "I don't like to be lied to."

Balak tried to interrupt but she quickly quieted him down.

"And I don't like to be interrupted. I know who you are. I know what you've done. I know that underneath that sleeve lies the mark of my enemy. But, with that said, I also know that none of that matters now. The Phayladin asked me to care for you and your family and that is what we intend to do. Your sins are no different than mine; they are just more severe in their implementation. However, in the Amari's eyes, you are my equal. I am no better than you, which means, I will treat you with the same respect that I ask of you. This is my calling. I encourage you to discover yours."

"With all due respect, I am here because I have nowhere else to turn. I know what my sins are and I deal with them every day. I want nothing more than to disappear into this world and begin my life anew. I have survived this long without the Amari and I do not need him now."

"Young man, this is not a matter of survival. My only concern is the state of your soul. There is a life after death and everything that we do here leads to our final destination. You can try all you want, but you will never be free from your past. Only the Amari can offer you redemption."

Balak was growing slightly agitated at the conversation, but he had thought more about this than usual.

"You are all the same," he declared. "No one has experienced the darkness of this life in the same fashion that I have. No one has found their way out of the depths of depravity in the way that I have. Yet everyone feels as though they completely understand and can relate to every aspect of my life. There will be no redemption for me until I give it to myself. Believe what you want, but I cannot be forgiven. There are some things that even the Amari cannot provide."

There was a moment of silence between the two of them. Sister Mary spoke first.

"All I know is this. The Phayladin specifically sought you out. You know in your heart that he is who he says he is. You might start asking yourself why your life is so important to him."

She turned and walked a few steps down the hall and stopped. She looked Balak in the eyes and said, "Redemption is real. I beg of you, please do not fight that which you can't see. For once in your life, follow your heart. For now, would you please come with me? This place needs more work than you can imagine, Balak."

Balak smiled. It had been a long time since anyone had stood up to him and gotten away with it. He couldn't see one bit of fear in her eyes and for some reason that intrigued him.

High above the orphanage, the Persuaders were watching him from above. Sister Mary was right, there was a plan for Balak's life and it had been set into motion. There was a war still coming and Balak's life was needed. But, more importantly, he was wanted. The Amari was working to restore Balak and the Amari never gave up.

Michael had begun to stir up quite a following. He loved his new position of authority and the power that came with it. In less than a week, he had made his way through village after village, declaring himself as the ambassador for the great Ozgul. His hands were healing diseases and calming fears. The fact that the Phayladin had all but disappeared only fueled the work that Michael was doing through the power of Sanathi's possession. The rumors had spread far and wide about the victory at Todere, but the Phayladin's identity had never been revealed. Michael was the talk of the moment and the glory was his to own.

In every village, there were some who decided to give up everything to follow Michael where he went. They would follow him for miles, pledging their devotion to him. Michael was just glad to finally be on Ozgul's good side. He had been doing everything that was asked of him so far. Ozgul must certainly be pleased. Michael needed to find a way to get away from the crowds that followed him. He had a meeting to attend. He needed to sneak away and he turned to the man in charge of his security to help him with that problem.

From the moment that Michael found his way out of jail, Tobiah had been skeptical of who Michael claimed to be. Tobiah had set out to bring Ozgul's army to justice. However, when Michael began healing everyone who was sick or injured, Tobiah feared that he would not be able to hold Michael captive without the people becoming angry. He was forced to let him go. For the next few days, he kept a close eye on Michael to make sure he remained honest.

Tobiah stood by as Michael proved that he was offering some form of hope. Life after life was changed in Michael's presence, and much to Tobiah's chagrin, he started to believe it as well. Tobiah had been deceived and never knew it. Michael instantly recognized Tobiah's talents and asked him and his men to help protect him and be his escort as long as he was keeping an eye on him anyway. Tobiah agreed.

Michael and Tobiah's men had managed to slip away from the crowds as they entered the forest north of the Great Divide. It was late when they decided to make camp and the men were tired. They really had nothing to worry about as most of them were convinced that Michael would protect them from any danger. The fires continued to burn deep into the night and the sentries that were stationed around the encampment had grown weary and their eyes began to close from the weight.

One of Tobiah's men laid his sword up against a tree and sat down beside it. He laid his head back against the trunk and rubbed his eyes to try to remove some of the sleepiness. He shook his head rapidly back and forth and waited for his eyes to adjust again but he was overcome with sleep. He closed his eyes and allowed himself to fade away. Within seconds of falling asleep, he was awoken by the sound of something breaking in the distance. He quickly jumped to his feet as he fumbled around for his sword. These forests were known for wolves and scavengers and he wasn't going to let himself get caught off guard. He scanned the forest but could not see

THE ACCOUNTS OF AMARI

anything in the darkness past a few feet. He held his sword out in
front of himself and waited for another noise to occur. His heart
pounded intensely as he heard a low growl come from behind the tree
he was leaning on. He was not a fully trained soldier and his fear
gave way to hesitation. Instead of immediately turning around to
face his attacker, he slowly turned his head but was fully unprepared
for what he saw next. A monster of a man, with a hideous face,
roared at the frightened soldier and it echoed into the night. He was
face to face with Shod.

Shod reached out and grabbed the soldier by the neck and
lifted him slowly off of his feet. The soldier was helpless to do
anything. With one hand, he grabbed Shod's arm to try to keep from
being strangled. With the other hand, he swung his sword at Shod
who removed it from the soldier's hand with force. The soldier was
defenseless and he knew it. He kicked and swung at Shod but his
blows did nothing. Shod held the soldier at face level with one hand
and, with the other, he slowly lifted the man's sword and held the
point into the man's stomach. The man tried to scream but could not
muster a sound as his own sword was plunged slowly into his body.
Shod allowed the sword to do its work and tossed the lifeless man
aside as though he weighed nothing.

Back in the camp, Tobiah's men were awakened by the roar
of something in the forest, but Shod was not their problem. They had
no time to collect themselves as an army of darkness invaded their
camp. These men hid amongst the shadows and they had every
intention of defeating Tobiah and his men. They quickly moved
throughout the camp and ended the lives of their opponents. Those
who were quick enough to ready themselves with weapons would
only get a glimpse of their attackers. They moved like shadows
within shadows as their dark clothing barely reflected the light from
the fire. Their speed and strength was overwhelming and, in the
darkness, their faces could not be seen. To Tobiah's men, this army
could have been nothing more than ghosts in the night for that is how
they appeared. It was impossible to tell how many men there were.
Their attacks were quick and soon Tobiah's men were dead, all
except for Tobiah.

They had captured Tobiah and dragged him to the light of the
campfire; his presence was no longer needed. They forced him down

to his knees and pulled his arms out to the side and back while they pushed his shoulders forward. Tobiah felt as though his arms could snap behind the pressure. One of them reached out and pulled Tobiah's head back so he could see what was happening around them. He finally saw the faces of his attackers and was surprised to see that they were only human despite their strength. Evil could be seen within their eyes as they stared down Tobiah. Tobiah's struggles were useless. He looked around the camp and saw all of his men dead and the faces of evil that had slaughtered them all. In the middle of it all, he saw a familiar face approaching.

"Tobiah, I am sorry it had to come to this," said Michael, "but, as you can see, there is no way that I could stop them, even if I wanted to."

"I knew it!" shouted Tobiah. "You have lied to us all! How could I have been so stupid?"

"I'm sure that is a question you have asked yourself before," replied Michael. "Fortunately, I won't have to hear you ask it again."

"What do you want from me? Let me die with my men!"

"You are in luck then. I am in the business of granting requests. Oh, and don't worry, you will have an eternity to find out whether or not the Amari will forgive you."

Knowing that he was defeated, Tobiah began to laugh before Michael.

"You think you have won," he said, "but you lost many years ago when you sold your soul out to evil. I at least have the hope of redemption. What does Ozgul offer you?"

"You fool," retorted Michael, "you are standing here on the brink of death and I have the whole world ahead of me. Power and riches are mine for the taking –"

"But I pity you!" shouted Tobiah. "You live only for this life and I hope you do enjoy it! As for me, I know of what the future holds and I shall be with the Amari forever!"

Michael bent down in front of Tobiah and said, "Then let me help you get there a little faster."

Michael stood up and moved to the side to reveal Shod standing behind him. As Tobiah prepared for his death, he welcomed it with an odd sense of joy. The last thing he remembered was not the face of Shod, or the army of men surrounding him, but a light shining in the distance that brought him peace. In that moment, he knew his soul belonged to the Amari and he was finally home.

11. IN THE DESERT

Ethan had been riding for what seemed like an incredibly long time. He was doing his best to get to Morgan as soon as possible, and, in order to do that, he had ridden day and night without stopping for food or water. To make matters worse, the desert was going to become his first major test as the Phayladin. Ethan came upon a small section of desert that was covered with large rock formations. This marked the edge of the Desert Lands. He pulled in close and stopped his horse. Even if he wanted to continue riding, the horse refused to go any further.

Ethan dismounted from his horse. He scanned the desert looking for something. He wasn't sure exactly what it was but he knew that he would recognize it when he saw it. He removed his sword from the saddle and reassured his horse that everything would be fine. The wind slowly began to pick up and swirled the sand around. Ethan pulled a hood up over his head and held it tight to his mouth and nose. He pressed forward toward the rocks to seek some shelter. As he did, he could tell that the lack of water was starting to get to him. His strength had left him and he was only going to survive this with the help of the Amari.

He climbed his way up to the top of one of the rocks and looked around. Before him was the end of a great plateau, and fifty feet in front him was a sharp drop to the desert valley below. He knew he would have to descend it in order to make his way forward. He looked for the best place to start, and, when he found it, he set out on his journey.

Riding through the desert was difficult enough for any man, but Ethan had set out on foot. It was impossible to know how long he had been walking, but, in his current state, it felt as though he had been out there for forty days. His breathing was becoming irregular as he would breath in some of the sand that was blowing around and cough it back out. The heat had taken its toll and Ethan was beginning to stagger as he walked. He had gone beyond the point of no return and was being led here for this moment. The Amari's test was about to begin. His legs gave out from under him; he fell to his knees, and collapsed, unconscious, to the ground.

The desert was quiet as Ethan lay motionless in the sand. Ethan's breath became staggered. His body took in one deep breath, slowly breathed it out, and Ethan stopped breathing. As he did, the world around him ceased all movement. The sand that was blowing stopped moving in the air. Time was standing still.

Almost as quickly as it had stopped, Ethan's breathing began. He stirred on the ground as his eyes fluttered open. His body still ached with exhaustion, he was still in the desert, but it seemed as though he was in another place and time. The scenery had grown slightly darker and a gray hue had taken the place of all the color in the Desert Lands. It was almost as though this world was the exact opposite of Eret. It took only a moment to realize what had happened. He had slipped into the other side of existence, the home of Persuaders and Destroyers.

He swore his eyes were playing tricks on him as all around him a haze began to form. The cloud encircled him as he lay in the sand and, one by one, the bodies of the heavenly beings appeared. As Ethan looked forward, he watched in amazement as the faces of Persuaders appeared in front of him in a way that he had never seen.

Their bodies had a glow that encircled them and light poured out from their eyes. The light was not obtrusive to Ethan's eyes, but rather it offered a calming feeling that seemed to overwhelm him. Each Persuader had their own unique features, from the shape of their faces to the length of their silver-like hair. Their bodies were covered in a metallic armor; each one identical to the rest. In the middle of their breastplates was the symbol of the Amari; a representation of the Orb of Pashii with wings stretching from the sides matching the wings on the Persuaders backs. There was a multitude standing before him and all of them were staring at Ethan. They were poised like an army waiting for their orders. However, in one motion, their eyes were averted to something behind Ethan.

Ethan was puzzled at the sight and slowly turned his head to look behind him. Before he could see it, he heard the voice.

"Welcome to the other side!"

The voice was unmistakably that of Ozgul's.

"Is this all that the Amari has to offer? All this time, I was worried that you would be a warrior. A monster of a human being whose body could be tested and not fail, but, here you are, weak and pathetic before me. So I wonder, what do we do now?"

Ethan pushed himself away from Ozgul as this was the first time he had seen this beast. Not only that, but behind him appeared a host of Destroyers, similar to the Persuaders, but void of any light. Their eyes were dark and it was nearly impossible to see the outline of their dark armor and skin. They appeared to be one dark object standing behind their leader. The black glow of each being consumed the light around them, and, they as well, were lined up in a battle formation. Ethan couldn't believe his eyes. He looked back at Ozgul.

"I could kill you, but we all know that wouldn't stop you and the Amari. He has the power to give life and he certainly won't let you die. Not today and not ever."

Ozgul paced his way around Ethan, sneering at him with every turn.

"If only your followers could see you now. They would certainly abandon you. 'The Phayladin cannot take care of himself; how can he ever take care of us?' they would say."

Ozgul threw himself to the ground so that he was inches away from Ethan's face.

"Don't you understand? You will lose this battle! In the end, you are still a human and you have your weaknesses. I may not be able to stop what you are doing but I will make it incredibly difficult for you to be alive!"

Ethan stared back into Ozgul's empty eyes and said, "You cannot win. The Amari is strong enough to save us all, and, if I must suffer, then I do it gladly."

"Where is he?" shouted Ozgul. "Look at you. Here you are in this weakened state and he cannot even provide for you! If he allowed it, you could have a feast presented before yourself. Don't you get it? He has forsaken Eret and left it in my hands. I am the god of this world and there is nothing you can do to stop me. You may be his chosen one but you are not him. If you are, prove it to us all, we are all waiting. Save yourself!"

Ethan slowly brought himself up to his hands and knees. He placed one foot out in front of him and used it to push off of in order to stand to his feet. He groaned as he straightened his body to stand before Ozgul. Without hesitation, Ozgul laughed out loud at the sight of Ethan's bravery and, almost instantaneously, he kicked Ethan squarely in the chest, sending him flying backward to crash into the sand once more. Ethan rolled on the ground, trying to catch his breath. He knew Ozgul could not kill him, but this had the promise of becoming the most painful experience of his life. The Persuaders never moved from their position. This was Ethan's battle.

"Where were your precious Persuaders for that one? Where were they to catch you when you fell like the prophets of old foretold? You see, you are alone in this world and we are here to stop you."

Ethan struggled to stand up again.

"How about this?" said Ozgul. "I will give you a choice. Bow down before me and I will surrender myself to you. That's right. You give me the honor that I deserve from the Amari and I will surrender everything over to you. All of their souls will be protected by your generous and humble offering."

Ethan stared him down unwilling to bow.

"Only the Amari is worthy of glory," he said. "I bow to him and to him alone."

"Do not be so quick to decide," said Ozgul. "Think of what I am offering. No more will I terrorize mankind. Your enemy will be gone, and I will be unable to hurt anyone, including, the ones you love."

Ethan reached out and unsheathed his sword from its place. He pointed it at Ozgul and said, "You will not tempt me any longer. I have made my decision. You have your place in all of this but, in the end, you lose."

"I may lose," answered Ozgul, "but can you live with the consequences?"

Ethan charged forward with his sword but Ozgul was ready. With a wave of his hand, he sent the sword flying from Ethan. Ethan watched in bewilderment as the weapon shot out from his hand and floated away from him. It spun through the air and landed in the sand. Ozgul laughed and approached Ethan quickly.

"You have no idea of the power I have on this side. I was created as the strongest being of my kind. In this land, I rule!"

Ethan managed to speak, "You have no power except what was given to you by the Amari. Unfortunately for you, the Amari and I are one."

Ethan lunged forward and punched Ozgul in the chest. The contact caused ripples to form in the air around it and the sound echoed into eternity. Ozgul's body went limp as he fell backward to the ground. He grabbed his chest where Ethan's fist had landed.

"So you are not as weak as I assumed you were," said Ozgul as he stood to his feet. "I won't make that mistake again."

"I'm not going to give you that opportunity," replied Ethan.

The two charged forward and collided. In the middle of the desert, a battle began that affected all of creation. As the two fought on the ground, the battle around them began as well. The Persuaders and Destroyers drew their weapons and charged to the fight. There was no foreseeable outcome to this battle as neither side would win at this moment. But there was a point that needed to be proven.

Ethan and Ozgul traded blow for blow. Ethan was able to muster up the strength to withstand the onslaught of attacks being delivered by Ozgul's hands. The battle raged around them but Ethan's eyes were fixed on the being in front of him.

Ozgul was on the move as his strength was close to that of Ethan's. He swung his fists in the air with the power of evil and, when the time was right, Ethan returned with attacks of his own, thrusting them toward Ozgul. He punched Ozgul in the face with his left hand, brought it back and hit him again with the same hand, and then followed that with a third strike using his right. The strength that he was missing had returned in the form of a supernatural adrenaline.

Ozgul stumbled backward from the strike but quickly regained himself. Ethan moved to deliver another strike on Ozgul, but Ozgul managed to grab Ethan's arm before it landed. He pulled on it hard, dragging Ethan around in a half circle, and hurling his body off to the side. He quickly ran over to Ethan and moved to stomp on Ethan's chest. Ethan rolled over and grabbed Ozgul's foot in the middle of its descent. He struggled under the force but managed to push it away from his body. He rolled over to his hands and knees but was not quick enough. Ozgul kicked Ethan in the face, and Ethan recoiled from the blow. Still on his knees, Ethan looked up momentarily to see Ozgul's fist collide with his face.

Dazed, Ethan managed to raise his arm to block the next attack. He forcefully stood up and drove his body into Ozgul's stomach. The power from the rush sent them tumbling over backward into the sand. Ethan grabbed Ozgul's body and pulled his upper half off the ground. In the same motion, he drove his head directly into Ozgul's. He let go and punched Ozgul in the face. Ozgul pushed off of the ground and flipped Ethan over his head and Ethan tumbled forward.

Ozgul rushed over to Ethan and pinned him to the ground. He loomed over top of him and attacked Ethan with his fists. He delivered three solid blows to Ethan's head and pinned him to the ground.

"I will give you one more chance to save the ones you love from pain. They will look back at all that has happened and they will blame you for their suffering and for their pain. If you bow before me, you will save them! Give me my honor!"

Ethan's mind flashed to all those that he loved: Morgan, Lillian, and King Hezra. He saw faces of the people who live in Bodain. They had already suffered through so much. However, the last image that his mind went to was that of his earthly father. He heard the girl scream as the horse raced toward her in the street. His mind went to a time when he and his father were smiling and playing with each other, and then returned to the girl as he saw his father run out into the road and grab the girl in his arms. He watched as the horse trampled over his father's body, and then as the little girl crawled out from underneath him. In that moment, through all the exhaustion, Ethan remembered what being the Phayladin was all about. His father had taught him the greatest lesson of all. He showed him a sacrificial love. He traded his life for another. Ethan came to his senses and focused his attention on the problem at hand.

Ethan yelled into the air, "I will never bow down to you!"

Ozgul screamed back and raised his hand into the air to continue the attack on Ethan, but he didn't get very far. At the moment of Ethan's declaration, a loud noise sounded throughout the heavens. The sound was so deafening that every being within range stopped what they were doing and held tight to their ears and collapsed to their knees. All of the Persuaders and Destroyers were momentarily unable to attack due to the pain from the sound. Even Ozgul and Ethan recoiled from the noise. It continued for only a few seconds but it seemed to last forever. The Amari had made his point clear; the battle was over, and the Amari had the final say in the matter. When the noise stopped, Ozgul and Ethan slowly turned over and stood to their feet.

"Remember this," said Ozgul, "you are only one man. You may win this battle in the end, but you cannot protect everyone you love. You can only be one place at a time and we are everywhere. Even your brother's life is in danger as we speak. Emperor Neroni is a possessed man who will do anything for me. But then, what about those you love in Bodain? What about the rest of this world? You can't save them all. You had your chance, Phayladin, and now you can regret it for the rest of your life. Believe me when I say, we will meet again."

With that said, Ozgul turned and he and the Destroyers flew away from the scene. Ethan took a deep breath and, instantaneously, his body left the heavens and returned to reality. He collapsed from exhaustion as everything returned to normal. The wind began to blow again and the heat returned to Ethan's face. Even his body was returned to its weakened state.

Out of nowhere, Persuaders began to appear and they were being led by Kitaan. Kitaan ran to Ethan's side and held the exhausted redeemer in his arms. The rest of the Persuaders rushed to Ethan's side and began to attend to him, helping him regain his strength. Even Ethan's horse had found its way back to him. Ethan's trial was over and he had proven himself faithful.

As soon as his health returned, he climbed upon his horse and rode further into the desert. He must hurry to get to Morgan.

12. THE DESERT CHILDREN

Just over the horizon, Ethan could see the Desert Kingdom begin to appear. It was surprisingly dark over this area of the desert and nightfall was a long time away. Ethan was not surprised. He knew that the current state of evil across Eret was at an all-time high. He could feel the selfishness of humanity beginning to grow. The times were becoming more and more perilous as the days went on with no relief in sight. This struggle would continue in this fashion until the time was right for the Amari to fulfill Ethan's destiny as Phayladin. It was something that Ethan had just come to accept. For him, it was impossible to fight the will of the Amari, and why would he want to? He knew what lay ahead and he was intent on fulfilling his mission.

Ethan knew that the Desert Kingdom was falling apart. He didn't have to be the Phayladin to figure that out. Emperor Neroni was losing his mind, not to insanity, but, rather, to the will of his possessor. He had all the power and wealth that he would ever need and he did not need the Amari any longer, or so he thought. However, his soul needed to be occupied by something and, if it wasn't the Amari, that left plenty of room for something else. Unfortunately, the only other alternative was evil.

He continued on toward the Desert Kingdom. From where he was riding, the kingdom sat below him in the lowest part of the Desert Lands. Surrounding the valley were large rocks and boulders that were scattered about but, for the most part, there was nothing but rolling sand dunes for as far as the eye could see. From time to time you would see low range mountains that had no dominance over any of the landscape. Many of these foothills contained underground tunnels that the people of the Desert Lands had used for protection and water for hundreds of years. Ethan knew immediately which way he was going to take and he headed off in that direction.

The caves were now being used as shelter for the outcasts of the kingdom. The poor, the sick, and the dying were usually expelled outside of the kingdom walls in order to maintain a society of high class. Living in the caves was primitive but it at least allowed them to have a life. They lived in the same way their ancestors lived before them and everything they needed, including water, was provided by the desert.

Ethan wanted to stop by the caves first. He desired to get some rest before he entered the kingdom and continued on his mission. He pulled his horse up to the edge of the valley and scanned the horizon for a cave to seek shelter. Just down the rim of the bowl was a cave that would do. He dismounted from his horse and led it to the mouth of the cave. He made it within a few yards of the entrance when the ground gave out from underneath him.

Ethan's feet fell out from underneath him as his body fell to the ground. He lost his grip on the reigns as his horse pulled away from the collapsing sand. Ethan had wandered into a trap. He tumbled down the sloping side of the hole and rolled to the bottom. He quickly closed his eyes and covered his head as sand poured down on top of him. Almost as soon as it began, it was over.

Ethan pushed himself up and started dusting off the sand. He soon noticed that he was buried in it up to his knees. He spit some out of his mouth and began to violently cough as he inhaled the sand left in the air. As it began to clear, he managed to wipe some of the sweat filled sand from his eyes to look above him. This was perhaps the most uncomfortable that he had ever felt in his life. Sand was everywhere. As he looked above him, the sun blinded his eyes. He strained to correct his vision as shadowy figures appeared all around him. As his eyes cleared, he saw exactly what he was looking for.

"We have you surrounded. Don't try to move."

Around the top of the hole, a group of children had gathered. Perhaps even more surprising were the spears that each of them held pointed directly at Ethan's face.

"We watched you coming in from afar," said one of the children.

"Who are you?" asked Ethan.

"My name is Ritga. I am the leader of this army. You will address me and me alone."

Ritga was a tall boy but his youth could still be seen in his face. From the looks of the other children who had gathered here, Ritga was probably the oldest. Ethan scanned the rim and saw a number of mixed faces staring back at him. Some showed of courage and honor, while others showed fear and loneliness. Ethan knew what was wrong.

"Where are your families?" asked Ethan.

"Don't act like you don't know," said Ritga. "We know that any adult roaming freely around the desert is one of Neroni's men and that includes you."

"I have nothing to do with the emperor. I come from a faraway kingdom called Bodain."

There were some whispers amongst the crowd of children. The mention of Bodain had apparently caused them to stir. Ritga noticed it as well.

"I don't believe you," he said quickly. "You are an adult, why should we trust you. If you had it your way, you would probably take us all one by one."

"That's where you're wrong," replied Ethan. "I have come here to help you. I want to help you."

The sides to the hole were slightly sloped and Ethan began to try and crawl out from the sand trap. His movements were quickly stopped when the children raised their spears higher. Ethan understood what they were saying. He raised his hands in the air and backed down to his original position.

"You are a liar!" shouted Ritga. "All of the adults, including our parents, have been taken to be slaves by the emperor and his people, and we have been left here to die."

The children began to whisper to one another.

"How many more of you are coming?" asked Ritga.

"No one else is coming," answered Ethan. "My name is Ethan, and I have been sent by the Amari to help you."

The whispering started again and even Ritga was involved in the secretive talks. Ethan could tell he was saying the right things.

"You may not know it, but I am here to bring you hope. Do you know about the Amari?"

"Don't be stupid," answered Ritga. "Of course we know the Amari. We have been waiting for him to answer our prayers, but he hasn't done that yet."

Ethan saw his opportunity, "Maybe you should consider the fact that I am here to answer your prayers."

The whispering began again only this time it had grown louder. It was obvious that not everyone was on board with the dispatching of Ethan's life.

"Have you heard of the Phayladin?" asked Ethan. "Because I am the Phayladin."

The whispering began furiously again and it was starting to bother Ethan.

"Ok, the whispering thing is really starting to freak me out," he said.

"We will whisper if we want to," declared Ritga.

Ritga waved his arm in the air and signaled someone behind them.

"You can't be the Phayladin," said Ritga. "The Phayladin would not be traveling alone in the middle of the desert, and we are done talking. One less adult means that we are one step closer to safety."

Ritga turned to the crowd and shouted, "Take the little ones away and get those dogs up here!"

The crowd began to disperse and those in the front were replaced by the dogs. Each animal was being held on a leash as the children holding on to the ropes gave their best effort to hold back the dogs. Their teeth were bared and they were barking in the general direction of Ethan. He couldn't help but feel sad for these children. Their innocence had been taken away from them and they were forced to survive. Ethan was growing angry, not at the children, but at Emperor Neroni and all of his men. Once out of this hole, he would make certain that the emperor received his punishment for this crime.

"Ritga," said Ethan, "I want to help you. I want to get your parents back and remove the emperor from power. You have to have faith in me that I can do that."

"I am sorry," replied Ritga, "maybe you are just in the wrong place at the wrong time, but I can't put my faith in what I don't see."

"But don't you understand," interrupted Ethan, "faith is believing in what you cannot see. It is how you can believe in the Amari, and it is how you can know that I am here to help you."

"We have talked long enough. I have to get these people back inside before anyone else comes. These dogs have not eaten in days. If you survive this, and, I do mean 'if', maybe we will talk again."

Ritga turned his back on Ethan and walked away.

"Release the dogs!"

The children let go of their ropes and the dogs leapt into the hole. A tear came to Ritga's eye as he walked away. This wasn't something he wanted to do, but it was necessary for their survival. He hoped.

One of the other children shouted, "Ritga! Wait!"

Ritga turned back to the hole as he could hear laughter coming behind him. He quickly ran back to the hole and his mouth dropped in shock. The laughter continued on as Ritga looked down to see his ferocious dogs playing with their captive. Ethan tried to hide his face as the dogs were licking his entire head.

Ethan looked up and smiled at Ritga, "You have some wonderful dogs here, and they seem to be great with children as well!"

For the first time, Ritga admitted to himself that there was something different about their prisoner.

"Get the spears ready!" he shouted.

Instantly, the dogs turned from Ethan and started growling at Ritga. They ran up the slope as Ritga backpedaled away."

"Down boys!" shouted Ethan.

One of the dogs looked back at him and whimpered.

"Oh, sorry," said Ethan playfully. "Down boys and girl."

The female dog was pleased and the dogs stopped their approach.

"How . . . how . . . did you do that?" stammered Ritga.

"I told you, I am the Phayladin. How about you throw me a rope and we will talk?"

Ritga didn't have time to respond as the other children were already one step ahead of him. They tossed Ethan a rope and helped pull him out. Once at the top, the children celebrated and moved in to embrace him. They surrounded him completely as each of them tried to cling to the legs of the Phayladin. The crowd grew as each one tried to move closer leaving Ritga alone in the back.

Ethan looked at Ritga and said, "Never let anyone steal your innocence. I am going to help you. You have my word."

Ethan felt a tug on his clothing and looked down to see a small child asking for his attention.

"Mister, can you help my brother? He's really sick and I don't want him to die."

Ethan's heart broke at the words of the child.

"Why don't you take me to see him?" said Ethan.

"There's more than one," said Ritga. "And we are getting worse by the day."

"Well, as their leader, will you give me permission to help?"

Pride entered into Ritga's face once again. He looked around at his tiny army and saw their faces pleading with him. He knew what he had to do.

"Follow me."

Ethan followed Ritga down the maze of tunnels. There were no lights on the wall, but there were children equipped with torches to illuminate the hall. After a few minutes of walking, they arrived at the mouth of a large cavern filled with beds, supplies, and children.

Ritga began, "Our ancestors dug out this part of the tunnels. This is the infirmary where we keep our sick. Go through that door in the back, and you will find the rooms in which we live. It gives us a place to survive, but it's nowhere near home. However, there is only one way out of those rooms and it is through that door."

"Tell me about the sick," said Ethan.

"It all started about a week ago," said Ritga. "Obviously, no one here is a doctor so we don't know what to do. They just started coughing and then collapsing."

"Take me to the sickest one first," said Ethan.

Ritga led him to a back corner where Ethan saw a young girl of maybe eight years. Her eyes were closed but Ethan could tell by her coughs that she was still with them. He knelt down beside her and took a deep breath. The scene was breaking his heart, but all of that was about to change. He took his hand and wrapped it gently around her neck.

Ritga jumped forward, grabbed his arm, and said, "What are you doing? Get your hand off of her neck!"

He pulled back on Ethan, but Ethan looked at him and said, "I'm trying to save your sister."

Ritga looked at him in disbelief and released his hold. He never said this girl was his sister.

"And," continued Ethan, "I am going to prove to you that I am who I say I am."

Ethan closed his eyes and said a prayer. The healing came instantaneously and the effects were just as fast. The little girl opened her eyes, looked at Ethan, and smiled.

"You have a very lovely face," she said. "You're someone special aren't you?"

Ethan smiled and said, "You are going to be fine."

All the children cheered behind Ethan causing him to smile. It was good to see some joy left in the world. This is where he needed to be. This was his inspiration to continue. After the healing of Ritga's sister, Ethan moved throughout the cavern healing all of the sick children. The children began singing and dancing, and, even Ritga, was having a good time. Once all the children had been attended to, Ethan called Ritga to his side.

"Thank you for your help," said Ritga. "I am sorry that I doubted you."

"You did what you thought was necessary to survive," continued Ethan, "but even that isn't worth taking the life of another. Self-defense is one thing, but murder is entirely different."

"I know you are right," said Ritga, "but I'm not sure what else I can do, though. The soldiers of the kingdom have been trying to kill us or take us ever since we moved up here. Our parents are gone and we had nowhere to turn. I may have made some wrong decisions, but I did what I thought was right."

"Listen," said Ethan, "you know the Amari and so you should know that our sins do not have to destroy our lives. Whatever you have done, the Amari can forgive you for it, and, when the Amari forgives you, it's like the things that you have done never happened in the first place. He makes you new."

Ritga thought about it for a moment.

"That's why I am here," said Ethan. "It's not what you have done but what you are going to do that matters. Things are going to get worse before they get better, but if you do exactly what I say, I promise you everything will be fine."

"I will do it," said Ritga proudly.

Down one of the tunnels they heard one of the child guards begin to yell, "There are soldiers coming! The soldiers are coming!"

Ritga stood up ready to fight.

Ethan grabbed his arm and said, "Relax, Ritga, you have trusted me this far, now do the right thing and continue to trust me."

Ritga sat back down and said, "What do you want me to do?"

"You need to get everyone to the back of the cavern where you call your homes and wait there."

"But, I already told you," objected Ritga, "there is only one way out of there into the infirmary. We will be trapped."

"You will be trapped," replied Ethan, "but I promise you they won't even know that you are there."

"But, what if you are wrong?" Ritga asked.

"You have to trust me. It's just going to take a little faith. You can either do what I tell you, or you can wait for them to come get you. As their leader, the choice is yours."

Ritga looked at the compassion in Ethan's eyes and knew that he was right. He stepped away from Ethan and yelled, "Tell everyone to get inside now! Move it! Move quickly!"

The children scrambled quickly. They didn't have to question their leader.

"Get everyone inside! The guards, the lookouts – everyone!"

He turned back toward Ethan and said, "How long do we have?"

"Not very long, we have to move fast."

The soldiers entered through the cave from its multiple entrances. They were given orders to take prisoner every child in the vicinity. The emperor had plans for each of them in the kingdom.

However, Emperor Neroni had ordered them to kill anyone who fought against them, and, as unbelievable as it seemed, the soldiers were willing to follow his orders.

The soldiers searched the caverns and were quickly discovering that there were no children in sight. They had searched for about fifteen minutes but found no one. The place was empty and quiet. Finally, the first group of soldiers entered into the cavern where all the sick children had been. Their feet came to a stop as they were surprised at what they had found. There were definitely signs that someone had been here but all they found was Ethan sitting on a rock. Ethan stood to his feet at the drawn swords of the soldiers but there was no one else in the infirmary with him.

"Who are you and where are the children?" asked the soldier in charge.

Ethan smiled and said, "My name is Ethan and obviously I am the only one in this room."

He was careful not to lie.

The soldier turned to his men and said, "Keep searching the caverns. They must be here somewhere."

"Now, settle down just a minute," replied Ethan. "Is there something I have done to deserve this?"

"It's nothing personal," the soldier said, "but I have orders to arrest every adult living outside of this kingdom. Between you and me, I could think of a hundred things that I would rather be doing than chasing down children and fulfilling the emperor's insane directives. Now why don't you tell me where the children are?"

As Ethan spoke to the soldier, the children were all gathered together in the hallway behind him. Ritga could not understand how the soldiers didn't see them standing there. Certainly, it was dark, but his men hadn't even checked down their hallway yet. He did his best to keep the children quiet while Ethan addressed the men. What they didn't know was that Ethan had used his power to alter the look of the infirmary. The entrance to the hallway had disappeared. The children could see out, but no one could see in.

"Listen," said Ethan, "if you have to take me in then let's just go. You obviously aren't going to find any children around here. You've looked everywhere and there's only one exit from this room." He waved his hand slowly in front of him and said, "These aren't the caves you are looking for."

The soldier paced around Ethan, "No, it appears as though these aren't the caves I'm looking for."

There was something suspicious going on, but he couldn't figure out what it was. He could clearly see that Ethan was right, and he was tired and ready to go.

"Very well, I may not have found the children, but I can at least bring you back with me. Congratulations," said the guard sarcastically, "you are the newest member of Emperor Neroni's delusions of grandeur."

"I'm going to be honest with you," replied Ethan, "it doesn't sound like you really mean that."

The soldier chuckled and said, "Am I really that transparent?"

"Well, you could say it with a little more feeling next time. Your delivery was way off."

From inside the hallway, the children were beginning to relax. The soldiers were moving away and none of them knew why. Everything was going perfectly as planned.

The man in charge looked at Ethan and asked, "Are you sure you don't know where these children are?"

"What do your eyes tell you?" asked Ethan. "I can tell you this. According to the Amari, it would be better for a man to tie a rock to his feet and be thrown into the water to drown, then to bring harm to a child. And I think that he was pretty serious when he said it."

The soldier thought over Ethan's words and said, "The Amari has long forsaken us and this land. Believe me; his eyes are not watching us now."

"The Amari has never forsaken anyone or anything, and I think you would be surprised to find out that he is closer than you know."

The soldier glared over at Ethan as silence filled the hall.

Ethan slowly and casually glanced over his shoulder to the hidden hallway and his eyes met Ritga's perfectly.

"However, if there were children in here, I would tell them the same thing I am telling you now. Be calm and stay low. Trust in the Amari and everything will work out in your favor. But until it does, trust in those you love and keep them close. This will all be over shortly."

Ritga heard the message loud and clear. They would have to sit tight and wait.

The guard looked at Ethan and said, "You are a very strange man, but I like you. It's a shame that I have to turn you over to slavery. I truly will regret this one."

"What are we waiting for?" replied Ethan. "The scenery has to be an improvement over this place and, maybe, I can get a semi-decent meal."

The guard laughed again and said, "Not even the Amari could fix that."

13. THE POSSESSED

In the days since Ethan had left to retrieve Morgan, the kingdom of Bodain had managed to run itself. Lillian was performing her duties as expected including meeting with the people and making judgments from the royal throne on the little matters that affected the people. She was quite thrilled that she had not even passed Lorcene in the halls and hoped to keep it that way. Up to this moment, things were running smoothly.

She had decided to take some time to herself and invited Emma to come out into the kingdom with her. She wanted to take the opportunity to visit the shops in the Merchant Circle and be amongst the people. Some of the finest products were imported on a weekly basis to Bodain and the Merchant Circle was part of the lifeblood of the kingdom. Every once in a while, Emma and Lillian would find themselves perusing the booths of fine cloths and beautiful jewelry. It proved to be an excellent way to forget about any of your worries

They were escorted by a covered carriage down through the streets of Bodain by the king's personal guards; some of the finest fighting men known to Bodain. Ever since being attacked by those people in the alleyway with Morgan and Ethan, Lillian was no longer allowed to travel alone without the proper escort. Tomar was with her always as well. His eyes may not be perfect but he had proven himself time after time and commanded the way as they traveled. They arrived at the Merchant Circle and began to clear a path as the royal escort drew the attention of many of the people. When the princess stepped out of the carriage, the people began to cheer. They had no reason to dislike her. She was kind and sweet to everyone she encountered and her beauty was talked about consistently inside the kingdom walls. Lillian took the time to greet some of the people and then the guards ushered her on.

Emma took Lillian by the hand and the two of them walked toward the fabric shop which was one of their favorite places. The guards took up their positions around them as the two of them moved from place to place. In the corner of the shop, Lillian saw a woman and her young daughter admiring the beauty of a fabric. The little girl kept hiding behind her mother while trying to sneak peeks at the princess. Lillian couldn't help but smile at the sweet child and went over to meet her.

"Excuse me," Lillian said, "but might I have the honor of meeting you?"

The mother quickly bowed toward Lillian as her daughter again hid behind her mother's tattered dress. Lillian had taken notice of the condition and quality of their clothing and thought she could help.

"Now, Cynthia," said the mother, "this is not how we treat our royalty. I'm sorry, My Lady, she is a shy girl."

"Do not think twice about it," replied Lillian. She bent down and got on eye level with Cynthia. "Cynthia, is it?"

The little girl gently nodded her head.

"How old are you, my darling?"

Cynthia held up five fingers to show her age.

"Five is such a good age," replied Lillian. "There are many days that I wish I could go back to being five years old. There wasn't a care in the world back then."

Lillian looked at the material that Cynthia and her mother were looking at. It was a fine silk dyed into an array of beautiful pinks and purples.

She looked back at Cynthia and said, "Are you two planning on buying this? It is beautiful!"

Cynthia looked up to her mom who said, "We could never afford such a thing, My Lady. We were just merely admiring its beauty."

Lillian stood up and smiled as she said, "Nonsense, such a beautiful pair of ladies need to have beautiful clothes to match. Please, take as much as you need for yourself and Cynthia and I will arrange for the bill to be sent to the palace immediately."

Cynthia's face marveled at the gesture but her mother objected, "My Lady, no. We were not looking for any handouts. We could not accept such an offer!"

"Please, ma'am," replied Lillian, "you do not have much of a choice in the matter for this fabric will find you one way or the other. It is my gift to you and it is an order from the princess."

The mother began to tear up. She bowed toward Lillian and said, "Thank you, Princess, for the undeserved gift! You are a testament to the fact that even in these dark days, there is still good left in the world."

After seeing her mother's approval of the gift, Cynthia ran to Lillian and launched herself into a hug. Lillian and her mother laughed as Lillian stumbled for just a bit and then bent down to hug the child as well. They said farewell and Lillian and Emma began to move on to the next shop. As they were being escorted out, a loud commotion began to take place across the circle. They stopped their movement to see what was happening.

A man was mumbling loudly as he fumbled his way out of a shop. The owner was kicking and shoving the man, yelling at him to leave. The man looked as though he was drunk as his speech was slurred and his movements were hindered. The owner knocked the man down and spit on him. He started yelling for the guards to take the man away, but the man staggered to his feet, his movements were rigid and not graceful. Guards were slowly moving in but did not seem to be in a hurry. As the man stood back up, he began to vomit onto the street. The guards stopped their pursuit so as not to be covered by the splash. Something was clearly wrong with this man.

From the other side of the circle, came another commotion, and, soon, there were multiple people showing the same symptoms as the first man. The crowd was growing uneasy and so were Lillian and Emma. Tomar grabbed Lillian's arm and commanded her security to begin getting them out of there.

They began to clear the way but, as they did, the first sick man called out, "Princess Lillian! Ugly, ugly, Princess Lillian!"

Soon the others who were ill began to do the same thing. Lillian stopped running and became still. Something evil was in the circle and the tension in everyone's demeanor showed that everyone felt the same. The Merchant Circle's guards moved to overtake the four individuals who were causing the commotion. They reached for the first man but as they did, all four of them turned their heads and hissed at the guards, a low growl was soon to follow. In a drastic turn of events, they charged at the guards and suddenly showed no signs of whatever was plaguing them. The guards tried to draw their swords but they were quickly overtaken by their strength and speed. The people stared as their bodies were frozen in fear at the violence set before them. Screams slowly began to overtake the area. Some people ran while others could not take their eyes off of the event.

Lillian looked at Tomar and said, "We have to help those men! Do something!"

Through his faulty vision, Tomar could only imagine what was actually happening, but his duty was to protect the princess at all costs.

"Princess, we have to get out of here. It is not safe for you to be here!"

As he said that, the attackers stopped beating on the dead guards and growled and hissed in the direction of the princess. Emma huddled close to Lillian and their security readied themselves for the worst. The attackers bared their teeth at the princess; their eyes were black as night. They stood together and lined up beside each other. As they did, they began to speak at the same time.

"Princess Lillian," the four voices were in exact synchronization with each other but they spoke in different tones and pitches. It was extremely eerie. "You are not the ruler of this kingdom- we are. We are taking over the lives of your people one at a time and we will not stop until Bodain falls."

The people cringed at the sound of the four voices together.

Lillian interrupted them and said, "Who are you? What do you want?"

The voices continued, "It does not matter. Bodain will bow at our feet as we possess the people you are trying to save and nothing can stop us! The possessed will overrun you all!"

These were the last words spoken by the Destroyers as they were each struck with arrows from behind where Lillian was standing. More guards had finally arrived. They moved in to protect the princess to allow her to flee. The arrows found their marks but it only infuriated the possessed. Using a strength given to them from the possession, they ripped out the arrows and began to jump from building to building; destroying whatever was in their path. It was inhumane and scary. Tomar yelled for Lillian's security to begin their evacuation. The guards moved back as they protected Lillian and Emma who were absolutely scared for their lives. During the retreat, one of the possessed sprinted toward the security forces and leapt high into the air. The soldier, with sword ready, plunged it directly into the body but the man would not die. He made sounds like that of an animal as he tried to grab the soldier. It took every ounce of strength that the soldier had to keep him at arm's length. Lillian had already made it back to the carriage and was on her way back to the palace with all haste. The possessed man knocked the soldier backward, and with the sword still embedded in his body, he ran away. The people who had not managed to flee the circle watched as the four possessed began to scale the walls of the nearby buildings and disappeared over the rooftops. Screams could be heard from a distance as the possessed continued their attack.

Lillian and Emma huddled together as they rapidly raced through Bodain. Lillian peered out the window but did not like what she saw. The circle was not the only place being ravaged by the possessed. She saw people running for their lives as they were being attacked. She could barely breathe or find the words to speak.

The Destroyers were not the only ones who were present in the moment. From above, the Persuaders were engaged as much as they were allowed to be. Sevron flew above the carriage, keeping his watch on the princess. It was easy to tell who the possessed were from his perspective. Black smoke trailed from the bodies of the humans that were possessed as if they were leaking it out. It was only visible to the Persuaders and Sevron could see many of them approaching from all directions. He swooped down closer to the carriage. He had no power to rescue those who were possessed but he could do everything in his power to protect the princess. His spiritual form landed on top of the carriage, unseen to everyone, and he waited.

Lillian clung to the side of the carriage to keep from being tossed about. She hoped to be back inside the palace sooner rather than later. Her fear rose to a new level as she witnessed one of the possessed running along the rooftop parallel to her carriage. She watched as the woman jumped from rooftop to rooftop with great ease. As she came alongside the carriage, the woman leapt from the rooftop and landed on the side of the carriage; rocking it back and forth. The monster of a woman tried to climb her way in through the window and Emma and Lillian screamed as they pressed up against the opposite side. Sevron drew his spiritual sword and used it to shatter the wood that the woman was clinging to, as the spiritual was allowed to affect the physical at any time. Her hand slipped as the wood mysteriously splintered and she struggled to regain her balance. It bought them just enough time.

As Emma and Lillian huddled together, Tomar climbed down into the back of the carriage next to Lillian and punched the woman in the face until her hands let go completely and she tumbled onto the ground below. Lillian looked out the back window and saw the woman roll to a stop, stand up, and begin to chase after them again. She saw the hatred within the woman's face and it was an image that would not go away.

Sevron scanned the road ahead for danger, however, he was instantly blindsided by a Destroyer. The two spiritual bodies collided and it sent Sevron tumbling off of the carriage top. As they rolled on the ground Sevron managed to use that momentum to throw the Destroyer out of the way. He drew his sword and stabbed the Destroyer in the torso. The Destroyer's wings flared out behind him as he roared in pain and then dissolved away. Sevron turned his attention back to the carriage which was already a distance ahead. He unfolded his wings and pushed off the ground and flew with all of his might.

As the carriage raced down the street, the carriage driver continuously whipped the horses to run faster causing the passengers to bounce around violently. The palace gates were directly within their sights, however, their destination would take longer to reach then they anticipated. Sevron looked ahead and saw a possessed man standing in the street in front of them. The carriage driver had no choice but to continue forward as he could not avoid the man but intended to run him over.

Sevron caught up with the carriage and soared past it to charge toward the man. He flew faster than the horses could run and, as he approached the Destroyer, it looked directly at him and screeched in his direction. Sevron was unfazed by the Destroyer's battle cry. He could not separate the Destroyer from the man's soul without much more of a fight, but he could still attack. He reached inside the body of the man and grabbed the spirit of the Destroyer. His momentum, along with his strength, allowed him to pull the Destroyer backward. Due to the strong connection that the Destroyer shared with the man's soul, it refused to let go. Sevron's pull lifted the man off of his feet and he threw him through a window of a nearby building. The carriage driver was in disbelief. He could not explain what he just saw but was thankful for any help that they could get. Sevron's efforts to protect the carriage were brave, but he could not be in multiple places at once.

One of the possessed stormed out of the alley and threw his shoulder into the side of the horses pulling the carriage. The collision was strong enough to knock the horses into each other and send them tumbling to the ground. Sevron turned around quickly to see the carriage begin to crash. The driver was instantly thrown off of his seat and into the street ahead of the horses. The axel holding the front wheels of the carriage snapped under the weight and the carriage began to flip.

The momentum of the carriage had brought it close to Sevron's position. He held his arms wide and braced himself. As the carriage began to roll, Sevron caught the top of the carriage in his arms. Even in his spiritual form, he could not keep the carriage from pushing him backward as his feet slid along the stone ground. He managed to keep the carriage from flipping further, bringing it to a stop. The passengers inside were disoriented from being tossed about like dolls. It was a violent collision and they felt a very violent pain.

The three of them unpiled themselves from each other and Tomar helped them make their way out. From outside, they could hear the screams of the possessed filling the street. Soldiers were yelling at each other as more than one of the possessed began to attack. Tomar kicked in the door of the nearest building, grabbed Lillian's arm, and dragged her in behind him. In an instinctive move, he kicked the door closed; accidentally leaving Emma out on the street. Sevron flew inside after them.

Emma stood up and instantly became dizzy. She had bumped her head really hard in the crash and was feeling the effects of it. She stumbled forward and watched the scene unfold before her. The horses broke free from their reigns and were running away. The possessed were overwhelming the guards who were retreating toward the palace. They were quickly losing the fight and quickly losing their lives. In a complete daze, she tripped over a body lying on the ground. Her head hurt too much to move her body. She lay on the ground breathing heavily; the sun was glaring into her eyes as it reflected off of the surroundings and her vision was blurry. However, she didn't have to see clearly to see what was happening. The possessed had turned back around and were headed toward her.

Emma had given up hope of surviving and couldn't find the strength to move. She watched in horror as the possessed grew near. However, someone else was watching the scene unfold as well. Her eyes turned to a man's hand picking up a sword lying on the ground. She couldn't see his face but he ran between her and the possessed and stabbed the first one through the heart. He fell to the ground, lifeless, and the Destroyer let go of its hold on the man and flew away to find its next victim. However, more possessed were already closing in on Emma's protector. She watched as the man moved swiftly to stand between her and the attackers.

The man turned slightly and pointed at her as he screamed something she couldn't understand to someone behind her. As he pointed, her eyes locked on to what looked like the Seal of Ozgul. It was Balak. She felt someone's hands grab her off the ground as the man braced himself for the attack. Her head spun around to see Tomar looking down at her. He picked her up in his arms and began to carry her inside the building.

Balak could no longer be concerned for Emma as he had bigger things to worry about. He had managed to kill the first one but more than one would prove to be harder to handle. He held his sword with both hands, suppressed his fear, and charged toward the possessed. The first one leapt into the air to land on top of Balak but he was ready. He rolled to the side and back onto his feet. The possessed man landed and tried to spin around but Balak's drove his sword through the man's back. He ripped it back out and turned to brace for the next one but the sword was knocked out of his hand.

He was quickly tackled by another one of the possessed and tumbled to the ground. The possessed woman rolled on top of him and began to slam her fists into Balak's chest. He frantically tried to push her arms aside and, as he did, she leaned in to try and bite him. He grabbed her by the neck and lifted his hips off the ground, rolling her off of his body.

He scrambled to get to his feet and saw the futility of his efforts. He turned his head to see more possessed racing toward him from all directions. There was no way he would give up without a fight. The world seemed to slow down as the possessed drew near. Balak knew this day would someday come. He let his guard down and braced himself for the inevitable.

14. TO REUNITE

The world of Eret was growing darker by the day. It wasn't just that evil was infecting the people of the land, but it also came because good people were becoming indifferent. With the rise of evil noticeably taking over their lands and villages, it became all too easy to hide behind the doors to their homes rather than fight. Hope was diminishing across the world, not from choice, but from fear.

The darkness was surrounding everything, from thoughts and emotions, to the skies above. They were falling upon difficult times and it seemed as though the Amari had forsaken them, but the world could not be more wrong. The Amari was speaking loudly to his children, but the darkness served as a wall. It was not impenetrable, but it was an obstacle that was poisoning the people. If they chose, the people could see beyond it, but it was easier for humanity's free will to move toward darkness. To accept darkness was easy and natural. To fight against it provided the struggle of life and the triumph as well. But the Amari knew what was coming and, after every nighttime sky, there comes a new day.

Emperor Neroni lay silently in his bed. His chamber room was one of exquisite quality. The four posts of his bed were decorated by skilled craftsman and made of the finest gold harvested from the desert's mountains. The sheets were made of the finest quality linens and enveloped his body within them as he slept. Tonight, however, his sheets were being tossed about. As he slept, his dreams were plaguing his mind. The Amari was telling him a story of his future.

Neroni awoke suddenly. The sweat poured from his brow and his chest heaved from the short and choppy breaths that his lungs desired. The dream had frightened him immensely, yet, he did not understand it. As he sat in his bed, the images unfolded in his mind and were clearly seen.

At the start of his dream, he stood on the highest point on Eret. The kingdoms had gathered before him, and the kings of each nation had ascended to meet him. Neroni addressed the crowd of rulers and turned to sit in his throne. Neroni looked around and, to his left, was a paradise of riches, but, to his right, was a cemetery of defeat. Spirits of the dead hovered around the cemetery, whispering Neroni's name into the air. The sky before him was glowing the color purple and its hue was coloring the world around it. The emperor summoned the first wave of kings to present their gifts to him. Three kings each ascended the steps to his throne with their gift in hand. Once they were at the top, they held their gift before them and descended to one knee.

Neroni stood before them once again and proceeded to the first king on his left. He reached out and opened the box containing his gift, but was appalled at what his eyes beheld. The box was filled with only sand from the desert.

The first king looked at the emperor, bowed his head, and said, "A gift fit for an emperor of your stature, My Lord."

Neroni ignored the box, appalled by its content, and moved to the next. He slowly opened the second box with anticipation only to be disappointed again. Anger built up inside of him as he saw a box filled with only rocks.

The second king looked at the emperor, bowed his head, and said, "A gift fit for an emperor of your stature, My Lord."

By now, Neroni was becoming furious. These gifts were hardly fit for an emperor. He knocked the second box out of the king's hand and sent it tumbling down the steps behind him, but the king still smiled at Neroni. Quickly, he moved to the third box and paused only to notice the poor quality of the box. It was not decorated at all, but rather a simple wooden box with an emblem of the Orb of Pashii upon it. He ripped open the lid to reveal nothing more than an empty box.

The third king looked at the emperor, bowed his head, and said, "A gift fit for an emperor of your stature, My Lord."

After the third box was opened, the emperor stepped back. He looked before him, as one by one, the kings and kingdoms before him began to disintegrate. They quickly disappeared until one man remained. As the man approached, fire behind the emperor began to grow. The spirits that were whispering his name were growing louder with each breath. He watched in horror as their arms were reaching out for him. He could feel the warmth of the fire behind him growing throughout his body, but he could not move. The light from the fire showed upon the man's face and, just as it was recognizable, the emperor awoke.

The same dream had been occurring every time he slept. He had no understanding of what it meant, but now he was determined to figure it out. In yet another measure of his growing insanity, Neroni issued a decree throughout his kingdom. One by one, the people of the desert kingdom would be given the opportunity to interpret his dream for him. The one who succeeded would be given riches and power, but those that failed would be done away with in a manner fitting Neroni's desire.

Neroni scrambled through the kingdom looking for his answer. He started first with those in close position around him. He turned first to his magicians and psychics. It was their job to perform miraculous feats for him. They entered into his presence with much intrepidness. They knew their emperor well enough to know that he was serious about his decree.

"Which one of you can solve my problem?"

The magicians turned first to the psychics and said, "My Lord, the psychics have been blessed with the power to see the future. We suggest that you seek their counsel first."

"I am in agreement," replied Neroni. "Solve these nightmares for me so I may sleep."

"My Liege," replied the psychic, "we are not able to tell of your dream for we are here only to tell of your future. We can tell you that your future is bright and prosperity is yours for eternity. But we cannot see into the past as that is not our gift."

Neroni was unsatisfied with their reply.

"I have had these dreams every night and I will have it again tonight. So tell me, what do you see in my dreams tonight, which is the future?"

The psychics were tensing up. No answer was being given and the emperor had grown impatient.

"Tell me, what do you see of your future?" asked Neroni.

The psychics could sense where Neroni was headed with his speech and they looked to each other for answers.

"Take them away and lock them in the dungeons!" shouted Neroni. "You are nothing but frauds! You and any family you have will be forever surrounded by darkness!"

The psychics tried to run from the guards but they were quickly overtaken. Emperor Neroni turned to his magicians.

"Tell me what I want to know," he said.

"With all due respect, My Lord, there is not a man alive who can tell you what your dreams are. Tell us of these nightmares and we will help you define them."

The emperor stood and said, "Blah, blah, blah! You have nothing but excuses! Take them away as well and start bringing in the prisoners. Someone will tell me of my dreams or everyone will die."

The guards immediately moved on to the task at hand.

The captain that had taken Ethan captive in the cave had grown to like Ethan very much. He even insisted that Ethan ride in on a horse instead of being chained and forced to walk. The captain had grown tired of doing the emperor's work but knew of no way out of his service.

"So tell me your name," the captain said.

"My name is Ethan," he replied.

"My name is Captain Ardone, son of the emperor and heir to a whole lot of sand."

"So, Neroni is your father, then? How did you come to find yourself as a captain in the army?" said Ethan. "Shouldn't you be holed up in the palace somewhere?"

"I can think of better things to be doing, but my father insists that I learn the way of a true warrior. Don't ask me how arresting children and murdering families has anything to do with being a warrior."

"You disagree with your father, then?" asked Ethan.

"Of course I do," responded Ardone. "This is not how a kingdom should be run. The people here live in fear and our slave population far outweighs the amount of citizens who belong to the kingdom, but he is my father and I shall respect that. There are moments when I actually wonder how he and I are related. However, things will be much different when I am emperor. I want for my children to know what it means to respect others."

"That sounds like a good goal, and I can understand why you would be frustrated," replied Ethan.

"Enough about me, though. I'm sure I have said too much already. What brings you to the desert?" asked Ardone. "You obviously aren't from around here."

"I am actually here because of my family," replied Ethan. "I have come to find my brother and bring him back to Bodain."

"It looks as though your search may be interrupted."

"Not at all," said Ethan. "He is a slave inside of this kingdom and I intend to go in there to find him and bring him home."

Ardone began to laugh out loud.

"You are truly an interesting man," he said. "Why do I get the feeling that there is more to you than I know?"

Ethan smiled and said, "Because there is. I have been sent by the Amari to rescue Eret from Ozgul's reign of terror. I am the Phayladin."

Ethan's remarks caught Ardone off guard.

"Just when I was getting used to you I find out that you are crazy," replied Ardone. "What will you tell me next? Can you read my thoughts as well?"

"I know that you have a heavy burden on your heart," replied Ethan. "And it pains you that you cannot be at home during this time."

Ardone looked over at Ethan and said, "You expect me to believe that you are the son of the Amari. The one who has been promised to redeem us all? That's impossible. The Amari left this forsaken place a long time ago. He has no reason to be here now."

"This place is filled with death and destruction," replied Ethan. "What better place for him to be than here? There is much that is happening in the world outside of this desert. The balance of good and evil has shifted and the time has finally come for the Amari to permanently intervene, and that is why I have come to the Desert Kingdom."

They were approaching the gate to the slave community and were interrupted by another guard.

"Captain Ardone," said the guard, "do you have any prisoners to report?"

Ardone looked at Ethan. He could tell there was something different about him and regretted having to turn Ethan over to this dungeon.

Ethan sensed his hesitation and said, "This is what must be done."

Ardone reluctantly pointed at Ethan and said, "This is the man I have brought. Take him in, but treat him with a level of respect."

Ethan climbed down from the horse and said, "I wish you well, Ardone. I expect our paths to cross again."

The guard to the slave's area began to escort Ethan inside, but Ardone was not done with him yet.

"*Wait!*"

Ardone climbed down with urgency from his horse and ran after Ethan and the guard. Ethan turned to face him.

"You know my heart is heavy," said Ardone, "so you must know that my daughter is dying. She is only a child of four years and is the light of my world. I can't bear the thought of life without her. I do not understand it but I believe that you are the Phayladin. You can save my child from this fate. I know you have your reasons for being here and, far be it from me to interrupt, but, if you just say the words, I know she can be healed. I would gladly trade my life for her chance to live."

Ethan looked at Ardone with compassion in his eyes.

"Your faith is strong," said Ethan, "and there is no need to trade in your life. You have a bright future ahead of you. I tell you the truth. Your answer is heading this way now."

That was all Ethan said and he turned to go find his brother. Ardone watched as the two of them disappeared into the prison. He didn't understand what had happened but he knew of nothing else to say. As Ethan entered in, he looked back over his shoulder to see a man quickly approached Ardone. The expression in Ardone's face had said it all. The man had brought Ardone the news that his daughter had been miraculously healed. Ethan smiled and continued inside. Ardone looked in the direction of Ethan, but could no longer see him. With much anticipation, he mounted his horse and rode off to his home to be with his wife and daughter.

15. OLD GRUDGES DIE HARD

The prison was located far on the outskirts of Emperor Neroni's palace. Once inside, there were rows of houses that the slaves shared with one another. The place reminded Ethan of the Shakack only a lot hotter and covered with sand. The amount of people in slavery under Neroni's rule far outnumbered the amount of people living in the Desert Kingdom but their oppression had made it so that the slaves did not know their size or what they were capable of doing. As far as they knew, there was no escaping this prison as the entire community was surrounded by guards, dogs, and a tall fence. Ethan was impressed by the size of the place, but quickly began to look for Morgan.

The community may have been impressive but the living conditions were not. The houses were no more than four walls and partial roofs, and it was not uncommon to find the number of people outnumbering the number of beds in each shelter. All around, men, women, and children were scattered throughout the area. For the most part, they seemed free, but the presence of guards with their whips at hand showed them otherwise. At the center of the prison, there was a large quarry that had been chipped away at for years. Neroni was using these rocks to build himself a palace that would stretch into the heavens. He looked around to see people chipping away at the rocks that made up the walls.

Captain Ardone had asked that the guards treat Ethan with a level of respect and the guards did just that. He wasn't mistreated at all as they got him situated into his new home. Needless to say, Ethan had no desires to stay here longer than necessary, and the guards had no intention of letting him get comfortable. They immediately walked him to his work spot and gave him his pick axe.

After explaining the type of work Ethan was supposed to do, the guard laid down the rules.

"The rules here are simple. If you do what you are told you will not be harmed by any of our guards. We don't want to be here any more than you do. If you step out of line, however, there's no telling what your punishment will be. So, I suggest that you just accept that you have no options but to do what we say. Escape is impossible so put those thoughts out of your head right now. You will be served three meals a day, be allowed six hours of sleep, and will be here for the rest of your life."

"Why would I ever want to leave?" said Ethan. "This place sounds magical."

Ethan's sarcasm never even fazed the guard who ignored Ethan completely. He gave Ethan a look of contempt, and said, "Dinner will be in less than an hour, but that doesn't mean you can't get to work now."

Ethan grabbed the tools and turned to go to work. As he walked through the quarry to his spot, he saw hundreds of warn out men and women slaving away, from young to old. It broke his heart to know that at some point in time, all of them were probably happy, raising their families without concern and, then in a moment, their world suddenly crashed to the ground. Countless lives had been lost at the hands of Neroni. This was the reason he was here and everything would soon come together, but the part that really got to him was that it all had to wait. At any point and time, the Amari could give him the opportunity to unleash his power on the world, but he wasn't there to dictate how people should live, he was just there to provide them with another option. He could think of a million other things that he could be doing with his life, but, for now, this was where he needed to be as it was where the Amari had led him. At least dinner was coming soon.

Morgan collapsed to the ground. He was partially ashamed at himself. He had done more work since he arrived in the Desert Kingdom then he had ever done before. He gently rubbed the palms of his hand in an attempt to massage the pain away, but they were too sore for comfort and blistering from the day. He rolled his fingers into the palm of his hand and clinched his fist to numb the pain. Unfortunately, he couldn't do the same for the welts on his back from the whipping he received. As far as he could tell, the skin only broke open in a few rare places but the pain was very real.

Nothing much could be said for the working conditions that Morgan found himself in every day. Every morning it was the same order of living. They were awakened early by guards with bad attitudes and poor pay. Morgan swore to himself that if he ever made it out of here, he would never force another human being to work for him ever again. However, the idea of him getting out of here was looking a little slim.

Time in the prison had given him the opportunity to evaluate his life. So much had happened in the past few weeks and it had begun to make him wish for home. Now that his father was gone, Bodain was probably spinning out of control. Not only did he destroy the lives of his family, but the lives of his people could be at stake as well. On top of it all, the last words he had spoken to Lillian were words of anger. He missed her severely, and, by now, she had probably made her way back home leaving him far behind. But no matter how often he thought about it, all of his problems came back to one person: Ethan

There wasn't much in the way of becoming clean in this pit, but there was a stream of water that flowed in from a nearby river. It wasn't good for drinking as no one could be sure what was in it, but it was at least a little cool to the touch and could get some of the dried dirt off of his skin before dinner. He knelt down, splashed some water on his face, and wiped it off the best he could with his shirt. He stood to his feet and made his way to the dinner line in a larger shelter inside the prison.

Morgan wasn't in a hurry either. The food would taste just as bad no matter how quickly he got it. He entered into the large area and immediately came to a halt as it felt like his heart had stopped.

He rubbed his eyes to make sure he wasn't seeing things. Standing directly in front of him was Ethan.

Morgan was instantly flooded with emotions. A part of him was happy to see him, but he was still caught up in the idea that Ethan had ruined his life. He stood there, frozen in time, and unable to speak. Ethan smiled at Morgan just a little bit. He had played this moment through time and time again, but now the moment had actually come.

"Morgan," began Ethan, "how are you?"

"What are you doing here?" asked Morgan. His voice was subdued and without emotion.

"I came to get you," replied Ethan. "It's time for you to come home."

That set Morgan off. He rolled his eyes and pushed Ethan out of the way and proceeded forward.

"Morgan, please," pleaded Ethan, "we need to talk."

"We have nothing to say to each other!" shouted Morgan. "You ruined my life, and now you want to come here and tell me what to do! I'm not going to stand here and just take that!"

By now, the people in the makeshift dining hall were staring at the two brothers. This was the most entertainment they had seen in days.

"Morgan, I didn't come all this way to fight with you," said Ethan. "I came here to help bring you home. So much has happened since you left. There's a lot I need to tell you."

Morgan had stopped walking away and turned again to face Ethan.

"Lillian asked me to come. She's worried about you."

Just hearing Ethan say her name was beginning to make him angry again.

"She's worried about you, and right now she is running Bodain by herself. You can't let her go through this alone."

"Leave her out of this!" shouted Morgan. "This is about me and you and nothing else. If it wasn't for you, none of this would have happened! You single-handedly ruined my life!"

"You know that isn't true," replied Ethan. "Look, bad things happened to us all, but life is about personal responsibility."

"Do not start preaching to me! I had everything that I wanted before you became the Phayladin. You spent your entire life living in my shadow and, in one moment, you try to take everything from me. I will never be able to forgive you. In fact, I don't want to even look at you. Just stay away from me."

Morgan turned to walk away, but Ethan wasn't done talking. He calmly walked up behind Morgan and put his hand on Morgan's shoulder. Unfortunately, that set Morgan off.

He spun around and lunged into Ethan, driving him back into a wooden post suspending the ceiling. The force was enough to jostle it just a bit from its original position. Ethan reached up and grabbed Morgan's hands to try and pull them off, but Morgan quickly pulled Ethan away from the post and threw him to the floor. Ethan fell forward onto the floor and quickly turned himself around. Morgan was beginning to circle him with his hands out in front of him.

Ethan slowly got up to his feet and said, "Is this what you want?"

Morgan glared back at Ethan and said, "This is what I want. And I'm not stopping until you get what you deserve."

"But there's much more that I need to tell you," replied Ethan.

"But I don't want to hear it anymore."

"Then do what you have to do."

The crowd was getting riled up for this fight. In a moment, they managed to encircle the two brothers, cheering for the fight to continue. It was time to handle this like brothers do.

Morgan shuffled his feet forward and took a swing at Ethan's head. Ethan pulled back as Morgan's fist swung in front of his face. He countered Morgan's attack and swung his fist back into Morgan's stomach, but Morgan barely flinched. He blocked Ethan's second swing and threw his forearm squarely into Ethan's chest. Ethan stumbled backward and was unprepared for Morgan's next attack. His fist collided with Ethan's face. Ethan fought to regain his balance and stood up straight just long enough to see Morgan running, hurling his body into his own. As Morgan pushed him backward, Ethan took his elbow and brought it down onto Morgan's back, but the attack turned out to be useless.

The two of them collided with the wall of spectators and were immediately pushed back into the makeshift ring. They separated as they fell but quickly found each other again and began to wrestle. Morgan got the upper hand and found himself on top of Ethan, pinning him to the ground. Ethan's arms were still free but the tumble to the ground left him slightly disoriented. He looked up as Morgan brought his hand back to hit Ethan again.

"Morgan, wait," said Ethan.

"I've done enough waiting already," came Morgan's reply.

Between breaths, Ethan managed to say, "Then you leave me no choice."

He quickly reached up and grabbed Morgan's shoulder. Using an unseen power, he managed to pop Morgan's shoulder out of place. Morgan screamed in pain and Ethan pushed him off from on top of him. Morgan squirmed and struggled to get to his feet. The pain was shooting through the entire side of his body. He searched for a nearby pole and, upon finding one; he reared back and slammed his shoulder into the large pole, screaming louder than the first time. He felt it pop into place and staggered backward. As he did, he heard a loud voice echo through the chamber.

"*That is enough!*"

The crowd instantly got quiet and began to quickly disperse.

"Grab those two men!"

Guards instantly rushed in and grabbed Morgan and Ethan. They were too tired to fight and went quietly to the guard in charge.

He looked at Ethan and said, "Is there a problem here?"

Ethan looked up and said, "No sir, we were just having a discussion."

"You've been here for less than two hours, and you are already causing problems on my watch! This makes me very upset. Tell me, by any chance, did you work out your differences?"

The two of them looked on without saying a word.

"Very well," continued the guard, "what do you suppose we should do about this? Rules are here for a reason and to break one of those rules should bring about some form of punishment. If I let one offense go, soon we will have a riot on our hands."

The guard stepped back to address the whole crowd.

"Let this be a lesson to anyone who thinks they are above the law! From here on out, anyone wishing to take matters into their own hands will be whipped immediately!"

With that, the guards pulled Morgan away from Ethan.

"Wait, no! Wait!" shouted Ethan.

"Don't worry, you will be next," said the guards.

Two men pulled Morgan's arms wide as another tore the clothing off of his back. The man in charge was handed his whip. He rolled up his sleeves and let the whip unravel to the ground. Morgan tried to fight back just a little but realized it was useless. He braced himself for the pain he knew he was about to face. Ethan caught a glimpse of the wounds on Morgan's back from his previous whipping as the guards prepared him for more.

"I beg of you, don't do this," said Ethan.

The guards continued to ignore him. "Think about your family!" he shouted.

The guard with the whip stopped what he was doing and turned his attention back to Ethan.

"Young man, are you threatening me?" he asked.

"Not at all," said Ethan. "I just thought you would want to know the consequences of your actions."

"Do you really think there is anything you could do to harm me?" replied the guard.

"I would never dream of doing anything to harm you," said Ethan. "I just thought that you should know that the man you are about to punish is Prince Morgan of Bodain. Imagine what the emperor would do to you and your family when he finds out what you have done to someone as valuable as this."

The guard paused momentarily and said, "I don't believe you."

"Is that a chance that you are willing to take?" asked Ethan. "Because I don't believe that you are. There's too much at stake."

The guard looked at Ethan and laughed. The others joined in as well. Ethan stood there staring at the man with the whip. The guard continued his laughing as he turned back to where Morgan was being held. As he raised the whip into the air, Ethan closed his eyes and said a prayer under his breath. The guard brought his arm back and, as he moved to strike the backside of Morgan, the leather in his hands burst into flames and was instantly consumed, turning to dust. His laughter ceased. His hand recoiled from the fire and he jumped back. The entire crowd became quiet as the event had left them all puzzled. Still in shock, the guard slowly turned his head toward Ethan. His body was beginning to shake. Ethan said nothing but looked at the guard with compassion.

"Wh– wh- what did you do?" asked the guard.

"Now, just relax," said Ethan. "I couldn't let you make that mistake. Someday you will thank me."

The guard looked at Ethan. He reached up and rubbed his eyes as though he needed a better explanation for what had just occurred and fear was beginning to take control of his heart.

"This man is one of Ozgul's!" shouted the guard. "He uses magic to control us all!"

Ethan began to object, "Not at all. I'm here on behalf of the Amari."

"No one on earth has that kind of power!" said the guard. "You are possessed by Ozgul himself!"

Ethan spoke again to the guard, "Albado, relax!"

At the sound of his name, the guard again became speechless.

"Please, I am the Phayladin. The one sent from the Amari to restore Eret back to what it was . . . what it could have been."

The crowd around them was getting more and more confused by the moment, but they listened intently to the conversation before them.

"How did you know my name?" asked Albado.

"I know a lot about you," responded Ethan.

He turned and looked at the faces in the crowd.

"I know a lot about all of you," he continued. "A thousand years ago, the Amari promised to send one in his name to free you all from the darkness that surrounds you. Look at this place. This is not how your life was supposed to turn out. Many of you here are without hope. You have been separated from your families wondering if you will ever see them again. Day after day, you struggle to survive.

"Once, you were proud warriors. The Desert Land was known for your fierceness. You fought hard to uphold the values set forth by the Amari, but evil had another plan. Faced with hopelessness, you gave up the fight to provide for you homes and your families. Even many of the guards who work for the emperor have given up that which they treasured most. And nothing in this world should be more important than our families."

Ethan was looking directly at Morgan at this point. Morgan was feeling the weight of Ethan's stare on him and he turned his head away.

"And that is why I am here," continued Ethan, "to restore that which you once had, that which you long for now."

"How do we know that you are the real Phayladin?" asked someone from the crowd. "What can you do to prove that you are from the Amari?"

The crowd erupted. The people were all wondering the same thing and they began to talk amongst themselves.

Ethan raised his hands up to silence the crowd and said, "This is my promise to you. Within the week, you will all be set free."

The crowd immediately erupted again. Some of them looked at him as though he was speaking nonsense. Others were wondering how much of this could be true. The idea of freedom was something that they had all longed for but knew they would never see. The guards quickly worked to control the crowd.

Ethan turned back to Albado and said, "Take me to the emperor and you will have back your dignity."

Albado could not deny that there was something different about this man.

He thought about it for a moment and said, "Take these prisoners to the throne room and let the emperor decide their fate. He wants me to send him prisoners anyways. He can have his own fun with the two of you. And if you two are any good at interpreting dreams, maybe I will see you again. Take them away!"

The guards pushed Morgan toward the entrance. As Ethan turned to go, Albado grabbed his arm and said, "You had better be right. If you have lied to us all here in this room, I guarantee you will be wishing for death."

"You have my word, Albado. Place your trust in the Amari. Wait and see."

As they walked, Ethan looked over at Morgan and said, "Look, things definitely haven't turned out the way either of us planned, but let's agree to talk about this the first chance we get."

Morgan looked over at Ethan with a blank expression on his face and said, "This isn't over. Not yet."

16. THE IMPOSTER

The possessed swarmed toward Balak running with nothing but complete rage. Their speed carried them quickly and Balak was ready for death. However, in an odd twist of events, Balak stood shocked as the possessed, all of them at the same time, collapsed to the ground. Their bodies became lifeless except for their heavy breathing. Balak released the tension in his body and began to laugh as he turned to look all around him. He slowly started to cheer at the victory he didn't earn.

"Haha! Take that you stupid beasts! Not today! Not today!"

He was so relieved to be alive still that he began rambling on like a fool. In his moment of joy, he never even noticed that he was no longer alone on the road. After kicking dirt repeatedly onto one of the possessed, he looked up and saw Lillian, Emma, and Tomar staring at his celebration. However, Balak's joy in that moment would not be ruined.

"Did you see that?" he shouted as he pointed to the possessed littering the ground. "Did you see that?" Balak laughed harder at the sight and said, "That's what you get when you mess with me!"

He bent over and placed his hands on his knees and tried to catch his breath. He pointed at Emma and said, "I'm sorry, I completely forgot. Are you three all right?"

Emma was the first to speak, "We are fine. Thank you for saving my life, good sir."

Lillian spoke up and said, "Yes, thank you. We owe you our lives. You, however, do not look so well."

Balak was confused until he saw where Lillian was pointing. Blood was rushing out of a deep wound on Balak's side. In the rush of adrenalin, Balak had failed to notice the severities of his injuries.

He placed his hand to the wound to try and stop some of the bleeding but it just continued to flow.

"This old thing," said Balak, "it's just a flesh wound."

Balak looked like he was about to pass out and collapsed to his knees. Tomar ran over to him to help steady him as Balak's eyes rolled back into his head. He held the limp Balak in his arms as the princess began to yell for help. Soldiers from the palace were already on their way to help rescue Lillian. As they drew near, Lillian waved them over to where Balak was standing.

"Quickly," she shouted, "we are all okay. Get this man into the palace, he has been severely injured and requires medical help."

As the soldiers laid him down and began to dress his wounds, Lillian's attention was drawn down the street in the other direction. A soldier on a horse was racing toward them, screaming to get their attention. He pulled on the reigns and slowed the horse as he approached the princess.

"My Lady, you must come with me quickly," he said. "You are not going to believe what just happened. I raced here as soon as I saw!"

"What is it? What are you talking about?" she asked.

"The Phayladin is here!"

Lillian's heart became overwhelmed with joy as she said, "Prince Ethan has returned! This is good news. Tell me, did you see Prince Morgan with him? Was the prince with him?"

"Forgive me, My Lady, but there is no mistaking it. The man I'm referring to is certainly not Prince Ethan. His skin is much darker and there is no way to mistake it."

Lillian was puzzled again and said, "Ethan is the Phayladin. This man is obviously an imposter."

The soldier's horse pranced about as he said, "If this man is an imposter, then he has great power. He is the reason the attack just ended. I saw it with my own eyes."

All the people in the street turned their attention to the soldier as he recounted the details.

"The gate to the kingdom was being overrun by these things; these creatures of darkness. I myself was fleeing for my life, but, then, this man came running through the gate and we narrowly missed a collision with each other. He shouted something at my attacker and the thing fell to the ground. The next thing I knew, the man raised his arms into the air and shouted another prayer of some sort and all the attackers just stopped attacking. It was truly a miracle! I thought he might be the Phayladin and I came immediately here to tell you. He is by the front gate as we speak. You must see for yourself!"

"Princess Lillian!" the voice came from behind her.

There was too much happening all at once and a frustrated Lillian yelled, "*What is it now?*"

The soldier who called out to her said, "We have a slight problem. This man has the Seal of Ozgul on his arm – his right arm, My Lady. Do you know who this man is?"

"Why would I know who this man is?" asked Lillian.

"Because, Your Highness, this man is General Balak; the man who is rumored to have led Abaylin's army to attack Todere."

The thought of her home having been ravaged by this man was a lot to handle. Lillian could not hold back the tears as she thought about her people and the lives that were lost. This was slowly becoming the worst day of her life.

"Arrest him immediately!" shouted Lillian. "This man is to be locked in the dungeon until further notice!"

Emma raced over to Lillian's side and said, "Please, Princess. This man saved our lives. Regardless of his crimes, I seek to repay the debt by saving his."

"Emma, this man could have been involved in killing our friends and families. We cannot let him have free reign within the palace."

"I'm begging you, allow me to take him to the palace and get him the help he deserves. Keep him under house arrest in the meantime. We aren't even sure that he is General Balak but we are sure that he is severely injured."

Lillian saw the compassion in Emma's eyes and said, "Very well, Emma. I will do this for you but he could be very dangerous. You must be careful. Take the man to the palace as planned and go quickly. Get him all the help he needs, but keep him under guard. The rest of you come with me! We are going to see what is going on with this miracle man."

The soldiers brought Lillian a horse and began to escort her to the kingdom gates. Emma ran back to Balak's side as the men threw his body over the top of a horse. The rider kicked his horse and they went as fast as they could. Another soldier helped Emma up on his horse and they followed.

Once inside the palace, they carried Balak in and made him as comfortable as possible while they waited for the king's doctor to arrive. Emma ran and retrieved some clean towels and water and the guards posted themselves at the door. The bleeding had slowed a lot but the wound looked very deep. This wasn't the first time she had ever dressed a wound. She quickly went to work but it looked infected. As she tried to clean it out, Balak began to wake up. He opened his eyes up and began to look around. Emma grabbed his hand to try and calm him.

He looked up at her and said, "Where am I?"

Emma leaned in toward Balak and said, "Lie still. You are in the palace. The princess has arranged for you to be taken care of until you begin to heal."

"And who are you?" asked Balak.

"My name is Emma and I am the servant of Princess Lillian."

Still in a daze, Balak said, "You are the one I rescued."

"Yes, it was me," replied Emma, "and I will be eternally grateful for the gesture."

Balak lifted his hand and placed it on Emma's face and said, "You are more beautiful than I thought."

Emma began to blush at the compliment and at the quirky smile on Balak's face. His eyes were starting to close again.

"My family . . ." said Balak, ". . . with Sister Mary. They . . . need to . . . know."

His voice trailed off as he lost consciousness again. His hand collapsed beside him. Emma could not help but smile at the last words he spoke, however, she also noticed that his fever was stronger than ever. She placed a cold towel on his head and said a prayer. All she could do now was wait. As soon as the doctor arrived and Balak began to heal, she would go to the orphanage to find out about his family.

As they approached the front gate to the kingdom, Lillian could see the large crowds that had gathered. Something was obviously happening.

"Make way for the princess!" shouted the guards.

Lillian followed behind her soldiers and in through the crowd as they moved apart to allow her to get to the Phayladin. In the middle of it all, stood Michael.

"My friends," said Michael, "I do not come to you empty handed. I understand that it may be difficult to believe in who I am but I offered you proof. You brought me your sick and I brought them healing. I have nothing more to offer you than hope and life. These times are difficult but you are not alone."

As she approached, Michael bowed his head toward her. She stopped her horse and dismounted.

"Princess, it is an honor to be in your presence," said Michael.

"Who are you and what are you doing here in Bodain?" Lillian wasted no time getting to the point as she was no longer in the mood to be trifled with.

"My Lady, my name is Michael."

Lillian glared at him inquisitively and said, "My soldiers tell me that you claim to be the Phayladin. Is this correct?"

Michael raised his hands up in front of him and took a defensive position to object to Lillian's question. "No, no, My Lady, I never claimed to be the Phayladin at all. I'm sorry if you were misled. I have no desire to pretend to be the Phayladin. I come with a new hope to offer you and your people."

"I am confused," said Lillian. "My men say that you are the reason the attacks stopped. How is that possible?"

Michael stepped back to address the whole crowd. "People of Bodain! You have all been witness to a terrible perversion today. None of the pain and heartache that has been brought upon you should ever have occurred. Unfortunately, many of your loved ones have been possessed by what you call Destroyers. I commanded them to release your loved ones and they did."

The people in the crowd began to talk to each other in hushed tones; some with trepidation, others with a glimpse of excitement.

"Again," continued Michael, "look around you. In just a few short moments, I calmed the attackers and immediately set out to repair some of the damage that occurred."

"What do you mean by 'you repaired the damage'?" asked Lillian.

"Before you arrived, Princess, I was healing those who were injured in the attack."

"Healing them with what?"

"This is where things get interesting," replied Michael. "Please let me explain before we go any further. I just want to remind you of all the good that has already occurred and I promise that what you have seen here today will not cease; not until all the needs of this kingdom have been met. I believe that you would refer to what I am doing today as nothing short of miraculous."

"By whose power do you do these things?" Lillian asked. "If these are miracles as you say, then the Amari must be involved, but you are not the Phayladin."

Michael smiled and shouted, "Exactly! I am not the Phayladin! What I offer you is better than anything he has ever done. In fact, where is he now? Let him come out and share with us his plans for you, the people."

The crowd eagerly glanced around for Ethan.

"He is not here," said Lillian. "He is out doing the work of the Amari."

"My Princess, perhaps you didn't notice but it looks like he should be doing the work of the Amari right here in Bodain. The people of this kingdom were almost destroyed by this random attack. What more important work is there than right here? Each and every day, more and more people are flocking to this city for shelter and medical attention. In these dark times, Bodain will be known as the center of hope. I've already begun to heal and restore and I have been here for less than one hour. It is I who brought an end to the madness that had just occurred. These people were all possessed by Destroyers and at the sound of my voice, the Destroyers fled before me. How else do you explain their end?"

"It's true," said a voice from the crowd. The man was wrapped in old cloths and covered in dirt. "I was one of the possessed people and I was completely unable to control myself. It used me to commit crimes that I will not speak of, but, now, I am free! It's a miracle!"

"And he's not the only one."

The crowd turned toward a woman cradling a young child.

"We just arrived here a few hours before he did. My child was barely awake and his fever was high. We waited for hours to see a doctor, but this man took his fever away instantly. He saved my baby."

Lillian watched as the crowd erupted with stories of how Michael had helped them. They all began talking over each other and Michael stared at Lillian and smiled.

"You see, Princess," said Michael over the noise from the crowd, "you have nothing to fear. I am simply here to help."

Lillian was unwavering in her stance, but, for the moment, she was baffled. She had to shout above the crowd just to be heard.

"But by whose authority do you do these things?"

Michael tried to silence the crowd in order to answer. "I must say, that is an excellent question, but it is not an answer that will sit well with you, at first. For a thousand years of history, you have been led to believe that there is a great battle that has been occurring since the dawn of time; between the Amari and Ozgul. However, the truth is not that simple.

"Ozgul is not the one who wants to hold you down and oppress you. You must understand that it is the Amari and his people who have been lying to you all this time. Ozgul is not the evil monster that you believe him to be and I am here today under his authority and by his power."

The crowd erupted again but this time in anger. They shouted back and forth at each other. Lillian could not believe what she was hearing.

"Arrest this man!" she shouted.

Michael did not resist as the soldiers moved in to seize him. The soldiers began to push back the crowd but the people were growing agitated.

Lillian approached Michael but she was feeling extremely uneasy about the situation and said, "Ozgul is nothing but evil! I'm sure he was the one behind all this today. If he is such a friend to the people, why did he attack and kill people in this kingdom before you arrived!"

"That is the problem with the people of Eret. You have blindly followed the Amari for so long that you have believed his lies! Ozgul is not a created being; he is a god amongst gods! Unfortunately, the Amari turned this world against him and, as with anything, if you suppress its power, the people that love it will become disheartened and turn away. These Destroyers that you claim are attacking you are just desperate and lost. The Amari is like a spoiled child. He doesn't care who he hurts as long as he gets to have his way. However, that all changes today because Ozgul has come to set us all free from the oppression of the Amari. You now have a choice of whom you can worship; the absent Amari or, Ozgul, the one who has already begun to heal this land and the people in it. Besides, it looks like the Amari does not love you as much as you believe he does."

The crowd was silent. Lillian stood in disbelief. As much as she wanted to disagree with him, she couldn't ignore all of the power that he had put on display. She looked around at the crowd who was waiting for a response from her. The thoughts in her mind kept taking her in different directions but she came to her conclusion.

"Leave this kingdom immediately."

That was not the reaction that the majority of the crowd wanted to hear but Lillian pressed on with her command.

"Escort this man out of Bodain, immediately!"

The guards began to take him away but were interrupted with something else.

"Make way! Make way!"

The crowd began to part again and Lillian waited to see why. She rolled her eyes out of frustration at the revelation of who it was. Apparently, Lorcene had heard the news as well. As Lorcene came forward with other members of the Senate, he ignored Lillian's presence entirely and faced Michael directly.

"Why is this man being held?" asked Lorcene. "I hear we have you to thank for relieving the kingdom of these monsters."

"You are welcome," replied Michael. "As I was just telling the princess, before she had me arrested, it is my honor to be able to aid this great kingdom in the fight against evil."

Lorcene turned to Lillian and asked, "Is this how you treat the hero of Bodain?"

Lillian objected, "Senator Lorcene, this man is not a hero. He is an agent of Ozgul."

"Yes, yes, I heard everything. However, I'm afraid I cannot share the same resolve as you," replied Lorcene. "Regardless of whose side he is on, who can deny the great things that he has done. We need a man like that on our side. I for one have had enough of the bickering between religions. My concern now is this kingdom and its people."

The crowd cheered again and begged Michael to continue his work. Michael raised his hands in the air to quiet the crowd.

"Perhaps the princess requires a demonstration in order to believe," said Michael. The crowd loved the idea.

"I volunteer."

Lillian turned to see Master Tomar stepping up through the crowd and looked at him with disbelief.

"Look at my eyes. Anyone can see that I have been partially blind since a child as my eyes look different than all men. No man's eyes have been as big as a curse as mine. If this man is who he says he is, then he can restore my vision."

"Master Tomar," Lillian said, "you don't need to become a part of this man's charade."

Tomar looked at Lillian and said, "What is there to lose, Your Highness?"

"Very well," replied Michael, "come here and close your eyes. This will not take long."

He closed his eyes as Michael held Tomar's head in his head. He lightly pressed on Tomar's eyes with his thumbs and said, "I will give you back your sight but you must promise to do me one favor when I call on you."

"If you do this for me, I will owe you my life."

"Then open your eyes and see what I have done."

Master Tomar hesitated and was almost afraid to open his eyes. If this worked, it would be the first time in a very long life that he was able to see the world again as it was intended with all of its beauty. The crowd grew completely quiet as they waited to hear the results. Tomar felt no different than he did before. He slowly began to open his eyes as light began to pour through them. He already noticed that the colors he was used to seeing had disappeared. It took just a moment to adjust but he could finally see the world the way he remembered it. Color was restored; definition returned. He fell to his knees in disbelief.

"I can see," was all he could say before the crowd erupted with praise.

"Look what I can do!" shouted Michael.

Lillian could not explain it, but she could not accept Michael either. She was happy for Master Tomar but she couldn't help but feel like he had just traded in his soul. The crowd began to sing an old Bodainian song. Michael lifted his hands in the air as a sign of victory and celebrated with the people.

As she stood there speechless, Lorcene yelled above the crowd, "I, for one, am convinced! This man should be considered a friend of Bodain!"

Lorcene bowed himself before Michael and stood beside him as though Michael was his champion.

"People, please! Listen to me!" said Lillian. "This man cannot stay here! He is the one who brought all of this with him!"

Her cries were falling upon deaf ears and those that did hear began to boo her. Her popularity was fading fast as she was soon the only one present who doubted Michael's claims. Lorcene leaned in toward Michael and said something that only they could hear. Michael nodded his head and addressed the crowd once more. The people almost instantly grew quiet.

"People of Bodain! I plan on being amongst you for quite some time. There will be a time for all of you to experience the blessing. Please don't blame the princess for her disbelief. These are difficult times and they may only get worse from here. However, in time, I will continue to show you that Ozgul is a friend of the people. If we are to survive these times, we must work together to help each other."

The crowd cheered in agreement with their newfound redeemer.

Michael quieted the crowd with a wave of his hand. The look on his face went from welcoming to serious instantly. The crowd waited to hear what he would say next.

"Understand this," began Michael, "there is a storm coming to this kingdom. Even I, with all of my power, could not stop it if I wanted to. Ozgul will not allow you to be mistreated by the Amari any longer and he will do whatever it takes to rescue you. There are those who have been lied to for so long that you cannot free yourself from the idea the Amari loves you. How could anyone, with all his power, leave you hurting and hopeless for close to a thousand years? I do not welcome the storm but it is a necessary storm. It is being sent to punish those whose allegiance lies with the Amari in an effort to set the people free."

The people were silent; hanging on every word that Michael spoke.

"This is my offer," he continued, "I will remain with you for seven days. I will heal the people of this kingdom as a show of good faith. In return, you will deliver the Phayladin over to me to be tried for his crimes against humanity!"

The crowd's silence ended. People began to argue and discuss amongst themselves; some furious and others in fear.

"Seven days!" shouted Michael. "Bring me the Phayladin and I will stop what is coming! If not, the judgment that he deserves will fall on all of you! Ozgul will save you from yourselves, one way or another!"

Lillian could see the emotions of the crowd escalating. She ordered Michael to be taken to the palace to continue the discussion which only riled the crowd up even further. Soldiers moved in to hold the crowd back as she climbed upon her horse and turned to leave. She had no idea what to do from here, but one thing was certain, this storm could not be good for anyone. She prayed for Ethan's return.

High above and all around, invisible to the naked eye, the Destroyers were doing some celebrating of their own. Everywhere Michael went, they followed him using their powers of persuasion to help convince human beings that Michael was a great hero. They had waited all of this time for an opportunity to conquer Bodain and, now, they had their opportunity. They surrounded the square and darted in and out of the crowd. There were Persuaders present in the marketplace as well, but they were becoming far outnumbered at this moment. On top of one of the buildings, looking down, Ozgul watched as his plan unfolded perfectly.

17. THE MAN IN THE DREAM

Ethan and Morgan said no words as they were escorted to the emperor. Ethan knew it was going to be difficult. Morgan had always been the more stubborn of the two, but, then again, he did have the weight of a future kingdom on his shoulders. Ethan looked over at Morgan and had compassion for him. He just needed to remind him of his honor and integrity, and, above all else, he needed to find time to tell him that his father was still alive.

The doors to Neroni's throne room opened before them and Ethan was impressed by the extravagant layout of the room. At the moment, the throne was empty as Neroni was not in the room. The guards led them right up to the bottom of the steps that ascended to the throne and they waited for the emperor to arrive. Minutes passed and there was still no sign. Even the guards were starting to get restless. Finally, the doors opened yet again and the emperor powerfully walked into the room. He looked toward the guards and ascended the steps. After a few steps, he flung his robe around to the side and spun himself around.

"Hello, young prince," he said, "I was hoping to never have to see you again. However, since you are here, there is much that I wish to discuss with you."

Neroni walked down the steps and stood within inches of Morgan's face.

"I have good news for you," Neroni said. "I have decided to let you live for the time being. I will be sending an envoy to your kingdom to discuss your ransom. If your kingdom will not negotiate, then we will go to war. We shall finally see whose kingdom is the greatest in a test of bloodshed."

If there was one thing that Morgan had never let go of, it was his desire to protect the people of the kingdom. The last thing he had wanted was for anyone else to suffer because of his mistakes.

"Leave my people alone," replied Morgan. "I abandoned my place on the throne; they will never come for me. You are a pathetic man who preys on the lives of the innocent."

Emperor Neroni flew into a rage at Morgan's remarks. He pressed his face up against Morgan's and yelled, "You will not speak to me like that, boy! I am the great Emperor Neroni and I will not be disrespected by anyone no matter their status! Is that clear with you?"

Neroni had spit all over Morgan's face with each word but Morgan was unable to clean it up as his hands were still bound. He leaned away from Neroni's face as best he could and said, "My apologies, what I meant to say was this."

And with that, Morgan slammed his head into Neroni's nose and sent the emperor reeling backward. Neroni tripped on the steps leading up to his throne and fell backward onto them. The guards behind Morgan and Ethan quickly rushed to help their emperor stand.

Ethan looked at Morgan who was smiling just a little and said, "Really, Morgan? That was your solution to the problem."

Morgan had nothing to say. He just smiled at Ethan and shrugged his shoulders. In some way, Ethan was just happy to see Morgan smile at all. Neroni pushed his guards away and scrambled to his feet, too proud to accept any help. From behind, one of the other guards clubbed Morgan in the back of his legs, just behind the knee caps. Morgan fell to his knees from the pain and laughed just a little. Neroni became furious at the sound of Morgan's laughter and grabbed the sword out of the sheath of the nearest guard. He rushed to up to Morgan and pointed the sword into Morgan's chest.

"Do with me what you will!" shouted Morgan. "I do not care! My life was over before I came to this wretched kingdom!"

"I will kill you!" shouted Neroni.

Ethan had never seen Morgan like this before.

"Do it then!" Morgan shouted. "I have nothing left to live for! I am already dead!"

"Do not test me! A dead prince is just as good as one that is alive!"

Morgan shouted with more emphasis than before as tears rolled down from his eyes and said, "I do not care!"

Neroni raised his sword over his head and prepared to plunge it down into Morgan's body.

"Emperor Neroni!" shouted Ethan. "Please wait! I can tell you what your dreams mean!"

Neroni stopped his attack and looked at Ethan.

"What did you say to me?" asked Neroni.

"The dream you've been having," replied Ethan, "the one with the boxes. I can tell you all about it and I can even tell you what it means."

Morgan began to sob uncontrollably on the ground. The guilt and the weight of his crimes had gotten to be too much to bear and he finally took an opportunity to release everything he had held back. It was true. He did not have a desire to live at this moment. He had taken an innocent life and felt that his life should be taken in return. Emperor Neroni lowered his sword and ignored Morgan for a moment.

"And who are you that you should know my dreams?" asked Neroni. "A psychic? A magician? What are you?"

"Emperor Neroni, my name is Ethan and I am the Phayladin."

"Really?" replied Neroni. "You expect me to believe that you are the Phayladin?"

He motioned toward his guards and continued by saying, "What is wrong with all of these prisoners? Have they all gone mad? First, I have prince who is crying like a baby and now I have a man who believes that he is the savior of the world."

The guards laughed along with Neroni.

"What I say is true," replied Ethan.

"Very well, but be forewarned, if you fail to tell me what my dreams are, I will have you killed."

Ethan began, "In your dream, there are three kings and each king presents to you a gift fit for an emperor of your stature. The first king opens his box to reveal nothing but sand and dirt. The second king reveals his gift and it is only filled with rocks. Finally, the third king presents to you an old and tattered box with the symbol of the Amari as its only decoration. Inside, you find that it is empty and you become furious at the insult."

Neroni interrupted him and said, "How could you know such things?"

Ethan ignored the question and continued, "After the box is opened, fire comes from behind you as evil spirits begin to call out your name. As they reach out for you, the fire grows stronger and a man's face begins to appear."

Neroni was captivated by Ethan's retelling of the dream and said, "Please, tell me what it means. Tell me why I have been plagued by this dream for so long."

Even Morgan was listening to Ethan speak at this point.

"Neroni, you have been a very wicked man. You may have power but it is only because the Amari allowed you to get this far to prove his strength to the world."

"You watch your tongue," said Neroni.

"Do not interrupt me," replied Ethan. "The first box of sand represents the kingdom that you have built. It is useless and will only return to sand when all is over. The second box represents your death. The rocks inside tell of how your life will end under the rubble of the kingdom that you have built."

"That is enough!" shouted Neroni.

Ethan was not fazed by Neroni's shouts. As he spoke, the very chains binding his hands fell to the ground and he began to move toward Neroni. Neroni saw the approach and moved backward up the steps to his throne. The guards in the room did nothing as they were captivated by the authority in which Ethan was speaking. The room remained silent.

"The third box is empty because that is what your kingdom will become! When you die, you will die alone and with no power and with no riches! Everything you have ever done will be forgotten and everything you have ever owned will be destroyed. The fire is the judgment of the Amari and the punishment that you deserve for the countless lives you have taken in vain!"

Ethan's intimidating approach had pushed Neroni back into his throne and he could go no further. Ethan stopped his approach and said, "And, finally, the man that you saw before you awoke. That is the man who will bring your life to an end, but that will not be revealed to you until the time comes."

"Guards! Guards! Take this man away from me!" shouted Neroni.

The guards in the room finally snapped back into reality and ran to restrain Ethan once again. Ethan did not put up a fight and allowed himself to be pulled back down the steps.

"Bring me Captain Ardone!" said Neroni. "Bring my son to me now!"

One of the guards took off running to find the captain. Neroni nervously ran his fingers through his hair and pulled at his skin. The sweat was pouring off of his brow and his breathing became heavy and at times sporadic. Ethan looked on as he could tell that Neroni was being severely infected by his worries. The guards pulled him back to Morgan's side as they pulled Morgan up to his feet.

Morgan looked at Ethan and said, "See, even he thinks you can be a bit of a jerk."

Ethan was relieved to see a bit of Morgan's sarcasm returning. However, everyone in the room had fixed their attention on their emperor as he had begun to start speaking to himself. Captain Ardone was not far from the throne room and came running in quickly.

"What is happening? What is wrong with my father?" asked Ardone.

Ardone slowed down as he saw Ethan being held by the guards.

"What is this?" he asked again. "Ethan, why are you here?"

"Captain, I'm afraid the emperor isn't too pleased with me," said Ethan.

Ardone looked at him inquisitively and continued up the stairs toward the throne. As he neared, Neroni leapt up and screamed, "Stay away from me! They are all coming to get me!"

Ardone stopped running at the words of the emperor. The guards in the room did not move at first for they couldn't believe what was happening. The Destroyers who had possessed Neroni had lain almost dormant for many years. Once Neroni had become emperor, he didn't need to do much. Neroni was insane and evil enough on his own. However, now that the Phayladin had arrived the Destroyers were beginning to get agitated.

Neroni charged and grabbed Ardone by his coat. The force of the two colliding pushed Ardone backward and he stepped back to catch himself from falling.

"Stop calling me your father, you half-blood! I am not your father and I should have had you killed years ago!"

"This is madness!" shouted Ardone. "What do you mean by this?"

"Your father was a coward and a tyrant! Even leading to his death, all he could do was scream like little girl. 'Please don't hurt me! Please don't hurt my son!'" Neroni pushed Ardone away and began crying as he said, "Mother! Mother! Where are you? I need you. *Mother!*"

Ardone was unable to explain his father's ramblings.

"You men," said Ardone, "take my father to his chambers. He obviously needs to get some rest. Quickly!"

The guards rushed in to restrain the emperor as Neroni began to kick and squirm. Neroni used his supernatural strength and threw the men violently to the ground but stumbled backward hitting his head upon the steps.

"Let me go!" Neroni shouted as he reached for his head. "You listen to me! There is not a man alive that can bring an end to me. I am stronger than anyone and my kingdom reflects me in every way. I shall destroy all that you love!"

Ethan was unmoved by Neroni's remarks and said, "Mark my words, Neroni. In three days, this kingdom will come tumbling down and the Amari will announce his judgment upon you as well. When the sun raises red on the third day, prepare yourself for you will have your reward! Unless you turn away from the evil within you and allow the Amari to save you, your name will be remembered no more!"

The guards removed Neroni from the throne room and all Neroni could do was cry and wail. Ardone turned to Ethan and said, "What did you say to my father? Why have you driven him mad?"

"All I did was interpret his dream for him," replied Ethan. "And I must say it was not what he expected at all."

"What was his dream about?"

"It was more than a dream, Ardone; it was a vision of the future. For all the evils that he has done, the Amari is bringing his rule to an end."

"What did you mean by three days?" asked Ardone.

"This may be hard to hear, but in three days, this kingdom will come toppling down. However, there is something else you should realize. When it does come to an end, you will have to step up in his place."

Ardone took offense and said, "Are you telling me that my father will die in three days?"

Ethan remained silent.

Ardone stared into empty space. He was surprised to find that the death of his father did not disturb him nearly as much as it should. However, as the prince, he felt as though he must remain faithful to the kingdom.

"Listen, Ethan. I am eternally grateful for what you did for my daughter. I have never seen that little child more alive than she is right now. You will forever have my thanks. However, what you are saying now is an offense against the crown of this kingdom. I have no choice but to return you to the dungeons and lock you up until the three days have passed."

"You will do what you must, Captain, but rest assured, I will not be the one who brings the emperor's life to an end. He will die by your sword and your hands."

"That is a bold statement to be making. You are taking a major gamble by saying that in my presence. I hope you are wrong," replied Ardone. "Guards, return them to the cells."

The guards dragged them out of the throne room as Ardone watched them leave. They were taken back to the prisons and each of them were placed into a separate cell made of metal bars and a stone wall. They threw Morgan to the ground. He pushed himself up to his knees and stared at the wall away from Ethan. His shoulders were slumped forward and his hands were lying pointlessly along the floor.

Ethan walked to the bars separating him and Morgan and said, "Morgan, I have to tell you something."

"Ethan, now is not the time. All I want to do is rot out in this cell," replied Morgan.

"But Morgan, I must—"

"Ethan, I understand that you want to fix things but things are beyond broken at this point. You can't fix something that wasn't to be fixed."

"Just listen to me—"

"Don't you see what happens? You bring destruction wherever you go!"

"I did not destroy your life and you know that!" shouted Ethan. "No one forced you to make the decisions you made."

Morgan said nothing in return but looked away from Ethan.

"Ever since we were kids, you've always wrestled with your pride and who could blame you. Your entire life was being led to one moment and that was to one day become king. Not just any king, but the most powerful king in the land. Your father did his best to teach you—"

Morgan approached the bars between them and stood face to face with Ethan.

"But now my father is dead!" shouted Morgan. The tears began to flow wildly. Ethan knew he needed to tell him regardless of the interruptions. Morgan continued through his tears. "And if I hadn't been so stupid, so blinded by hatred, he would still be alive today and I would be by his side right at this moment. It is my fault that he is dead, and I am not fit to be a king in his stead."

"Morgan—"

"Ethan, I am tired of talking to you!"

"Your father is alive!" Ethan shouted.

Morgan's heart felt like it had exploded inside of his chest. He looked at Ethan with wide eyes, like a child. He became completely numb to everything. He stopped hearing. He stopped seeing and, for a moment, he had stopped breathing as it seemed impossible to function properly. What Ethan had said continued to replay over and over in his head.

"Morgan, say something. Say anything."

Morgan's mouth was dry and he did his best to find his words.

"What . . . did you say?"

"Your father is not dead. He did not die after the fall. I mean, he was dead, but by the grace of the Amari, I was able to bring him back to life."

Once the reality of Ethan's words had set in, Morgan began to weep uncontrollably. All of his fears were taken away from him in one moment. He hadn't felt this much peace since the day of the accident. Tears formed in Ethan's eyes as well. He reached through the bars and pulled his brother's head in as close as he could. The two of them wept together; forehead to forehead.

"He's alive," said Morgan. "He's still alive."

"Yes he is," replied Ethan, "but he probably is going to be pretty upset with you."

Morgan laughed just a little.

"I am such an idiot," replied Morgan. He backed away from the bars and looked at Ethan. "I have blamed you for everything and I had no right to do that. You're right. I'm going to get yelled at when I return!"

"Morgan, I know you don't want to hear this, but even though you feel like you have failed, you have never been alone. There is a purpose to all of this and I hope you are now willing to see this through."

"What could that purpose possibly be?" asked Morgan. "Was it just for me to finally realize that I am a fool and a coward? You could've prevented all of this. Why let it happen?"

"I couldn't Morgan. Some things are just fixed points in time and cannot be changed. In some way, you needed this to happen."

"Ethan, I don't know what to think. In the end, what does it matter? We are stuck in this prison regardless."

"Not for long," replied Ethan.

"I suppose you have some magical powers to get us out of here, then?"

"Seriously, Morgan, it has nothing to do with magic and you know that."

"Aw, come on, Ethan! When we get back you can use these powers of yours to entertain me. The jester position after all is still available."

"You should be careful what you say," said Ethan. "I may not have 'magical powers' but I can make life very difficult for you if the Amari wills it to be."

"Oh really?" asked Morgan. "Life is already difficult for me as the only thing I have to look at is your ugly mug."

The two of them laughed at each other for what felt like the first time since before Ethan had become the Phayladin. The laughter slowly trailed into silence.

"Ethan," began Morgan. He began to stutter as he tried to get the words out. "I just wanted to say . . . I mean, if you were in my position . . ."

"Morgan, it's ok. You don't have to say it. I know. All is forgiven."

Morgan looked up and smiled.

"So, what do we do now?" asked Morgan.

"For now, we get some rest. It's going to be a long couple of days."

18. HIDDEN NO MORE

Balak awoke and sat up quickly in the bed. His first reaction was to reach for his sword but he could find one nowhere. It took him just a moment to realize that the room he was in was unfamiliar to him. He calmed himself down and tried to remember what had happened. The last thing that he could remember was saving those people in the street. He couldn't remember many details but he definitely remembered the face of the girl he saved. He lay back on his bed and smiled. He would not forget her face anytime soon.

Balak looked down at the wound on his side. It had been bandaged rather well but the pain still remained. He was still bleeding a little as the white bandages were stained with his blood. He pulled the sheets off of his legs and gently swung them over the side of the bed. The floor was cold beneath his feet as the entire room had a chill about it. He scanned the room for his shirt and shoes but could not find them anywhere. He stood slowly and gripped the wound on his side. Where ever he was, the room was decorated well and contained some of the finest things he had ever seen. His back was to the door and he was startled as it opened behind him.

Balak turned to see two Bodainian guards standing inside the doorway. From in between them, the girl from the street appeared carrying a stack of clothes and some medical supplies. Emma was surprised to see Balak up out of his bed. She stopped her approach and bowed toward Balak.

"Good morning, sir," said Emma. "I am glad to see you are up and walking around."

"You," said Balak, "you are the girl from the street, the one that I saved, are you not?"

Emma smiled and said, "Yes sir, I am. And I am incredibly grateful for the gift, but I am afraid that you were severely wounded in the fight."

The two of them stared awkwardly at each other as neither one of them said anything. However, when the silence was broken, they found themselves interrupting each other.

"If I may—" said Emma,

"I just wanted to—" said Balak. The next words were hard to hear as they spoke over each other again. Emma smiled at the confusion as Balak said, "I'm sorry for the interruption."

"Not at all," replied Emma. "It is I who should apologize."

Balak conceded and said, "Please, say what you wished to say."

Emma moved to a table in the room and set her things down as she said, "I brought some new bandages to redress your wound and I took the opportunity to mend and wash your shirt." She picked the shirt up from the pile and walked it over to Balak. "However, I'm sure the shirt has seen better days as blood is incredibly difficult to remove, and there certainly was a lot of that."

Balak reached for the shirt and said, "Thank you. This will be more than sufficient."

"What is it you were going to say?" asked Emma.

"Unfortunately," said Balak, "I do not remember much of anything that has happened in recent events. I'm not sure as to where we are or how I managed to get here. However, I'm fairly certain that your name is Emma, correct?"

"Yes," replied Emma. "That is my name and after the accident, you passed out on the road. I asked the princess to bring you to the palace until you were well and she agreed."

Balak's demeanor went from relaxed to slightly agitated at the mention of being inside the palace. Of all the places he could have been taken to, this was the last place he wanted to be, but he didn't want to draw attention to himself any more than he already had.

Balak slid his shirt on over his head as he said, "Thank you for your hospitality, but I really must be on my way. My family will be worried about me."

"I'm sorry but you cannot go anywhere."

Balak looked at Emma and said, "I beg your pardon, Emma, but there is no reason for me to stay. I appreciate all you have done for me."

Balak walked past Emma and headed for the door.

"No," objected Emma, "you don't understand. You cannot go anywhere because there are guards at the door." Emma grimaced at the thought of telling him what had happened, but continued on anyways as Balak stopped his departure. "When you passed out in the street . . . well . . . I'm afraid that the markings on your arm became exposed and everyone saw the Seal of Ozgul. You were immediately identified as General Balak."

A mix of emotions ran through Balak's mind but he knew he had been caught. The charade he had hoped to play was losing its purpose. In the end, he knew he couldn't keep this up forever. He rubbed his face with his hands.

"Is it true?" asked Emma. "Are you the same General Balak that led the attack on Todere?"

Balak let out a deep sigh and turned to Emma as he said, "It is true that I am that Balak, however, I was not at the battle of Todere. I fled with my family to save their lives long before that battle had begun. I am certainly not proud of whom I have been, but that's why I took the risk of coming here to Bodain. I'm just looking to start over. All I want to do is return to my family and disappear."

"My home is in Todere and my family has been through so much," replied Emma. "I'm not even sure what their current status is at this moment. Abaylin's army destroyed so much of what I loved in that kingdom."

"But that wasn't me," declared Balak. "No one will ever be able to pin that sin onto me. I was not there."

"But what about the other families that you have devastated? I mean, are you the monster that everyone believes you to be? Should I be worried about being in the same room with you? I think I would like to understand."

Balak looked at Emma. She could see the brokenness in his face and she couldn't help but feel some kind of compassion for him.

"Believe me, My Lady, you do not want to understand. You couldn't if you tried because even I cannot. All I can offer you is a declaration that I am no longer that man. I will not pretend to be something that I wasn't, but, if there was a way to change it all, I would gladly take that route instead."

"So you've allowed the Amari to redeem your soul then?" asked Emma.

Balak laughed and said, "What is it with everyone being so concerned about my status with the Amari? Can't a man change his life around without surrendering everything he is to some distant god?"

"Actually," replied Emma, "no, he cannot truly do so. Anything less is nothing more than a covering that will slowly fall apart. You said it yourself. You came to Bodain to hide away but look at where you are now. I am not here to debate with you on the condition of your soul. I am here because you saved my life and I am indebted to you for that reason. Consider this a clean slate, at least with me. If you have truly changed, then I shall delight in getting to know the real you. Now let me redress that wound before it becomes infected all over again and, maybe, in the process, I will be able to show you how compassionate the Amari can be."

Balak could not help but to be intrigued by Emma. She maintained a compassionate look about her even during the revelation of who he was. He allowed her to begin to change the bandages.

"Thank you," said Balak.

Emma smiled and said, "Please, this is nothing. It will only take a moment."

Balak grabbed Emma's hand and squeezed it tightly and said, "No, I mean thank you for not judging me. You have already shown compassion that goes beyond most."

"Everyone deserves a second chance," said Emma. "However, I can't very well change the bandages if I don't have the use of my hands."

Balak paused for just a moment and then let go. Emma smiled back and began to get to work.

"So how long am I trapped inside of this room?" asked Balak.

"I cannot give you that answer for I am just a servant to Princess Lillian. You will have to wait until she returns and decides what to do with you from there."

"My family will be worried," said Balak.

"While you were sleeping, you woke up long enough to tell me where to find them. I have already visited with them. They seem to be incredibly jealous of the fact that you are staying in the palace, but I didn't tell them you were being held here just yet."

"Believe me, they will not be surprised to find out," replied Balak. "My life has been one disappointment after the other. The real question is how do I get out of here? From the looks of things, I am the least of the problems here in Bodain."

"I must admit," replied Emma, "what just happened out there was the scariest moment of my life. I'm not sure how we survived the crashing of the carriage. It was odd. As the carriage was flipping, it felt like something was holding it up. If that wasn't enough, those people were certainly not themselves. They were so vicious and evil. In all of your battles, have you ever seen anything like that before?"

"I cannot say that I have. However, if I had to guess, I would say that those people were possessed, but even I have never heard of so many beings possessed at one time."

"Now, that is something that I wish upon no man. The depths to which evil will go seems to have no end."

Balak lowered his head and said, "If only you knew. If only you knew. Did you stitch me up?"

Emma laughed a little and said, "I may be able to change bandages with the best of them but I have never been good with a needle. You were visited by the king's very own doctor, Dr. Forthen. He said you should make a full recovery, which I'm sure will leave many people severely disappointed."

Balak laughed out loud at Emma's sarcasm. She was the first person outside of Balpa and his family that had taken the time to be real with him, and, to Balak, Emma was much better looking than Balpa was.

Balak let out a heavy sigh and said, "It won't matter much anyways. I'm sure I will be executed by the morning. This wound will be the least of my worries anyways."

"Do not say that," responded Emma. "The princess is a woman of mercy and there is always hope."

"That is kind of you to say but I'm sure I do not have much time left. Honestly, I have come to grips with the fact that death is the least of the punishments that I deserve. My family is being taken care of so they no longer need me, and evil seems to follow me wherever I am. I can only hope that the Amari can find enough grace to cover my sins."

"But, if the Amari is real, and I believe that he is, then there is more than enough grace to go around. Besides, he has no desire to see you perish."

"Now, there is where you miss the point," replied Balak. "I have no doubts that the Amari is real. I have seen enough evils and things that are completely unexplainable to know that he is real. But, I also know that there is no way he could love me. I am resigned to my fate. If he wishes to punish me for my sins, who am I to argue?"

Emma had nothing to say in return. She stared at Balak who was now a broken man before her. He sat down on the side of his bed and buried his face in his hands. He was exhausted and had no desire to fight the current situation. Their conversation was soon interrupted by the door opening as guards entered into the room.

"It's time. You must leave the prisoner now," said the guard.

"I don't understand," replied Emma, "what is happening?"

The guards moved in to bind Balak's hands. There were four guards altogether and they knew whom it was they were escorting.

"The princess has returned and we are escorting the prisoner to her to determine what to do with him now," said the guard. "This man is the most wanted man in the area, if not the world, and we need to make sure that he does not slip through our hands while he was on our watch. He will most likely be dead by the morning."

Balak stood to his feet and said, "I have no desire to run. Let's just get this over with. If I am to be dead by morning, then I wish to sleep in peace tonight."

Balak placed his wrists side by side and waited for them to be bound. He looked over at Emma who had clenched the remaining bandages in her hand as she held them close to her chest.

The man tying Balak's hands together looked up at Balak and said, "My father lived in the village of Dunfre. Do you remember Dunfre, General?"

Balak said nothing.

The guard moved in closer and said, "Yes, of course you remember. That was the place where you locked all of the villagers in the town storehouse and set the place on fire. My father died in that fire trying to rescue the villagers; men, women, and children."

Balak looked at the guard and said, "I am sorry—"

The man punched Balak in the face before Balak could finish the sentence. The other guards quickly jumped in to pull the man back before he attacked Balak again. Balak recovered from the blow but did not retaliate. He knew he deserved that and much more.

The guard fought against the pull of the others as he shouted, "Do not apologize to me! My father was a good man and you killed him! For what? *For what?*"

Emma could not believe what had just happened. When the fight began, she had moved as far from it as she could. She nervously stared at the ground only to glance up every few seconds or so. Balak stood broken before them all. In all of his conquests, he had never stood accused by anyone he had brought harm upon. The guard broke loose of the others and continued again toward Balak who did nothing to protect himself.

The man swung and his fist landed squarely on Balak's jaw. Balak braced himself as the onslaught continued. The man tackled him to the ground and, as Balak's hands were tied, he was unable to brace his fall. His back absorbed most of the fall and Balak wrenched from the pain. The man climbed over Balak and began to punch him repeatedly, leaving Balak's face bloodied and quickly bruising. Balak's mind had drifted away into a state of numbness. He had buried deep all of the guilt and shame inside of his soul from the things that he had done, and all of that was rising to the surface.

"Stop him!" shouted Emma. "Somebody stop him!"

The guards rushed forward again to pull their friend off of the defenseless Balak.

"Get him out of here!" shouted Emma.

In the chaos, one of the guards yelled back, "Do not tell us how to do our job, servant!"

Emma retreated back to the wall where she was standing and minded her own business for the moment. As the guard was dragged out of the room, Balak rolled to his stomach as blood dripped from his face. In his heart, he knew things would never change. From now on, everywhere he went, he knew he would find someone whose life he had helped to destroy. His life had bottomed out and it seemed as though he had nowhere left to turn. So, in that moment, he did the only thing that made sense. Lying on the floor next to him was a knife that had fallen from the belt of the guard that had attacked him. Balak grabbed the knife and sat up on his knees. He raised the knife above his head with the tip pointed down at himself. Hope had abandoned him. If he was going to die, he wanted it to be on his own terms.

He closed his eyes, and said a prayer, hoping that the Amari was listening. "Forgive me."

He rose up to plunge the knife into his body when hope finally revealed itself. Once Balak had grabbed the knife, Emma ran to stop him from fulfilling his goal. She grabbed his hands and knelt down before Balak. She said no words as Balak stared into her eyes. His heavy breathing quickly turned to sighs of relief. Emma reached up and slowly pulled the knife from his hands.

"You saved my life and now I have saved yours," said Emma. "There is always hope."

Balak felt himself lifted up from the ground as the guards began to lead him out of the room. Balak turned his head to look back at Emma as she sat unmoved from the floor. For the first time, Balak had found a reason to live. That reason was Emma.

19. WHEN OLD FRIENDS UNITE

As the soldiers dragged Balak down the halls of the palace, his feet kept stumbling underneath his weight. His face was bleeding a lot and Balak could feel it beginning to swell in multiple places. He did his best to keep pace with the guards who didn't seem to care whether or not he did. Every once in a while, he would stumble as blood would drip down over his eyes and the guards would quickly respond with some kind of blow to his body. A few times, Balak tried to push back but was equally met with more resistance. He soon found it was easier to go along with the guards than to put up a fight.

They arrived at the throne room and took him directly to a side of the room where prisoners were required to wait for justice. The large room was not empty as officials and some curious onlookers were waiting for the princess to return but it was nowhere near full. The buzz in the room had been centered on the attacks of the possessed but, as Balak entered the room, the voices became hushed and Balak felt as though all eyes were on him. Balak looked at the ground mostly but did look up long enough to see Emma come walking into the room. She made her way toward the throne and took her place on the side and waited for Lillian to return.

Murmurs began to echo through the halls and some of those murmurings became shouts of insults directed toward Balak. Soon the room was filled with all sorts of screams in his general direction. The crowds started pressing in as things began to be thrown at the one who had murdered thousands. The guards were reluctant to help but knew that they must keep order, so they called for more men and pushed the crowd back even further. Finally, a yell was heard over the noise and echoed through the room.

"Announcing, Princess Lillian and the honorable Senator Lorcene!"

The crowds quickly lost interest in Balak and looked toward the entrance of the room. Lillian was the first to enter and a look of annoyance was on her face. Her walk was quick and determined. She was so overwhelmed with the arrogance of Lorcene and his newfound devotion to Michael. During the entire ride back to the palace, she kept trying to come up with some form of a solution to this problem. She knew Michael was up to nothing good as he had already promised to bring destruction, however, the things that Michael was doing certainly gave him some kind of authority. She couldn't argue with the fact that the things he did were miraculous, but if he was lying about who he was, then there was no telling what else he could be lying about. She headed straight for the throne and ignored the crowd of people as Michael entered into the room. News had traveled fast.

Balak watched through half open eyes as Lillian made her way to the throne, but, like everyone else, his attention was turned toward the throne room entrance. However, his current condition quickly turned to rage. His heart began to pound as he saw Michael enter the room. He could not believe his eyes as Michael was being celebrated while he was bruised and bound awaiting a trial for crimes he didn't commit. In Balak's eyes, Michael deserved nothing less than death.

Senator Lorcene shook hands with the people as any good politician would. Unconcerned with the previous threats, he made sure that he stood by his newfound champion. Even Michael was enjoying the moment as he had never been this close to a throne room before. He went from one of the most hated men to one of the most beloved and he loved it. He was so caught up in the moment that he never saw Balak standing on the side of the room, however, Balak was going to make sure that he knew.

The guards were caught completely off guard as they had been locked into the moment. Balak used the opportunity to do something stupid yet again. With hands bound together, he rushed toward Michael. The guards saw him running but responded too late. Balak's approach was unhindered except for one man. Senator Lorcene never saw it coming as Balak knocked him to the ground.

Lorcene's body flailed around as the impact sent him sliding across the polished marble floor. The guards yelled, the people in the room gasped, and Michael turned just in time to see his fate. Balak, with hands bound in front of him, swung his fists directly into the side of Michael's face. The blow made Michael stumble backward into the crowd behind him. The guards reached out for Balak as he tackled Michael to the floor. The look of horror in Michael's eyes pleased Balak immensely but the fun was soon over as the guards began to beat up Balak and dragged him away.

Lillian turned around and was just as shocked as anyone to see the scuffle but, inside, she smiled at the sight of Lorcene on the ground, scrambling to stand back up. She watched as the guards pulled Balak back and helped Michael to his feet. The room was alive with screams and yelling as chaos ensued. Balak was screaming ferociously at Michael and Lillian decided that it was enough. She needed to try to bring order back into the room. She motioned to the guard who had moved in to protect her and told him to clear out the room. He began to bark out orders to the other guards and for reinforcements. The room was soon filled with soldiers as they pressed the crowds against the wall and funneled them out of the room. Balak was pressed to the ground by a group of soldiers while Michael and Lorcene regained their composure.

Balak screamed, *"You coward! Let me go and fight me like a man!"*

Michael was unprepared for this moment and had nothing to say. He was stunned and speechless. The last time he had seen Balak was when he participated in the order to have him and his family captured. He had always been a little fearful of Balak and had hoped to never see him again.

Lorcene quickly jumped to Michael's defense and said, "Guards! Teach this man a lesson! He needs to be punished for his crimes!"

The guards began to beat Balak again; kicking him in the sides. Balak absorbed each blow in extreme pain, especially the ones that reopened his wound. The blood began to flow.

"Enough!" shouted Lillian.

The people in the room slowly grew subdued.

"You will not give such orders in my throne room!" she shouted. "Pick that man up and bring him before me!"

As the guards lifted Balak to his feet, the princess could not help but wonder what it was that caused Balak to attack Michael. She needed to know if he knew who Michael really was. Balak was brought before Lillian and forced to kneel before her. They grabbed him by his hair and pulled his face up toward her.

Michael wanted to control the situation and said, "Princess, do you know who this man is? This is General Balak from Abaylin's army. He helped misuse the name of Ozgul! What is he doing here in your kingdom? He seeks to kill you; I'm certain of it!"

Emma who had been sitting by watching things unfold came to Balak's defense, "That is not true, My Lady!"

Another argument ensued between the people left in the room. The guards looked around at each other; confused as to what they should do.

Lillian's head was starting to hurt and she shouted, "Stop it! All of you!"

Her voice echoed off the walls but managed to get everyone's attention. They stopped fighting and looked toward her. She turned toward Emma and calmly said, "You need to stay out of this. This is not the time and you do not have the right."

Emma saw the look on Lillian's face and knew she was serious. She graciously bowed her head and stepped back away from the throne. She had overstepped her bounds and did not know why. Her concern was only for Balak but she had forgotten her place.

Lillian waited until the room was silent and then turned her attention toward Balak. This had gotten out of hand and she was not about to let it continue any further. She looked at him and saw that blood was everywhere.

"Call the doctor back to the palace," she cried, "and get something to start cleaning this man up. What happened to him?" She examined the fresh wounds on his face and realized that they were not formed here in that short amount of time. She looked around the room and said, "Who did this to him?"

The guards were silently looking around for the perpetrator but no one was taking the credit. Lillian looked toward Emma and asked, "Do you know who did this to him?"

Emma lifted her head long enough to point at the guard who had given him the original beating but did not say a word. After realizing that he could no longer hide, the man stepped forward to take responsibility. He lowered his head before the princess. Lillian was done with playing games.

"Did you beat this prisoner?" she asked.

The guard replied, "Yes, My Lady, it was me."

"What was your reasoning for delivering this punishment to him? Who gave the order?"

The guard puffed up his chest and said, "This man was responsible for the death of my father last year at Dunfre. I suppose I let my anger get the best of me. There were no orders. I acted alone."

Lillian paused, pointed at the guard and said, "Seize this man."

The guards were hesitant at first but she reaffirmed her previous statement and they moved in. They removed him of his sword and held him by the arms.

"I understand your frustration," she said, "but this man was under my protection until such a time that he could be questioned. You will be removed of duty for one week's time without pay, but, understand, it could have been worse for you."

The guard bowed his head and was escorted out of the room.

Lorcene spoke up and said, "Your Highness, if this is the fearsome General Balak then he deserves any punishment he has received and more!"

Lillian fired back, "Not until I say so!"

"With all due respect," replied Lorcene, "you are not fit to make these decisions on your own. You are letting the emotions of the day cloud your judgment. We should be thanking that guard, not sending him away disgraced."

Lillian was done listening to the senator ramble on and said, "One more word, Senator, and I will have you restrained as well."

The senator held his tongue for the moment.

She turned her attention back toward Balak and asked, "Are you General Balak? The general that led Abaylin's army to attack Todere – my home?"

Balak kept his head bowed and replied, "Your Highness, I am General Balak and I have led many armies through the years but I did not lead the one that attacked Todere." He turned his head to look at Michael and said, "He is the one who did that!"

Michael objected, "This man is delusional! Obviously he would lie to save his own neck!"

"My Lady," said Balak, "I know that I am deserving of all my crimes and even the crimes of others I have commanded. I am not trying to stay out of trouble, I have no need to. I speak honestly when I say that this man, Michael, took my place when I fled from Abaylin's army to protect my family. If it pleases the princess, you should ask Emma. She has already visited with them. They are staying with the sisters in the orphanage."

Lillian turned toward Emma and she confirmed what Balak had said.

"Your Highness, how can we be sure that he hasn't manipulated this poor girl into believing something that isn't true?" asked Michael. "It wouldn't be the first time, I'm sure."

Lillian looked at Michael and said, "At this moment in time, I trust her more than I trust anyone else in this room. If what General Balak says is true, then you should be arrested and tried the same as him."

Michael responded by saying, "This man has done nothing but evil his whole life. He cares for no one but himself. I believe I have already shown you that I am who I say I am." Michael composed himself and remembered the power that was within him. Balak was no match for that now. "I have already laid my intentions out before you. I am not hiding the fact that I serve Ozgul but I have already explained how Abaylin acted on his own authority when he led those armies. However, this man acted on his own desires and did things so vile that no one should speak of them."

Balak began to laugh out loud. "This man is incompetent and is probably just a tool in the hands of Ozgul himself. Princess, you may do with me as you wish, but, please, believe me when I say that if Michael is here, then no good follows him."

Lillian processed what Balak was saying before giving her response. She was in quite the position. The world's most notorious criminal was slowly becoming the most honest man in the room.

Lillian was hesitant about trusting him but they shared one thing in common – a dislike of Michael.

"A thousand pardons, Princess," began Lorcene, "but we do not have to listen to any more of this man's lies. He is a criminal and has already confessed to being such. You must have him put to death immediately."

Lillian looked at Lorcene and said, "We have seen him commit no crimes and just a while back, he saved my life and the lives of Tomar and Emma. To bring down the sentence seems unjust."

Lorcene was being polite to try and get what he wanted.

"My Lady, I do not wish to speak back to you in your position, but you must uphold the law at all cost. I understand that you may be unfamiliar with all of our laws so I will educate you in this matter."

"If I am missing something," responded Lillian, "please fill me in. As of right now, I wish to stay this execution until Ethan and Morgan return."

Lorcene moved closer to Lillian's position and said, "I'm afraid you have no choice in this matter."

"There is always a choice," responded Lillian.

Lorcene lowered his voice and sternly said, "Not in this matter. According to Bodainian law, any criminal that confesses directly to his crimes must be instantly brought to justice. Failure to do so could result in the forfeiture of the throne because the king, or acting queen in this case, must adhere to the laws of Bodain at all times. That is why we have the senate in place to prevent such a thing from happening."

Lillian knew he was right but her thoughts were interrupted by pleads from Emma.

"Please, My Lady! Do not bring this sentencing down upon him. He saved my life and I owe him mine."

"Emma, I'm sorry," replied Lillian. "I don't think I have much of a choice in the matter."

Lillian looked over to see Michael and Lorcene smiling with delight at her words. Their demeanor was enough to make her angry all over again. She looked down at Balak and tried to figure out if there was a loophole that she could use without giving Lorcene the kingdom. Her mind raced with options as she stood before a broken Balak. His hand was pressed hard against his side to try and subdue the pain he was feeling. It was in that moment that Lillian found her loophole.

She smiled at Emma. It was a smile of victory. She knelt down in front of Balak and asked, "Do you wish to continue your fight against the Amari and those who have surrendered their lives to his presence?"

"Your Highness," began Balak, "I just pray that one day, people will have completely forgotten who I am. If I could believe that the Amari would take me back, I would surrender myself, but I have done too many wrongs to be loved by him. I do not wish to fight against anyone any longer." Balak turned his face away from Lillian and looked at Michael. "However, I would not mind a chance at him."

Lillian stood to her feet and said, "Very well, according to Bodainian law, I have no choice but to place you in the dungeons until such a time as a proper trial can be held for the crimes you may or may not have committed."

Lillian smiled as she watched the senators face switch from happy to confused, all in one moment.

"You cannot do that!" he shouted. "According to the law you must have him executed!"

"You are wrong, Senator! According to Bodainian law, any man proved to be of nobility is automatically given the right of fair trial before sentencing can be passed. To act outside of this law would lay aside hundreds of years of practice."

"This man is of no nobility!" shouted Lorcene. "He is a common criminal!"

"What proof do you have of that?" replied Lillian. She knew exactly what she was doing.

The senator fumbled his words and said, "I – I – I have no proof. However, what proof of nobility do you have?"

Lillian had him right where he wanted him.

"The proof I have is right there upon his right hand. He bears the ring of a noble."

Balak himself was shocked at all that the princess was doing. He looked down at his hand at the ring on his finger. He had almost forgotten about it himself but was now thankful for the dead man in the woods that he had taken it from before entering into Bodain with his family. Maybe the Amari was up to something after all. He smiled at Lillian and then at Emma who returned the same sentiment. Tomorrow would not be the day of his death after all it seemed. He looked at Michael and took personal delight in the fear that was resting on his face.

"Do not be an idiot!" objected Lorcene.

Lillian quickly responded by saying, "You will not speak another word against me or this throne or I will have you arrested for treason."

The senator laughed at her empty threat and said, "You cannot do that—"

"Guards! Place the Senator under arrest."

They moved in and restrained him.

"Perhaps a night in the dungeons will remind you of your place in this kingdom," said Lillian. "Perhaps you and Balak would like to share the same cell?"

The senator was speechless. In his mind, he had forgotten that she was the ultimate authority and he had over stepped his boundaries. The guards began to pull him out and closed the doors to the throne room behind him. Lillian had complete command of the room. She felt like a different person altogether.

She called another guard over and said, "Do not actually lock him away. Let him go free, I think he learned his lesson. However, I do not wish to see his face again for the rest of the day."

The guard ran off after the senator. Lillian could not believe what she had just done as she just made a very powerful enemy, but she felt great about it nonetheless.

She looked to Michael and said, "I cannot deny what you have done but I can see right through your lies. I do not know your motives but I do know that you are not welcomed in this palace any longer. You may either leave willingly or by force."

Michael desperately wanted to use his new power to teach the princess a lesson but he knew he would have to face Ozgul if he did. He would not dare interrupt but he had become very angry.

"Princess, you will listen to me! I came here of my own free will to aid you and your people."

"You came here to threaten our people!" shouted Lillian.

Michael yelled back, "No! I came here to warn your people! Bring us the Phayladin and this kingdom will be spared! Refuse and watch this kingdom burn!"

"I should have you arrested for treason against the throne and these people!"

Lillian was interrupted by screams through the hall in support of Michael. He had only been here a short time but had already turned the hearts of the people. She quickly realized that she couldn't arrest Michael without causing a riot in the streets. The worst part was the look on Michael's face. He knew it too.

He stepped up and addressed the princess and the crowd.

"I have offered you nothing but respect and civility, even bringing healing to your people, but you reject me at every turn. Hear me very clearly!" Michael's voice grew deeper and more menacing as he continued. "I will leave your presence and continue the good work of Ozgul but my giving has its limits. Ozgul will rescue the people from the Amari's evil grip one way or the other and I will not be held responsible for what happens next. Do you understand what I am saying? You have seven days. Seven days!"

Lillian was taken aback by the tone of his voice. The look in his eyes made her very nervous and she wanted him gone.

"We will just have to take our chances and see what happens then," responded Lillian. "Enjoy your stay but get out of my palace – now."

Michael had no choice but to leave, but he left as a hero of the people. They already began to call for the Phayladin's surrender. Balak glared as Michael turned and exited the room.

"Stand to your feet, Balak."

Balak struggled to find his footing but managed to stand on his feet.

"Understand this," said Lillian, "you deserved to be punished for your crimes. My staying of your execution is not because I sympathize with you, but because I owe you my life. I do not know what will happen to you in the future, but as for now, I cannot in good conscience let you go free. Do you understand?"

"Yes, My Lady," was all Balak could say.

"You shall have no access to any visitors and will be secluded from anyone else."

Balak interrupted, "Please, My Lady, do not take my family away from me. They are all I have and my mother is very ill. This could possibly kill her."

Lillian thought it over and said, "We will tell your family of your situation but my decision stays the same. Who knows how many family members that you have kept from ever reuniting with their loved ones while on Eret. Their only hope is one that is to come after death, and I'm afraid that may be your fate as well. It is only fair."

Balak looked toward Emma as she implored him to not argue with the princess. Balak realized that there was no use in arguing and conceded the point to Lillian. As she motioned for the guards to take him away, she turned to exit out the back of the throne room. She asked Emma to not follow her and Emma obliged. Lillian really needed to be alone at that moment. She walked through the door leaving the crowd behind her. As it closed, she collapsed to the floor sobbing uncontrollably.

20. THE BEGINNING OF THE END

Morgan and Ethan had spent their hours in their cells catching up on lost time. Morgan had only been gone for a few weeks at the most but the emotional toll had made it feel like ages. They hadn't heard from the emperor since Ethan confronted him in his own throne room and they had been confined to their cells ever since. Not a second between the two of them was wasted. The burden of his father's death had been lifted from Morgan's shoulders and all he wanted to do was to be brought up to speed on what was happening back home. The very first question he asked was about Lillian. Ethan brought him up to speed on her promotion to queen and it caused Morgan to squirm. He kept going on and on about how Lillian would hate him when he returned.

The laughter between the two had grown quite serious as Ethan filled him in on Lorcene and his desire to overthrow King Hezra. He had come to terms with the fact that Ethan was the Phayladin and his pride had taken a secondary role to his admiration. He kept teasing Ethan about having super powers but was glad to have his brother at his side again. After all that was said, Morgan had only one question that remained and he had failed to ask it up to this point.

Morgan sat up against the wall and fiddled with the hay on the ground. He looked over at Ethan and said, "So, what do we do now?"

Ethan was sitting cross-legged in the middle of his cell and responded by saying, "We wait."

His answer perked Morgan's interest and said, "Really? That's the big plan. We just wait."

"We wait," responded Ethan.

Morgan sat up and said, "That's just not good enough. I know that you know more than you are letting on. What are you hiding? Better yet, why are you hiding it?"

"Morgan, being the Phayladin is not just some cheap parlor trick. To put it as simply as I can, the Amari speaks to me only that which I am supposed to know."

"That doesn't make sense," interrupted Morgan. "You two are supposed to be one and the same."

"We are," replied Ethan. "It's incredibly complicated to explain, but, essentially, I can only do what the Amari allows me to do, and right now, the Amari is saying that we have to wait. It's so easy for us to think that today is the only thing that matters because we live in the moment, however, today is just one part of the larger story. Besides, in the end, he does what he wants. I'm just here to serve in love."

Morgan smiled and shook his head, "Now, you're just talking nonsense! Are you sure you are the Phayladin? Shouldn't you be smarter than that?"

Ethan grabbed a handful of hay and threw it at Morgan and said, "Here's what I do know. We will get out of here and return to our homes, but it won't exactly be easy for both of us."

Morgan stared out the bars to the world on the other side. His smile slowly faded away as he said, "I'm not expecting any favors. I deserve to be punished for what I have done. I will suffer as I must regardless of the pain that comes with it."

"Morgan," began Ethan, "he's not out to punish you for your arrogance or stupidity. That's not the way it works, however, adversity is not such a terrible thing. It can make us stronger, more refined. You see, here's the thing, all that has happened to us – to you – is not without a reason. It's making you a better man, a better friend, and a better king. However, we have to ignore the situation that we are in and all that comes with it and look to the one who is still in control of it all. Think about it this way. Our sufferings teach us how to persevere through trials, perseverance brings about character, and character will lead us to hope because it allows us to put things in perspective and if this world needs anything right now, it is hope. Trust me on this one."

Morgan laughed as he said, "Then let's just skip all of that suffering stuff. I'm hopeful already! Besides, I'm sure that there will be enough of that to go around."

Morgan stood to his feet and walked to the cell door and began to examine it for any sign of weakness. The crude cell may not have looked like much but it was sturdy in design.

"Can you at least unlock the door?" asked Morgan.

Ethan stood to his feet as well and sarcastically said, "Where's the fun in that?"

Morgan looked at him with discontent and turned his attention back to the lock. He looked out into the area of the quarry and saw guards approaching quickly.

"Look at that," said Morgan. "I guess we will soon find out our destiny."

Leading the way was Captain Ardone. As they approached the cells, Ardone motioned for the other guards to stop and set up a perimeter. He needed to speak with Ethan alone.

Ethan spoke first and said, "Captain, to what do we owe the pleasure?"

Ardone came within a few feet of the cells, looked over at Morgan and then back at Ethan as he said, "You must tell me what you have done to my father. Phayladin or not, I demand an answer. I have never seen him like this before. It seems as though he is out of his mind and I want to know why. Tell me of the events that led up to his insanity."

"Ardone," replied Ethan, "I provided the answers that he was seeking."

"What do you mean by that?"

"His dreams were driving him mad and I explained to him what the dreams meant."

"And what of his dreams?" asked Ardone. "What did they mean? He has been plagued by these for such a long time."

Morgan spoke up and said, "It means your father is crazy. No offense."

Ardone did not respond but merely glanced in Morgan's direction.

Ethan answered his question by saying, "His dreams were given to him by the Amari and, unfortunately, his dreams were showing him the end of his life and the end of this kingdom. After that, he became infuriated; however, it is not he who is in control."

"What do you mean by that?" asked Ardone.

"Emperor Neroni is possessed by multiple Destroyers," replied Ethan. "It has been that way since he conquered Fosteria twenty-five years ago when you were just a small boy. Neroni lost control a long time ago and now it is coming to an end in just a few days."

Ardone's expression did not change at the revelation.

"You don't seem to be surprised," said Morgan.

Ardone looked at him and said, "No, I'm not surprised at all. In fact, it all makes perfect sense." He paused for a moment to collect his thoughts and said, "But it does not matter. He may have lost his mind but he has not lost his the strength that lies beneath his larger exterior. I am here to inform you, tomorrow, he is opening the Gauntlet and you two are the main attraction."

"What is the Gauntlet?" asked Morgan.

"It is a cruel and vicious game that my father began long ago. It has a two-fold purpose: the first is to entertain, and the second is to watch you die." Ardone began to pace as he continued. "The Gauntlet is not a typical arena and is the centerpiece of a day of celebration. It is a narrow path that must be completed from start to finish or you will find death in the process. You will face three obstacles down that path that range from man to beast, from simple to more difficult. If you make it to the end, you will be granted your freedom, however, do not get your hopes up for your chances are slim."

Morgan looked at Ethan and said, "So this is what you meant by suffering leading to hope, huh?"

Ethan shrugged his shoulders at the question.

"What's to keep us from just standing there and doing nothing?" asked Morgan. "If we don't go forward, there can be no games."

Ardone looked toward Morgan and said, "Behind you will be a giant wall of fire. That wall would be pushed forward by a handful of slaves. If you should choose to stay where you are, you will be pushed forward by the approach of the wall, burned alive in the flames, or impaled by the three foot spikes protruding from the wall.

THE ACCOUNTS OF AMARI

Once you are in the Gauntlet, there is no turning back. You will play my father's games or die."

Morgan puffed his chest up with pride and said, "Well, then, why wait? Let's do this now."

Ardone pointed at Ethan and said, "You told him that he would be dead in three days and he wants to prove that you were wrong by watching you die on the third day instead. This way he proves that he is stronger than the Amari and his messenger." Ardone began to beg with Ethan. "I implore you, please; many men have died in the Gauntlet. It is a suicide mission. Tell my father that you were wrong and maybe he will show you mercy."

"I can't do that," replied Ethan.

"But you must!" countered Ardone. He reached through the bars, grabbed Ethan's hand and placed a ring of keys into his palm. "If you won't do that, then take these keys and set yourselves free once we walk away. You are too important to die here!"

Ethan handed the keys back to Ardone and said, "This is how it has to be."

Ardone was speechless but managed to say, "Very well, but I don't know who is more insane: you or my father."

Ardone pushed himself away and began to leave. There was nothing else to say.

"Ardone!" shouted Ethan. "Is there something else you wanted to ask me? About your father?"

Ardone stopped once again. He had wanted to avoid the next question but knew it had to be asked. He turned back around and addressed Ethan's question.

"What about his claims that he is not my father? What do you know of that?"

"He was telling the truth," said Ethan. "He isn't your father."

"Then who is?" asked Ardone. "Why does he claim me as his son?"

"Twenty-five years ago, your real father was murdered by Neroni when he conquered this kingdom," replied Ethan. "Your father was the king of Fosteria. The stories that you have heard about Neroni's conquest are not exaggerated, however, it wasn't just your father but your mother died as well."

REDEMPTION   194

Ethan gave him a moment to process all of the information. He could tell by the look on Ardone's face that his emotions were running wild.

"Deep inside," continued Ethan, "you know I'm telling you the truth. Your father – your real father – was a good man. When he ruled, this land was different and, soon, you will be given the opportunity to stand in his place as rightful ruler of this kingdom."

Ardone said nothing in return. It was hard to believe that his entire life was a lie. If what Ethan said was true, then he had given his love and respect to the man who murdered his family.

Ardone's voice was broken as he said, "You should prepare yourselves for the worst."

And with that, he turned to leave.

21. AN ACT OF TREASON

Balak had been alone with his thoughts. His cell was dark and the food was terrible but it had given him plenty of time to process his life and his current situation. He couldn't help but to be worried about his family but he knew that they were safe and that gave him great peace. No visitors were allowed to see him and his cell was secluded from the rest of the criminals held beneath the palace. However, he was allowed to see one person and she came with his meals three times a day. He found himself looking forward to her arrival and a break from the loneliness he was experiencing.

Emma had volunteered to serve Balak his meals. Oddly enough, she felt as though she needed to repay him for what he had done for her. She knew his days were numbered but she felt an attraction toward him that compelled her to see him. Emma smiled as she descended the stairs that led to the dungeon. It was time for Balak's supper and she was on her way to deliver it. She walked down a long corridor that took her past the other prisoners that were being held there. The prisoners heard her coming and began to holler at her as she walked past. Emma felt extremely uncomfortable with their words and looked straight ahead and walked faster. As she came to the end of the corridor, a lone guard stood in front of a locked wooden door. He waited for her to stand directly in front of him and then proceeded to inspect the tray of food for anything suspicious. After he was satisfied, he turned and opened the door that led to Balak's cell.

Balak heard the door creak and quickly stood to his feet hoping that it was Emma walking through the door. He dusted himself off and straightened up his tattered and bloody clothes. He ran his hands through his hair trying his best to straighten it. He knew he looked terrible and cringed at his foolish attempts to clean up. He felt awkwardly embarrassed at the emotions he was feeling and found himself staring at the ground. Emma approached the cell door and paused a few feet in front of it. She slowly lowered her head and bowed in Balak's direction as she smiled.

"I know it's not much," she said, "but I did manage to sneak out some extra meat for you." She held the plate in front of her and waited for Balak to approach.

Balak moved forward and reached through the hole in the cell door that was big enough to pass the plate through.

"Your kindness means a lot to me," replied Balak. "It is more than I deserve. Have you any news of my family?"

Emma clasped her hands behind her back and said, "Your mother is doing much better. The sisters are taking very good care of her and her health is returning."

"That is good to hear," replied Balak.

"She tried to get me to bring you a coat," continued Emma. "She is worried that you will be cold down here. I tried to calm her fears but she insisted. She only stopped insisting when I told her that there was no way I would be allowed to bring one down to you."

Balak smiled and said, "That sounds exactly like her actually."

Emma moved closer to the bars and pulled up the side of her dress just enough to reach underneath. Balak stood puzzled as she began to fiddle with the hem of it. She pulled out a bundle of cloth and straightened her dress out again.

"However," continued Emma, "I managed to sneak one in for you."

She unfolded the cloth to reveal a light coat for Balak.

Balak reached out and took the coat from her and said, "Emma, you shouldn't have done this. Who knows what type of trouble you could have gotten yourself into? It's not worth it. I'm not worth it."

Emma smiled at him and said, "I guess we all have our bad side."

Balak smiled at her innocence and said, "Obviously, my presence here is leading you into a life of crime. I can see you are becoming a vicious criminal."

"Is it that obvious?" asked Emma.

Balak laughed at the look of pride on her face and swung the coat around to wear. As he lifted his arms above his head to slide into the sleeves, Emma saw that his left sleeve was stained with a lot of blood. Her joy quickly turned in to concern.

"What is wrong with your arm?" she asked. "Do you need medical attention?"

Balak did not pause as his arm disappeared into the sleeve.

"I'm fine," he said. "I was merely trying to erase my past."

He rolled the sleeves back ever so slightly to show Emma the damage done to his arm. Emma gasped at the sight. The exposed skin revealed that Balak had been trying to rid himself of the Seal of Ozgul tattooed to his forearm. It was bloody and the scars were beginning to form where it was healing.

Balak placed his hands on the bars in front of him and said, "If I must die, I choose to do it knowing that I am no longer a slave to Ozgul and the evil that plagues this world. I will die free."

Emma had no words to say. Her heart broke at the thought of Balak's death. She couldn't believe that the man who was once the most feared man in Eret was now standing before her broken and remorseful.

"At least, you do not have to die feeling as though you are alone," said Emma. She reached out and placed her hands on top of Balak's. "I promise that I will be there every step of the way."

Balak looked into her eyes and said, "Thank you. Your kindness is overwhelming at times and definitely undeserved."

"It is the least I can do," replied Emma. "Besides, I can—"

Emma was interrupted by the sound of the door opening behind her. She pulled her hands away and looked at the ground in front of here as though she were ashamed.

"It's time to leave," demanded the guard. "You've been here long enough and the prisoner has other visitors waiting. Let's go!"

Emma smiled once more at Balak and bowed. She turned on her heals and exited through the open door. She paused on the other side as she saw who the visitor was. Senator Lorcene was waiting for his turn to see the prisoner. Emma quickly bowed before him and hurried along the way. Lorcene entered into the cell after her. Balak looked toward the door and became indifferent as Lorcene approached. He pressed himself up against his cell door and gripped the bars tightly.

"Guard!" he shouted. "I do not wish for any visitors!"

Lorcene spoke louder and said, "Relax, General. I've come only to speak for a moment."

Balak's eyes grew fierce as he said, "I am nobody's general. You will not refer to me by that title any longer at risk of your own life."

Lorcene was frightened by Balak's words and stopped his approach. He was within arm's length of Balak in his cell. Balak stared him down for a moment and then lunged forward, grabbing Lorcene by his coat and pulling him tightly against the bars. Lorcene's face was smashed between the bars and, for the moment, his heart raced within his chest. Every beat felt like a drum within his chest.

"Please!" Lorcene managed to beg for his life. "Please! Just hear me out! If you don't like what I have to offer, I will walk away!"

Balak enjoyed the rush he was feeling from the fear in Lorcene's eyes. There were some things that were harder to let go of than others. He finally snapped back to reality and released his grip on the Senator.

"I have nothing to offer you," replied Balak. "My sentence is sure. You and your new friend, Michael, saw to that today."

Lorcene straightened up his clothes and backed away from the cell. He cleared his throat and tried to regain some of his dignity.

"I understand that we may have put you in a position in which you would be a bit angry with us, however, I am here on my own with my own interests at heart. Michael has nothing to do with this, however intriguing he may be."

Balak stared at Lorcene, unmoved by his words.

"You see, we both have common interests," continued Lorcene, "we are both concerned with our freedom: yours from this prison cell and death, and mine for the people of this kingdom."

"The people of this kingdom are already free," replied Balak. "What are you offering them freedom from?"

"Freedom from their mindless surrender! Freedom to experience life without the fear of repercussions from a dying religion! I offer them a chance to make a life for themselves and to choose their own destiny!"

"And what of you?" asked Balak. "What do you get out of all this? I mean, no offense to you, but you are an idiot."

Lorcene was unfazed by Balak's insult and continued, "I may be an idiot but you, my friend, will soon be a dead man. I can change all of that for you. I can get you out of this cell and back with your family but I will require your services in order to make that happen."

"So, what did Michael offer you? Whatever it is, Senator, I'm sure you should think twice before you completely agree to go through with it. Michael has a track record of stabbing people in the back."

"I have spent my entire life seeking wisdom above everything else and wisdom tells me that it is always better to join the winning team. You see, Michael, has promised that I will become the ruler of this land and that is an offer I cannot refuse."

Balak placed his hands on his hips and laughed out loud. He couldn't stop laughing as he said, "I get it. You are just as much of a coward as Michael is, or was for that matter." The laughter continued. "You two make a great couple!"

"You can make jokes all you want but what about your family?"

Balak snapped to attention at the mention of them and instantly reached out for Lorcene but he pulled back just in time.

"You will leave my family out of this or I will kill you," said Balak.

"I have no desire to harm your family as they will soon be under our rule anyways," replied Lorcene, "but I know that you desire to be with them and that is something that we can make happen in exchange for your services."

"What is it you want from me?" asked Balak, releasing the tension from his body.

"It's simple," replied Lorcene, "we need you to kill the king."

Balak was shocked at the request. "Isn't the king already dead?"

"Not at all. He is alive but is not awake. However, if he does wake up, it will be too late for us. We both know you are capable of fulfilling this request and I believe the stakes are high. Your freedom comes from his death, a full pardon."

"So all I have to do is kill the king of Bodain and you will let me go?" asked Balak.

"That is all," replied Lorcene.

"Obviously, there is only one choice for me," said Balak.

Lorcene waited for his response.

"I would rather die than help you with anything!" shouted Balak. "And there is nothing you can do to change that!"

Balak spit on the ground at Lorcene's feet to show his disgust for the request. Lorcene stood with a look of disappointment on his face.

"Very well. I gave you a chance, Balak. Your freedom will be lost! If you are still alive when I am king, I will make sure that you and your family's executions are the first thing that I do. Now, your only choice is to rot in this cell until it is time."

Balak refused to get angry but said, "Senator, your delusions will be the end of you. If you think for a moment that you are fighting for the strongest side, then you deserve everything you get."

Lorcene ignored Balak as he exited the room. The guard closed the door behind them and Balak was once again alone. He knew he had to do something but, at the moment, he had no answers. However, he would not stop trying to find a way. There was no way he was letting Michael win again. He kicked the plate of food that Emma had brought him in a moment of frustration. As it rattled around the small cell, it occurred to him. His only option was to wait.

THE ACCOUNTS OF AMARI

22. THE GAUNTLET

The third day had arrived. As the sun broke over the horizon in the desert, it burned an eerie shade of red just as Ethan had predicted. The guards had arrived being led by Captain Ardone to take Ethan, Morgan, and a handful of other prisoners to participate in the Gauntlet. Emperor Neroni loved his games and he shared that love with anyone in the kingdom who was not a slave. Ardone motioned for his men to place Ethan and Morgan in shackles and they did. First they shackled their wrists together, and then connected those to shackles on their feet. The rusty chains clanged together as they walked and were long enough to only allow their feet to shuffle.

Ethan looked around and took a quick count of the prisoners going with them to the Gauntlet. He counted only eight people not including Morgan and himself. These prisoners ranged in size and age and some were already suffering while a few seemed to be incredibly fit. It was a long walk to the Gauntlet and the midday sun was hot.

Whenever Neroni arranged for the Gauntlet to take place, it was announced all over the kingdom. It was an affair to remember and one that was not to be missed. The streets were lined with people from the kingdom who were celebrating the games. As the prisoners turned the corner to the street that led to the arena, they were greeted with a long lane known as the 'Walk of Shame'. Ethan and Morgan held their heads high as they walked the street. To the people of the kingdom, these prisoners were a random group of criminals who deserved their time in the Gauntlet. They shouted insults and threw food at the group as they walked past. A few times, the soldiers had to violently push people back as they lunged out for the prisoners. Ethan could not help but feel compassion for these people. Their time under Neroni's rule had hardened their hearts and chipped away at their humanity. They weren't necessarily violent people, but they were desperate. He could see it in their eyes.

Aside from being hit in the head by rotten food, the walk turned out to be fairly uneventful and they arrived at the gates to the arena. The soldiers had cleared the way for the prisoners to enter as the crowds to get inside had grown quite large. Directly behind the arena was the tower that Neroni was having built for himself. It already towered over the kingdom and it was only half way done. The arena looked small compared to the tower but it managed to hold a large amount of people. The crowds could be heard singing and chanting as they entered through the doors. The guards led them down a dark corridor to the holding cells as they waited for the games to begin. Some of the prisoners took a seat on the ground while others paced the floor. The tension in the room was high.

Ethan looked at Morgan and said, "You know you are going to survive this right?"

Morgan laughed a little and said, "Actually, I kind of assumed that you didn't come all this way for us to die together. It seemed to make sense to me."

"Your part in the Amari's plans is not quite fulfilled yet. Unfortunately, I cannot say the same for everyone else. People will die in here today."

Ethan did not wait for Morgan's response but stood to his feet and began to speak to the other prisoners. Morgan sat back and watched as Ethan talked about the Amari with each of the prisoners. His mind raced back to the moment when they found out that Ethan was the Phayladin. He was so foolish to react the way he did. He was proud of his brother and, if there was anyone who deserved to be the Phayladin, Morgan could think of none better. His presence in the room commanded attention but the way he held himself was so humble.

Ethan made his way around the room, praying with some and praying for others. When he was done, he sat down next to Morgan and said, "We need to pray hard for that guy over there."

Morgan looked over at the large man and said, "Why him?"

Ethan shook his head and replied, "When I started talking to him about the Amari, he became very opinionated. Let's just say he colorfully disagreed with me. I think he needs more time to live so that he can change his mind. We should watch his back."

Morgan chuckled and said, "How do you do that?"

"Do what?" asked Ethan.

"How can you be so concerned about saving his soul when you know that we are about to face our own impossible task? You've always been able to do that and it has always impressed me."

"My father's death taught me a lot about life," said Ethan. "He gave his life to rescue that little girl in the street. She was a stranger to us but yet he sacrificed everything leaving me behind. His example taught me early on that this world is not my home. It's just a brief moment in an endless saga. Once you see that, all that matters in this life is what you do to affect the life that is to come. And once you get to that point, you can face anything at any time. Think about it, if the Amari is on our side, who can honestly stand against us?"

As he finished, the door to the holding cell was flung open and in walked Captain Ardone.

"Everyone on your feet," he said. "It's time."

The prisoners shuffled forward, still shackled in their chains. As Ethan was about to leave, Ardone stopped him.

"Are you sure this is what you want?" Ardone asked. "The world needs you to live."

"The world does not need me to live, Ardone. Besides, everything will be okay. Just be on your guard today. You never know what choices you will have to make."

Ethan nodded at Ardone and continued out the door with Morgan close behind. Ardone had nothing more to say. They were led down a dark tunnel lit only by torches and the light coming from the end. As they drew closer to the light, they could hear the roar of the crowd growing louder. They came to their entrance into the arena and the guards led them out into the open. Most of the crowd booed the prisoners as they came, but there were some who cheered for the underdog. Morgan was incredibly impressed by all that he saw.

As they entered the arena, they saw that it was not much of an arena at all. To their right was the giant, spiked wall that Ardone had told them about. At the moment, there was no fire burning on it but Morgan was sure that was about to change. To their left was the Gauntlet. The stands reached high on each side of the path that made up the game. The people were positioned well enough to see all of the events at all times. The path had walls that stretched ten feet tall to keep anyone from trying to escape while competing in the game. At the end, the narrow path that they would fight down opened up into the circular part of the arena. On the backside of that ring, directly in front of the path, Emperor Neroni's chair was waiting for him to be seated. It was a very elaborate and vicious set up and that was something that Neroni took great pride in. Above the Gauntlet's main path, was a series of rope bridges suspended in the air. They were designed to allow Neroni to watch the games from above and not miss a bit of the action. Morgan looked ahead and saw that Neroni was already on one of the bridges and ready to address the crowd.

Neroni lifted his hands in the air and delighted in all of the excitement at hand. He motioned for the crowd to grow quiet and said, "People! People!"

The crowd grew quiet as they waited for the emperor to speak. The arena was built in such a way that the sound of his voice would travel around giving most people the opportunity to hear him clearly. The loud roar of the people had been subdued.

"People! My people! Today we have quite the event in store for you! Ten prisoners have been chosen by myself to run the Gauntlet!"

The people cheered again and then quieted down.

Neroni turned to address the prisoners below and said, "As most of you know, the Gauntlet is a test of strength and endurance! No thinking is necessary to complete this task. All you need to do is know how to survive. The Gauntlet is made up of three challenging and breathtaking tests! These tests will seem to start off easy and become more difficult as you move forward. And to make sure that you are a willing participant, we have a bit of motivation for you. *Light the Fire Wall!*"

Two guards with torches came out and began to light the wall on fire. It did not take long to flare up at all as the whole thing had been covered in a highly flammable liquid. The prisoners could feel the heat coming from the flames. The crowd cheered as the Fire Wall was lit. There was no way to get around the wall. Its width matched the width of pathway that they must fight through. There was no going back. The slaves behind the wall would push it forward to keep the competition moving.

Neroni continued, "In the twenty years since the games first began, many people have tried to defeat the Gauntlet to earn their freedom. Perhaps one of these prisoners will make it through! Regardless of the outcome, you will surely be entertained." The crowd cheered and booed yet again. "If one should try and escape, their immediate punishment will be death! Three events! Only one will survive! Welcome to the Gauntlet and let the games begin!"

The guards came out to unlock the shackles from the prisoner's hands and feet. Once the shackles were removed, they left out the same door they came in from. A horn sounded the start of the Gauntlet and the prisoners began to move.

Morgan's training in military strategy flooded back into his mind as he tried to find the upper hand quickly. Before them were a group of warriors armed with various weapons including spears, swords, and shields. Morgan began to realize that even the first task would not be easy to get through but he trusted Ethan. The prisoners began to spread out to try and avoid Neroni's warriors. The fire behind them began to push forward as its flames grew larger by the moment. The wall was so large that it required more than a handful of slaves to get it to start rolling. Morgan knew that their only means of survival was to help each other.

"Ethan!" shouted Morgan above the noise. "We will have to work together! There is no way to get past these shields unless we do!"

Ethan nodded at Morgan and they pressed in closer. Their attention was stolen by a cry of death as one of the first prisoners had already fallen. There would soon be others. The warriors already outnumbered them by at least two people and the difference would only increase. Ethan and Morgan carefully moved forward as they were confronted by a warrior of medium size. His face was covered in war paint and he grinned from ear to ear. He inched forward toward the two brothers and hit his sword on his shield to taunt them.

Morgan held his hands out in front of himself as Ethan stood behind him with one hand on his shoulder. The warrior took a swing with his sword and Morgan jumped back to avoid the tip. Ethan's movement was fluid and exact as he mimicked Morgan's every move. After a few more swings, Ethan realized that they were getting a little too close to the flames behind them.

"Morgan," shouted Ethan, "we must do something now!"

Morgan knew they were getting close but he had the warrior right where he wanted him. The warrior raised his arm high and brought it down diagonally to strike Morgan. Instead of moving backward this time, Morgan dove in the opposite direction of the swing. He rolled off to the side as Ethan stepped up to draw the man's attention away from Morgan. The man was no longer paying attention to Morgan and took a swing at Ethan. He put all of his might into the swing that his arm swung high above his head again. From the side, Morgan rushed up under the man's arm and lifted him off of his feet and planted him firmly into one of the side walls. The impact caused the warrior to lose his grip on his sword and it fell to the ground. However, the warrior's shield became trapped between the wall and his body and he used it to push back against Morgan. The man spun around to find his sword but it was too late. Ethan had picked the sword up and was tossing it over to Morgan. Once the man had realized what was happening, Morgan was already landing his finishing blow. The blade found its mark and the warrior collapsed to the ground.

"Ethan, take the shield!"

Ethan picked up the shield while Morgan yielded the sword and they scanned the area ahead of them. Including Ethan and Morgan, there were six prisoners still alive as they had managed to subdue the warriors and get the upper hand. Once the last warrior had met his death, it was time to move on to the next challenge. The wall of fire pressed forward as to give them no chance for a break. There was a gap underneath the wall just large enough to pass over the dead bodies on the ground. One of the prisoners saw an opportunity to escape and ran toward the flames and fell to the ground. Ethan called out to the man to stand back up but it was too late. Some guards appeared on the wall above and aimed their bows at the prisoner. Ethan turned away as the arrows took the prisoner's life. The guards disappeared behind the wall again. They were down to just five.

The prisoners moved forward with their newly acquired weapons in hand. Ethan picked up a spear to go along with his sword and they approached stage two of the games. In the wall on the left side, there was a series of random holes placed throughout it, both high and low. The prisoners looked around to each other for answers but no one knew what was happening. The crowds began to cheer as this was their favorite part of the games.

From behind the walls, there was a hissing sound that appeared and, in moments, they watched as fire and smoke began to pour out from within the holes. Seconds later, their next task appeared. From within the holes, fireballs shot across the path at high speeds. Once they hit the opposite wall they immediately exploded, showering the path in sparks and flames. Morgan could not believe the speed of which they were coming out of the walls. The explosions created quite the display for the crowd to rally behind and they stood to their feet in excitement. One of the prisoners began to panic. He bounced up and down for a moment to prepare himself for the trial and then bolted down the pathway. He did not make it very far, however, and was hit directly by more than one fireball. The explosion knocked the man off of his feet, the collision being too much to absorb. His body lay dead on the ground.

Morgan looked at the four of them remaining and realized they must do something. The wall behind them was growing ever close.

"Quickly! Grab whatever weapons are left and throw them to the other side of these fireballs!" The prisoners picked up the remaining swords and spears and tossed them away. "Everyone pick up a shield!" he shouted. "We can create a wall between us and the explosions! It's only a few yards to travel and we can make it if we stick together!" He pointed at the two other prisoners and said, "One of you needs to be on each side; blocking all shots that go high! We will watch for the ones going low! We must move as a unit. Do not lose a grip on your shields!"

The prisoners did as they were commanded and, together, the group formed a wall for protection.

"Morgan, look!" shouted Ethan. "There is an exact pattern every time and a few seconds of delay after each shot. If we time this right, we may be able to move virtually unscathed!"

Morgan nodded in agreement and said, "It's your move! Take us through! But you better hurry because that wall is closing in fast."

As Ethan timed out the pattern, it was as though time was slowing down. He felt the Amari's power stirring inside of him and he could see each fireball as though it was a single shot. He played the image out in his mind, waited for the right moment and shouted, "Let's go!"

The prisoners began to move forward. Ethan had planned it out perfectly so that they fit directly in the gap between shots. Fireballs shot past them in front and behind, but Ethan's pace kept them safe. Half way through, one of the prisoners stumbled and fell. Ethan paused to go back, but Morgan pressed them on as he feared if they stopped to help, more of them would die. Ethan moved forward with them as they were almost through. The prisoner on the ground laid flat against the ground and held his shield at the ready. The fireballs were soaring just inches above him but were not hitting him. He tried to stand but as he moved one of the fireballs landed directly on his shield and exploded, knocking the shield from his hands. He froze in fear.

The other three made it through with precision. Ethan looked back and saw the man lying on the ground. The fire wall was quickly approaching this portion of the Gauntlet and Ethan could not let the man die. This was too much for him to bear. He ran over to the nearest hole in the wall and planted his shield firmly in front of it, covering it up completely. He braced himself for the impact that was to follow. The mechanism inside of the wall that was producing the fireballs loaded the next shot and sent it flying. The fireball and the shield connected at the wall and the explosion was devastating. Ethan's body was thrown backward through the air and landed hard on the ground. Inside the wall, the explosion caused a ripple effect to occur as each hole began to explode from within. After the first few explosions, the entire wall blew up. People tried to duck and hide as ashes and debris began to rain down on them leaving some people with minor injuries. Neroni had been watching from above and even he had to cling to the ropes after the explosion rocked the bridges.

Ethan rolled on the ground in pain, unable to move. Morgan jumped into action and looked at the other prisoner and said, "Help me get them out!"

The large prisoner shook his head, grabbed some weapons from the ground, and moved down the path to get away from the approaching wall. He had no desire to die. Morgan rolled his eyes at the selfishness of the prisoner and turned to get the others. The prisoner that Ethan had helped stood to his feet without Morgan's help and began to run to the next stage of the games. Morgan ran over to Ethan who wasn't moving. As he approached, he could tell that Ethan was really hurt.

In his daze, Ethan smiled up at Morgan and said, "Check that out. I didn't even have to use my powers to do that."

Realizing that Ethan was in no condition to move on his own, Morgan lifted him off the ground and over his shoulder. Morgan struggled under the heavy load but he would certainly not leave Ethan to die. As he turned to move further down the path, he heard Neroni yell from above.

"Release the Chee-Ti!"

The prisoners that had gone before Morgan stopped in their track as two doors opened at the end of the path leading to the arena. As they did, two large cat-like creatures leapt out from within. Their momentum caused them to collide with each other and they snapped at each other's necks revealing their large and vicious teeth. Their fur was thick and long and dark throughout. Even from a distance, Morgan could see the muscles in the creature's legs as they were ferociously strong. The Chee-Ti sized up their prey and quickly became poised to attack.

The prisoner that had left first was caught unaware and frantically tried to back away but tripped on his feet. The first Chee-Ti leapt forward to attack and swiped at the man's head. Its brutal attack ended the man's chances for survival.

"Morgan," said Ethan, "set me down. I will be alright."

Morgan moved over to the wall and set Ethan down again. Ethan winced at the pain he felt. Morgan quickly ran over and grabbed a spear from the ground. The other prisoner now faced two Chee-Ti. He held a shield in front of him and managed to keep the Chee-Ti at bay, but they were merely waiting for an opportunity to strike. Morgan held the spear up next to his ear and horizontal to the ground. He ran forward a few steps and flung the spear through the air. The first Chee-Ti never saw it coming and the tip of the spear entered in to the creature's neck. The creature collapsed to the ground as it slowly died from the mortal wound. The remaining Chee-Ti focused on the prisoner before it and pounced on his target. The man lost the grip on his sword but did his best to keep his shield between him and the Chee-Ti as it fiercely tried to get through with its claws. The mindless beast began to tear up the shield between them.

Morgan reached for another spear lying near him and readied it for launch. He threw it again hoping to strike the Chee-Ti but the creature saw it coming and ducked out of the way. He had missed his mark but at least the prisoner was safe for the moment. Bloodied and bruised, the man dragged himself away.

The Chee-Ti's focus was on Morgan now and the two paced back and forth within the Gauntlet's path. Morgan knew it was now or never. He had two swords in the ready. He remembered back to Ethan's promise that they would make it through alive and he found that his faith in Ethan had filled him with a new found courage.

"Come on!" he shouted. "Come and get me!"

The crowd roared in approval as Morgan taunted the beast. In all of the years of the Gauntlet, they had never been entertained so much by the competitors. They were in full support of Morgan as he attempted to live. Morgan did not wait for the attack to come. He charged forward with swords in hand. The Chee-Ti responded in like manner and the two raced at each other. Morgan studied his opponent as he ran forward, ready to make a move. The Chee-Ti planted its paws firmly into the ground and leapt into the air at Morgan. Morgan reacted quickly and slid beneath the creature, passing underneath it. As he did, he took both swords and drove them into the creature's body but not before the Chee-Ti's front paw took a swipe at him. The claw tore into Morgan's chest leaving him in pain, but the swords had done their work and the Chee-Ti collapsed dead on the other side of Morgan.

Morgan grabbed his chest in pain but quickly turned to make sure the Chee-Ti was dead. He scrambled to his feet and saw the Chee-Ti was no longer moving. He looked up to see Ethan on his feet as the wall had forced him to move or be burned. The main tasks were over and there was no need to hurry. The last remaining prisoner had scooted his way into the arena and decided not to move any further.

Ethan stumbled his way forward and said, "That looks like it hurts."

"I thought you said that we would make it through this without the pain," replied Morgan.

"I said we wouldn't die," said Ethan. "Remember the part about suffering. Besides, Lillian is going to be mighty impressed with those wounds. You may win her back after all!"

Morgan grabbed his sword from the Chee-Ti's body and said, "I think I will keep this as a souvenir." He helped Ethan hobble along and said, "What could possibly be next?"

The entire arena was sold on Morgan's heroics. Everyone except for Neroni. He was furious. No one was supposed to make it this far and here he had three people survive. At the sight of the last Chee-Ti's death he knew he had to change the rules and act fast. He made his way down to the arena floor. A horn sounded to quiet the crowd down as Neroni planned to speak and guards moved out around him, including Captain Ardone. The noise from the crowd slowly subsided and Neroni began to speak.

"People of the Desert Kingdom! Never before have we had such a show in the Gauntlet!"

The crowd roared in approval and once again the horn was necessary to demand silence.

"However, the rules state that only one prisoner may survive and here we have three."

The guards moved Ethan and Morgan into the center of the ring and dragged the last remaining prisoner and threw him on the ground near Neroni.

"In times like these, the burden now falls on my shoulders to decide the outcome. He turned to the prisoner before him and said, "You fought well, my friend, but I hereby announce that all that you have achieved for yourself is a delayed death!"

"*No!*" shouted Ethan. His cries fell on deaf ears as Neroni snapped the man's neck. His body collapsed to the ground as the crowd booed in defiance but the emperor was unfazed.

He pointed at Ethan and Morgan and yelled, "As for you two! I think your time in the arena is far from over! I demand that we have one last battle. A battle to the death! Brother against brother!"

23. DREAM FULFILLMENT

Ethan and Morgan were not at all surprised at Neroni's request for them to fight to the death, but they both knew it wasn't going to happen. As the crowd cheered on, Neroni moved in closer to where the two were standing.

"How about that?" asked Neroni. "You didn't think you would both be getting out of here alive did you?" He pointed at Ethan and said, "What do you think of your dream interpreting skills now? Three days have passed and here I am still fully alive while you could very well find your end here today."

"Nothing has changed," said Ethan. "You will still die here today but it will not be by my hands. You will die and the Destroyers that have claim to your soul will perish along with you."

"Live long enough and we shall see," said Neroni.

"You're a fool if you think we are going to fight each other," Morgan interjected. "It just won't happen."

"Of course you will, Prince! If you don't, you will both die here in this ring together."

Morgan looked at Ethan and said, "Then I wish to die with him."

"Do not think that you can ruin my day, boy! Prince or no prince, this is my kingdom and you shall do as I command or there will be swift punishment!"

"Stop fooling yourself!" shouted Morgan in return. "We've played your game and we won. We have earned our freedom and you must let us go now. It is the only honorable thing to do."

Neroni fired back at Morgan and said, "I do not care about honor! I care about power and wealth; the things of this world that actually benefit a life."

The crowd began to grow restless as chants for freedom began to spring up around them. The people were not interested in more bloodshed and felt that the prisoners should be allowed to go free. The pressure of the crowd was making Neroni even angrier than before.

"No, no, no, no, no! This is not how this will end!" Neroni pointed at Morgan and said, "You will fight your brother now or else!"

Morgan stood his ground and said, "We will not fight!"

Neroni's insanity was revealing itself in the moment. He was alone and it felt as though the whole world had turned against him.

"Very well," said Neroni. "If you will not fight each other then I will just have to take matters into my own hands. I will not let you go free! Guards, seize these men!"

The guards quickly rushed in and pushed Morgan and Ethan down to their knees as they restrained the arms. Swords were drawn and the tips were planted at their necks. Ardone looked on, unsure of what to do at that moment.

Neroni pointed at Morgan and said, "Drag him off to the side, but leave his brother here."

The guards began to drag Morgan away as he fought to get free. He struggled with all that was left in him but he could not gain his freedom. He had no choice but to watch what would happen next.

The horn sounded again as Neroni motioned for the crowd to be subdued.

"People of the Desert Kingdom, these two prisoners have openly committed crimes against the throne and their acts of treason cannot go unpunished. Let this be an example to everyone that this is my kingdom and I am the law!" He motioned toward Ethan and said, "Because of your crimes, I now sentence you to receive thirty-three lashes!"

The guards followed the orders of their emperor as they always had before. They tied two ropes around Ethan's wrists and stretched his arms out to the side, pulling tightly on the ropes. Another man came up and tore Ethan's shirt to expose his back. Ethan was too tired to fight back, even if he had wanted to do so. Morgan began to fight harder to protect his brother but more guards moved in to pin him down. The guard with the whip slowly moved forward and paused in front of Ethan. Ethan looked up and saw that Albado was standing in front of him. The look in his eyes told Ethan that he did not want to go through with this. He made his way around to the back and let the whip unravel to the ground. He snapped it a few times to warm up his arm and looked over at Emperor Neroni.

"Begin!" barked Neroni. Albado hesitated and Neroni shouted, "I said begin!"

Albado slowly reared back and, with one swift movement, he brought the whip down upon Ethan's back. The wound instantly appeared as contact was made. Ethan's whole body tightened up under the pain and he clinched his fists to help fight it off.

A sinister smile appeared on Neroni's face as he said, "Again! Again!"

Albado reluctantly continued and brought the whip down again. Wound after wound appeared upon his skin as blood rolled down his back. With every snap of the whip, Neroni would squeal in glee. The Destroyers living inside of him were taking pleasure in being the one who helped destroy the Phayladin. Ethan could barely breathe but his body was becoming numb to the pain. Albado was halfway through when he stopped.

"Why are you stopping?" Neroni demanded an answer. "You are not done!"

Albado looked at Neroni and said, "Do you know what we are doing? Do you know who this man is?"

"Of course I know who he is! Now carry out his sentence."

Albado had made up his mind that he would not continue. He threw the whip on the ground and stepped away.

Neroni rolled his eyes and said, "It does not matter. I will do it myself."

He walked over to where the whip was and raised it to the ready. He smiled as the whip cracked down on Ethan's back. He quickly built up momentum and continued one snap of the whip after the other. He was no longer counting out the punishment and, in this moment, he did not care if Ethan lived or died. Ethan collapsed under the pain and was barely holding on. He managed to look over at Morgan who had stopped struggling and stared in disbelief at his wounded brother.

As the emperor's insanity raged on, the crowd was completely silent and many of them turned their faces away at the sight. The emperor raised his hand into the air one more time and brought it down with all of his might. However, the whip's progress was interrupted as it wrapped around an arm of Captain Ardone.

"Enough!" shouted the captain. Neroni was caught completely off guard by this attempt to rescue Ethan and Ardone ripped the whip from his hand. "I will not let you continue this assault! Guards, let this man go and get him some medical attention."

Neroni was furious, "How dare you defy me? My own son defies me!"

"I am not your son," fired back Neroni. "I am the son of a murdered king and the rightful ruler of this empire!"

"Who fed you such lies?" asked Neroni. "Of course you are my son! He is not our son, he deserves to die!" Neroni was arguing with himself.

"It's over!" declared Ardone. "You have lied to me all these years. I gave you my love and my devotion as any child would and you withheld the truth from me. This ends here and it ends now. You are no longer fit to be the emperor."

The emperor continued arguing with himself as the people watched. Finally, Neroni drew his sword from his side and shouted, "You fool! You cannot stop me!"

He ran toward Ardone with his sword drawn. Ardone drew his sword, dropped to his knee, and plunged it into the stomach of Neroni. The emperor's momentum came to an abrupt halt and a look of shock came over his face. Ardone stood to his feet as Neroni collapsed to his knees. His hands wrapped around the sword in his stomach. He looked at Ardone.

"I . . . did love . . . you," was all Neroni could say.

He sat back on his heels, dropped his head, and his hands fell to his side. Ardone was breathing heavily as he couldn't believe what had just happened. He had killed the only father he had ever known. He looked around at the faces of the people in the arena who were looking at him as if he knew what would happen next.

In all of the confusion, the guards had let go of Morgan and he raced to Ethan's side. He fell to his knees and slid in toward Ethan who was lying on his side. As Morgan lifted Ethan's head, he was relieved to see that Ethan was still alive. The wounds on his back were deep and many. Ethan reached up and attempted to pull Morgan's head down closer to his to be heard.

Morgan listened as Ethan whispered, "He . . . isn't dead."

His eyes immediately looked over at Neroni. Morgan instantly noticed that Neroni was still breathing. From behind them all, Neroni began to laugh. All eyes were glued on the emperor as he, once again, slowly placed his hands on the sword and began to pull it out of his body. His laughter grew louder and deeper as he did and, when the sword was free, he looked up at Ardone who stepped back away from the sight. Emperor Neroni's eyes were filled with darkness and he began to stand to his feet.

With a voice that was not his own, Neroni said, "You cannot kill me. I have existed since long before you were born and I will continue to exist long after you are dead. Neroni is gone, but we Destroyers shall live on in his place. The Phayladin can do nothing to help you!" His voice grew deeper and louder still as he said, "I will bring death to you all!"

He threw his head back as his battle cry rang out into the arena. The crowds began to panic and flee. The Destroyers living in Neroni had complete control of his body and their strength would be unmatched. Using Neroni's body, they reached out, grabbed Ardone by his clothing, and threw him across the ring. As he landed on the floor, the momentum of his body slid him through the dirt and slammed him into the wall causing it to splinter and break from the collision. Other guards began to flee. One unlucky man ran too closely behind Neroni who ferociously swung his arm into the fleeing soldier. The impact sent the man flying off of his feet and his body collided with the Fire Wall still burning behind them. His body broke through the wall and the fracturing caused the wall to fold over on itself. The already large flames quickly began to catch fire to everything nearby it as the wall was just a burning heap of wood.

Morgan dragged Ethan off to the side as Neroni looked around for him.

"Ethan, what should we do?" asked Morgan as panic was setting in. He had faced a lot of different enemies in life but even he knew he was outmatched. Neroni's strength was just too much.

Ethan found enough strength to say, "We do nothing." He pointed to the sky and said, "They will take care of everything."

Morgan was confused and looked to where Ethan was pointing. There was nothing there but empty space. He scanned the area once more and that's when he finally saw what Ethan was pointing at. A team of Persuaders appeared in physical form as they flew down to the earth with their wings spread wide. They landed in a circle around Neroni and the impact broke up the ground underneath their feet and caused Neroni to stumble. No words were spoken as the Persuaders attacked. One by one they flew toward Neroni's body. They were trying to separate the Destroyers within Neroni's soul from his body. Neroni swatted at the Persuaders who entered into his body and grabbed at the spirit of the Destroyers. They seemed to go in one way and come quickly out of the other. The attacks came continuously and caught the Destroyers completely off guard. After the assault had worn them down, the Destroyers finally released their grip on Neroni's body. Morgan watched as one by one, the Destroyers appeared from within. He counted six of them as they left Neroni's body in their physical form. The body collapsed to the ground as Morgan watched in awe as they fled from the Persuaders. The fight was over. It was time to leave.

The Persuaders let the Destroyers flee and got on with their mission. Morgan stood to his feet as two Persuaders made their way toward him, their physical forms towered over him.

"It's time to get out of here," was all they said.

One of the Persuaders bent down and lifted Ethan off of the ground while the other wrapped his arms around Morgan. In one swift movement, the Persuaders launched into the air and carried them away from the arena. They landed safely on the ground just outside the kingdom. As they arrived, Morgan noticed that Captain Ardone had been rescued as well. It was completely unbelievable.

Back in the arena, the final Persuader remained. He drew his sword from its sheath, turned it upside down, and held it firmly with both hands. He waited just a moment and then drove the tip of his sword into the ground below. The impact of the blade in the ground began to shake the earth. It started off as a small rumble but soon began to grow larger and larger. The ground began to crack and a large crevice began to form. The crack moved forward, splitting the walls of the arena and causing it to collapse. It was only the beginning as its target was the tower that Neroni was building for himself. As the crack arrived at the base of the tower it disappeared underneath it. The foundation started to break and the walls began to tumble.

Morgan watched from afar as the building toppled down on itself. It was not long before the ground opened up and started swallowing the tower whole. The hole beneath the tower grew only large enough to take down the tower but the shaking of the earth could be felt far away. The desert floor was collapsing and burying itself. The earthquake continued until the entire tower had been buried beneath the sand. Once it had accomplished its purpose, the rumbling ceased and peace washed over the land.

Morgan wasted no time. He turned to where Ethan was lying and ran to his side. The wounds were all over his body and his breathing was soft and shallow but he was alive nonetheless. He reached his hands out to help Ethan somehow but he hesitated and never allowed his hands to contact his brother; the damage was too severe. Morgan stood there helpless until a hand touched his shoulder. He looked back to see the Persuaders still present and waiting.

"Prince Morgan," spoke the Persuader, "we cannot stay here. We have to get the Phayladin to safety."

Morgan shook his head slowly and said, "Yes, let's get him inside so—"

"No, we cannot stay here. Destroyers are on their way as we speak and this is the perfect time for them to fight us for him. We don't have enough men to fight them. We have to leave for the sake of the world."

Morgan looked at Ethan again and realized that the Persuaders were correct. His face conceded to the point.

The Persuader continued, "You must take Ethan and ride with him to the Bendor Forest."

"The Bendor Forest?" asked Morgan. "That's just beyond Methir, the giant's kingdom."

"Yes, it is, but it will provide you with a place of refuge. The people there are loyal to the Amari and that is becoming a rare thing in this world."

"I can't ride all the way there. I have to go home. Bendor is a few days past Bodain. I have to return to Bodain!"

"We don't have time for that now. There is nothing you can do for Bodain that is more important than this. Their fate rests in our ability to get Ethan to safety."

"That's not good enough," said Morgan. "I can't just leave Lillian there on her own and my father is alive. I need to return home. Is there any other way?"

The Persuader glanced over at the others and said, "Bodain is too far away for you to help at this point. You wouldn't make it there in time."

"In time for what?" asked Morgan.

"Ozgul is planning something evil, but by the time you arrived it would be over. Ethan is injured and you cannot ride fast enough with him on your horse. I know this is hard but you must believe me, this is the only way."

"Can you all stop it?" asked Morgan. "There must be a way for you to intervene."

"We have Persuaders stationed all around Bodain and they will do all they can to protect as many lives as possible, but all of that is in vain if you do not get Ethan to safety."

Morgan didn't like this at all. If he hadn't run away to begin with, things would be different. He was conflicted between what he wanted to do and what he needed to do. He looked over at Ethan and knew what he must do. No more arguing.

The Persuader caught on and said, "As soon as you reach the Bendor forest, you can return to Bodain but not a moment before. Do you understand what I am asking you to do?"

Morgan was finding it difficult to think. In his mind, he knew that he had to do what the Persuader asked but, in his heart, he longed to hear his father's voice and to embrace Lillian again. For once in his life, he would put his selfishness aside.

"What do we do then? How do we travel without being seen?" asked Morgan.

"You will ride with Ethan under our cover. There are no Destroyers at this moment who are close enough to see what we are about to do. All you have to do is stay on course and trust us. The Amari will take care of the rest."

Morgan nodded his head in agreement. The forest was at the foot of the mountains that provided the backdrop for Bodain. They would have to ride around it and even then the Bendor forest was large and fairly unknown to him. He tried to calculate in his head how far out of the way they might be but without a map for reference, he was lost.

"Prince Morgan!"

Morgan turned to see Ardone walking toward him and gave him a half-hearted smile. He imagined that Ardone was probably just as lost as he was.

"How is Ethan?" he asked with urgency. "Is he still alive?"

Morgan could see the concern in his eyes.

"He is fine, Ardone, severely injured but he will make it," said Morgan. "I don't know what to say to you, however, I am sorry for your loss."

"Never mind that," replied Ardone. "Neroni may have raised me and called me his son but that man was not my father. I only hope that my actions do not reflect poorly upon me. Ethan has done more for me than any other man I have known, and I have only known him for this short time."

"He has that effect on people," responded Morgan and quickly changed the subject as a Persuader motioned for him to leave. "Listen, I have to get Ethan out of here and to safety. I suppose as the new emperor, you have a lot of work ahead of you."

Ardone cringed at the sound of that new title and said, "I am a warrior and not a dictator. I will oversee the rebuild, but I will change the way we rule to include more of the people, let them have a say in what happens next."

Morgan reached out to shake Ardone's hand and said, "You would make a fine emperor. This kingdom needs a man like you to lead them."

"Thank you, Your Highness, and I know we are not much to look at but the fight against evil is far from over. If you are ever in need of our services, please do not hesitate to send word. Our people owe you and Ethan a great debt and we consider Bodain to be our ally."

The pleasantries ended there as Morgan said goodbye. The Persuaders had already arranged Ethan on the horse and Morgan climbed into the saddle. While he was talking with Ardone, someone had managed to do their best to bandage up Ethan but the blood was beginning to show through. Ethan was strong but the wounds on his body were enough to kill any normal man. *This is what he gets for trying to save the world,* thought Morgan. *He doesn't deserve this.* Morgan said a prayer and began to trot away from the Desert Lands. The Persuaders followed him on all sides and for the first time, Morgan felt like everything would be alright. Their journey would take them near Bodain, however, and Morgan was certain it would break his heart not to be there.

24. DESPERATE TIMES

Lillian stood on a balcony overlooking the kingdom. This used to be her favorite place to get away from all of the stress but these past few weeks had consumed any ounce of free time she could have wanted. As she looked out from the balcony, she felt the weight of Michael's warning on her shoulders. There were just two days until the coming storm, as Michael put it, would be upon them. She had no idea what he could be referring to but it had to be terrible. However, at the same time, she felt a sense of peace knowing that Ethan could be back at any minute to set all things right again. They just had to hold on for another day as this one was almost over.

Lillian pulled her shawl tighter around her shoulders. Night was falling and the air, although warmer than it had been, was bringing in a definite chill. She turned to retreat back into her room to retire for the night as Emma would be there soon to help her get ready for bed. She was grateful for Emma as she was the only connection to a simpler life before all of this. Lillian had sent a letter to her mother and father, detailing all that was happening, but had not received a reply. She knew that there was a chance that her letter never made it but she longed to hear her father's voice, to let him take charge and solve these problems before her, or her mother's gentle touch that seemed to make every care just disappear. Unfortunately, she had come to learn that she couldn't have everything she wanted.

She entered the room and closed up the doors behind her. She placed her shawl on the old bed post nearest the door and sat down at a desk against the back wall. She grabbed the brush on the desk and began to brush her hair. The door opened behind her.

"Oh, Emma," said Lillian with a simple glance over her shoulder. "Could you start a fire please? It is awfully chilly outside and I want to go to sleep completely—"

Lillian was cut off as a hand quickly wrapped around her mouth and lifted her from her seat. She instantly grabbed the attacker's arm and began to fight back. Lillian may have a small build, but as a princess she was trained to fight. She squirmed under his grip until she found an opportunity to strike back. She bit down on one of his fingers and he released his grip long enough for her to slide away from him. She turned to see her assassin's face which was obscured by a mask. The eyes of the mask were darkened and the outline looked like that of a skeleton, covered with bone fragments. His face looked like that of a monster but he was obviously human. He shook his hand as Lillian poised herself into a defensive stance. The man rushed her again. This time all she could do was brace herself for impact as his weight was too much for her. Their momentum carried her back into the desk. She shoved her hands into his face as an attempt to block his vision. He reached up to grab her hands but she wasted no time punching him directly in the throat. He gasped for air and reached for his throat. Lillian pulled her feet up and pushed him off of her and he tumbled to the floor.

Frantically, Lillian searched the desk for some kind of weapon. She slid off the desk and pulled out the drawer on the top left side to obtain her knife but the assassin had already recovered from the blow and was slowly standing to his feet. Lillian saw an opportunity to reach the door to the hallway where she could call for help. She held the knife and ran. The assassin lunged out and grabbed her foot and she fell to the floor as the knife fell from her hand. She kicked back at him and managed to free her foot from his grasp, however, he was quick to recover. She crawled across the floor and was able to grab her knife just before the man pulled her back and flipped her over. She tried to sit up but the man punched her in the face. The impact rattled her and she became disoriented as another blow followed that one. She could feel the warm blood running down from her mouth. She looked up as the assassin reached for his knife and pulled it from its sheath. Instinctively, she took the knife in her hand and jammed it into his side. The man yelled from under the mask and reached to grab the handle protruding from his body.

Through tear filled eyes, Lillian grabbed his hand with the knife in it and, before he could react, she pierced the other side of his body. The assassin grabbed Lillian's head and slammed it into the floor and then he rolled off from on top of her. The knives had found their mark and the assassin was bleeding profusely. He pulled one of the knives out and collapsed onto his back. Lillian's head was throbbing from the impact. She managed to scramble away and backed into the side of the bed. She brought her knees up to her chest and wrapped her arms around them as she began to sob. She watched the man lying on the floor in his own blood and knew that it was over. Her chest heaved as she audibly wept, afraid to move. Her face hurt so badly.

Someone began pounding on the door to her room and she heard the voice of Emma coming from behind it. The door was locked and Emma could not get through. Lillian snapped back to the reality of the moment and quickly stood to her feet to cross the floor. She reached the door, undid the lock and pulled it open. Emma stood shocked at the sight of the princess but all Lillian could do was collapse into her arms. The sobbing continued.

A confused Emma tried to decipher what had happened and said, "Princess! Princess! What has happened? Are you alright?"

Lillian tried to compose herself and said between breaths, "This man tried to kill me. He tried to kill me!"

Emma surveyed the scene and said, "Princess, there isn't a guard on this entire floor. I came as soon as I saw. I don't know where they are but they aren't anywhere that I could find them. I don't think it is safe to stay here."

Lillian nodded and tried to stand to her feet. They made their way back into the room and Emma locked the door behind them. Lillian looked over at the dead assassin and thought to search for any information she could find. Emma helped her roll the body over. Lillian stared at her attacker for a moment. She reached out toward the mask but hesitated right before touching it. She needed to know for sure that it was just a man. After a moment, she pulled it back to see that her suspicions were correct. It was enough to relieve some of her fear and she continued the search. On the man's belt was a leather pouch. She untied it and pulled it away. The pouch contained a handful of silver coins and a piece of paper. She dropped the coins to the ground and began to unfold it.

Kill the princess and then help dispose of the king's body.
You are paid in full.

"What is it? What does it say?" asked Emma.

Lillian looked up at her with fearful eyes and said, "They are going to kill the king!"

Emma stared at her, unable to move.

"I must go to him," said Lillian. "Emma, you have to find us some help."

"But, Princess, there is no one out there," she replied.

"Then keep going until you find someone! I will head to the king's room and you can meet up with me there. Bring as many as you can."

Lillian stood and reached for the knife that fell from the assassin's side and, without any hesitation, she ran for the king. Emma exited the room and ran the opposite way. She knew exactly where she was going.

Lillian ran down the hallway and toward the king's chambers. She saw no guards and in her panic, it never occurred to her to call for help. The palace seemed eerily quiet. She ran for what seemed like minutes until she rounded the corner and saw the first sign of Bodainian guards. Their bodies were lumped together on the floor, dead. She slowed her pace and cautiously walked over to the entrance. She could hear someone talking to themselves from within. She held the knife close to her and peered around the edge fearing the worst. As she looked inside, her heart welcomed a bit of joy as she saw a familiar face standing over the king. Master Tomar.

"Thank the Amari that you—" began Lillian as she entered the room. She was interrupted by what she saw. Master Tomar turned his body just enough that she could see the knife in his hands, suspended just above the king's body. He was the assassin.

Emma ran as fast as she could to the only place she could think of for help. The palace's prison cells were down below and as far away as possible, but Lillian's room was at least on the same side. She descended the stairs hoping that the king was okay. She needed a plan and was running out of time. As she turned the corner, she saw the prison guards sitting at their post in front of Balak's cell. She decided that maybe the truth was the best option in the moment.

"Help me!" she shouted. "Help!"

The guards stood to their feet and asked, "What is wrong? Are you okay?"

Emma ran into the closest guard and wrapped her arms around him and started to cry. *This has to work,* she thought. The guard pushed her back just a little and grabbed her shoulders to try and calm her down.

"The princess was just attacked by an assassin and the king is now in danger!" she shouted. "You must help them! All the guards are missing! You are the only two that I have found!"

"Calm down, young lady! What do you mean by an assassin?"

This was taking longer than Emma hoped it would. "I mean, a man broke into her room and tried to kill her. What else could I possibly have meant? She managed to kill him though and his body is still in her room. She sent me to find help and you two are the only two guards that I have found in the whole palace. Something is obviously wrong! You must protect the king!"

The guards hesitated and one of them said to the other, "What do you think? We can't leave our post."

Emma's frustration was growing as she said, "Where is the prisoner going to go? He's locked up tight in a cell behind another locked door! Do you want to be remembered as the guards who let the king die?"

Emma knew that was a low blow but it worked. The guards believed her story and took off running for the king's room. She just hoped that they would make it in time. She waited until she was sure they were gone and then ran to the door guarding Balak's cell. In her hand were the keys to his freedom, she lifted it from the guard's belt when she had run into his arms. She fumbled through the keys, found the correct one, and threw the door open. Balak had been resting on his bed and was startled by her approach. He could see in her eyes that something was wrong.

"Balak, please," started Emma, "I need your help and I need you to promise me that you will not lie to me."

"What is it? What's going on?" asked Balak.

"Promise me that you will not lie to me!" shouted Emma.

Balak saw the seriousness in her eyes and said, "I promise. What do you need?"

Emma continued, "Because I am about to release from prison the most wanted man on this side of Eret and I do not want to be wrong about you!"

"It's the king, isn't it?" asked Balak.

Emma was taken back and said, "How did you know that?"

"Senator Lorcene visited me recently and asked me to be the one to assassinate the king."

"What did you say to him?" she asked.

"Obviously, I told him no. I have no desire to kill the king or help the senator take over this kingdom. I just want to make my family proud again in whatever way necessary, even if that means dying for my crimes."

Emma stared into his eyes and knew she had no choice. She grabbed the key to his cell and quickly turned the lock, securing his freedom. Balak stepped back as she opened the door.

"Emma, why are you doing this?" he asked.

"The princess was just attacked by an assassin. She is okay but the king is in danger as well. All the guards are missing and she sent me to get help, and, for some reason, you were all I could think of. Will you help me save the king?"

Balak shook his head and they left the cell. This could be a chance to redeem himself for some of his past crimes. They ran to a wooden box locked up tightly on the wall that contained extra weapons for an emergency. Emma fumbled through the keys looking for the right one when Balak pushed her aside. With one swift kick, he attacked the box at its hinges and the wood began to crack. He kicked it again and the box fell open. Balak reached inside and grabbed himself a sword and they took off to rescue the king.

"We must hurry," shouted Emma. "I fear that we are his only hope!"

25. TO SAVE A KING

Tomar looked at Lillian for a brief moment and then turned his attention to the king. Lillian was afraid to move. She could tell by the look on his face that he was sent here to kill the king. It was the perfect cover. The king's most trusted protector could have easy access to the king whenever he wanted. Even Ethan left Tomar in charge of protecting the family and, now, Lillian found that thought to be very puzzling. He should have known this would come to be. Lillian needed to stop him but she didn't know what she could do.

"Tomar, please, I know what you are planning to do but you can't. You can't do this!" she shouted.

Tomar hesitated and Lillian took this as a sign that he really didn't want to do this, however, something was off about him. Lillian moved closer to the end of Hezra's bed so that she could see his face. He stood there with both hands on the hilt of the knife with the blade pointed down just over Hezra's chest

"I have to do this," replied Tomar.

"No, you don't," agued Lillian. "You can put the knife down and walk away." The pitch in her voice escalated as tears began to form in her eyes. "Why? Why are you doing this?"

"Because I can see," replied Tomar. "For the first time, I can see. All my life I have begged for the Amari to bring me this healing and he has ignored my every cry."

"That's not true," responded Lillian.

"It is true!" shouted Tomar. "All the things that have been hidden from me- colors, faces, shapes and intricate designs- they are all so beautiful and so real. Why have I spent so much time suffering under the Amari's cruel thumb when he could have taken it away from me so easily? I spent my whole life serving him and his cause, and it was all for nothing!"

Lillian could see the pain on his face and said, "I am sorry, Tomar. I do not know what you have been through but this isn't the way to go. Michael may have given you your eyesight back but I still know that he is evil. Ozgul cares for no one."

The muscles in Tomar's face clinched tighter at Lillian's words. He gripped the knife tighter within his hands.

"You don't understand!" he shouted. "If I don't do this, I will lose everything! Michael is holding this against me and my sight will be gone forever. I cannot return to that existence. I need to see! I need to see!"

"But Master Tomar, if you do this, you will lose everything else, including your soul!"

"I do not care!" he said. "I will not go back!"

He raised his hands to plunge the knife into Hezra's body and Lillian instinctively reacted. She threw herself into Tomar but her small frame could not do enough to cause him to even stumble. He took his arm and threw her to the ground behind him and immediately turned back toward the king. Lillian scrambled to her feet and leapt on to his back. Tomar grabbed onto her arms with his free hand and tried to pull them off from around his neck. Lillian held on as tight as she could to try to keep him from getting a good grip. Tomar grabbed her arms and ran backward into the wall behind him. The air rushed out of Lillian's lungs and she released her grip on Tomar's neck. He swiftly bent over at the waist and threw her over his head and onto the floor in front of him. Lillian felt pain rush through her body as she collided with the stone floor.

Tomar walked slowly around her with the knife in his hands. He towered over her and Lillian saw a look of emptiness in his face.

"I am truly sorry, Lillian, but you are not supposed to be alive either."

Lillian sat up and began to slide across the floor away from Tomar. She cried knowing that there was nothing she could do to stop him. Her end was drawing near. She leaned back against the wall and pushed herself to her feet. Tomar held the knife in front of him ready to strike.

"I will make this as painless as possible," he said. "It is the least I can do."

Lillian could no longer see through the tears streaming from her eyes. She closed them tight and waited for the knife to enter her body. She thought of nothing else but Morgan. She wanted him to be here so badly. As she sobbed, she heard the knife drop to the floor. She opened her eyes to see Tomar standing in front of her. His face was twisted in pain and it was then that she saw the sword protruding from his chest. Tomar's hands hovered around the tip of the sword as he looked down. Slowly, he turned himself around and, as he did, Lillian saw a frail, white bearded man standing behind him. King Hezra was awake and his sword she had placed there at Ethan's request had saved her life. Her jaw dropped and she lifted her hands to cover her mouth in shock. Hezra showed no emotion and stared at Tomar.

Tomar turned to face Hezra completely. The shame in his eyes said everything. King Hezra reached out his arms and took hold of Tomar's shoulders as he collapsed to his knees. Tomar could see that he had clearly chosen the wrong side. His perfect vision proved only to be temporary and his old eyesight was starting to return. He looked at Hezra and the tears began to flow.

"Quiet now, my old friend." Hezra's voice was soft and compassionate.

Tomar looked the king in the eyes and wept. "I am sorry. I am sorry. I have been a fool." He wheezed and coughed between sentences. "Please, forgive me, My King."

"It is alright," said Hezra. "You have been a faithful friend all these years and I will not let this come between us now. We all make mistakes. Just rest. Just rest."

Tomar collapsed again to his side and his eyes turned to Lillian. The old colors were returning and his eyes had almost returned to normal. The beauty of her face began to fade away. He could manage no more words as life was leaving him. He looked back at Hezra to see him smiling at him and still could make out the tears falling down the old man's face. Hezra embraced the old warrior as he died.

"I will see you again, soon, Master Tomar. Soon."

"To glory?" asked Tomar.

"To glory," repeated Hezra.

With that, Tomar's eyes closed and he was gone.

The weight of the moment pulled Lillian to the ground. She could no longer control her weeping. Her body convulsed and she wept loudly. King Hezra gently laid Tomar's body on the ground and moved toward Lillian. He quickly wrapped his arms around her and she buried her face in his chest. He brushed her hair lightly and just let her cry.

"Now, now, my dear," said Hezra. "You are safe. You are safe."

Lillian clung to him but pulled her head away to look at Hezra's face.

Hezra smiled at her and said, "I am sorry that I have been unavailable. It was not my intention to abandon you."

Lillian managed a smile back and said, "I did miss you, My King. Thank you for saving me." She looked over at Tomar's lifeless body and said, "I tried to change him. I promise I did, but he wouldn't listen to me."

Hezra hushed her and said, "I know. I know. I heard everything from my bed. In fact, I have heard everything that you have said for a long while now. In fact, it is I who should thank you for visiting me every day. My body was not cooperating but my mind was fully aware. Your voice was so pleasant to listen to."

Between sniffles Lillian said, "So, you know everything: Morgan, Ethan, and the Senator?"

Hezra shook his head, "You were very informative. I also know enough to know that we are not safe here and should be on our way."

As he stood to help Lillian to his feet, he recognized that his body was still not cooperating well with him. Lillian helped to steady him instead as they heard footsteps in the hallway. They both froze in place as Emma came around the corner followed by Balak.

Emma looked at Tomar on the ground and immediately stopped her approach. She quickly turned her attention to Lillian and King Hezra. She was shocked to see the king awake and on his feet but instantly remembered to curtsy. Balak watched what she did and then awkwardly bowed his head as well.

Lillian looked at her in shock and said, "Emma, I sent you for help and this is who you return with. What is he doing out of his cell?"

"I searched for a guard but none of them are at their posts. I know that he is a criminal but I do trust him," replied Emma. "And right now, he has a particular set of skills that we could really seem to use. What happened to Master Tomar?"

King Hezra answered by saying, "His life came to an unfortunate end but his soul shall live on." He walked over to Balak and said, "I do not believe we have had an opportunity to meet. If I may ask, what type of criminal are you?"

Balak looked at Emma as if he was looking for direction as to how he should respond. She gave him nothing to work with. Here he was standing in front of one of the most powerful kings in all the land and he was once the most feared man in all the land. *This could not go well for me,* he thought. So, he lied.

"Uh, Your Majesty," he began, "my name is Benjamin."

Emma stomped a foot and cleared her throat. Balak quickly caught on.

"No, no. That is not true." Balak started over. "Your Majesty, my name is Balak and, by your reaction to that name, I can tell you already know what type of criminal I am."

Hezra stared at Balak for a while. Balak felt the weight of that stare and grew uncomfortable at the silence. Hezra always tried to make sure that he thought things through before he spoke.

"In terms of struggle, the enemy that I cannot trust bears stronger than the closest enemy that does not ask for trust. Therefore, I must give favor to the enemy of my enemy to trust that he hates my enemy more in this moment than he hates me."

The room was silent. Everyone was confused.

Hezra looked at them coyly and said, "Don't any of you ever read?"

He stood closer to Balak and said, "Do you hate my enemy more than you hate me?"

"Absolutely," Balak said, "and in my defense, I've never really hated you at all. It's a long story."

"One that I hope to hear someday," replied Hezra. "For now, our lives are in your hands and it seems we have a problem. I assume that the guards did not just wander off on their own, so what has happened to them?"

"We do not know," responded Balak, "but if your attackers have already gotten this far we should assume that there must be more. We need to go and we need to go now."

The air in the room began to stir and almost instantly a group of Persuaders appeared. Lillian smiled as she recognized Sevron from before but, for the others, this event was a complete shock. None of them had ever had an encounter like this before.

Hezra grabbed Lillian's hand and said, "Are we sure I'm not still asleep on my bed because, if this is a dream, it's the most exciting one I have ever had."

Lillian smiled at the king and laid her other hand on top of his.

Sevron spoke first and said, "We've been given permission to help keep you alive and we need to move quickly."

"What is wrong?" asked Lillian. "What kind of danger are we in?"

Sevron tensed up as he said, "The palace is under attack. There are Possessed coming this way now and we are all outnumbered. You will need our help if you have any chance of making it out of here but we must hurry."

"Why now? Where were you before when I was being attacked?" asked Lillian.

"You will have to ask the Amari that someday. Our obedience allows us to only do as we are told and not to interfere with the Amari's plans. Besides, look at you; you managed to save yourself and the king. Perhaps the Amari knows you are stronger than you think."

"Well, I'm sure we would all like more answers," said Balak, "but if the Possessed are coming, then we need to leave now."

"But if the Possessed are on their way," began Emma, "and we have a team of Persuaders with us, why don't we just stay here? It will be like a stalemate with neither side winning, right?"

Sevron continued, "Not before you suffer immensely. Persuaders and Destroyers can die just like you and, as I mentioned already, we are severely outnumbered. I can't explain it all to you as the Amari's plans are his own and it probably wouldn't make sense even if I could, but, if we die, then we die with honor, fulfilling our last duty on Eret. We go now and die if we must. We have a small army outside to stop what they can and we are in here with you.

"You need to know that we are not permitted to take human life. The Destroyers do not abide by the same rules. You will need your weapons to help keep us all alive so arm yourselves. All we can do is slow them down and attempt to separate Destroyer from human. If we cannot, then they will die together. A lot of life will be lost here today but, remember, this isn't about staying alive it is about freedom, freedom for all of Eret. Death is just the beginning."

26. RUN

The group headed out of the king's room and into the hallway. The Persuaders were very limited in their makeshift human bodies and could not retain this form for long. They would have to get creative if they were to make it through this battle.

The battle between Persuaders and Destroyers had been raging since Ozgul helped break the Amari's perfect creation a millennium ago. Hundreds of millions of them were created to be helpers to the human race; their numbers seemed limitless. They could die in this world but there would be no redemption for those who had rebelled. Persuaders carried their duties out with great humility in honor of the one who gave them life. They lived fearless in his hands.

The group ran cautiously down the hall and toward the main steps. Persuaders guarded the front and the rear and kept the humans safe in the middle. Emma looked down at two guards lying dead on the floor as they ran by. She recognized them as the guards from the prison. She had sent them to their death.

The goal was to make it to the secret entrance set up for the king and his family in case the kingdom was ever attacked. The tunnel was in the back of the palace which meant they had a lot of ground to cover if they were to make it there safely. Their speed was crippled, however, by King Hezra, his body still recovering from not having moved for so many weeks. Balak took on the role of the king's helper when necessary.

Lillian watched as the Persuaders each took turns disappearing into thin air. They would take that time to recover their strength in order to maintain their human forms before those bodies wasted away. Once those bodies were gone, the Persuaders would not be able to materialize again for a while. They took turns darting in and out of rooms looking for signs of the Possessed.

As they ran down the hall, Balak felt an eerie chill in the air. He couldn't tell if it was his own paranoia or something else. It was surprising, though, that they had traveled this far and had seen no evidence of the Possessed, until now. The group all looked in the same direction and paused in their run as they could hear glass breaking in the distance. At first, the sounds were few and far in between but the sounds soon began to grow louder and closer. Emma clung tightly to Balak's arm and jumped at each noise.

The palace was especially dark as the sun had set outside. Sevron waved to one of the Persuaders to go scout out what was happening. He vanished into the air as he jumped through the wall next to him. He was gone for just a moment and as came back, his message was clear.

"Run!" he shouted. "The Possessed are upon us!"

The group started to move but stopped abruptly. Down the long hall, doors began to burst open as the Possessed struggled to break through. The group turned to look behind them and saw more. The doors began to give way and, not one, but multiple possessed started to pour into the hallway. There was no time to wait.

Sevron called for them to move and they turned down a hall that was secluded from the outside. This would only buy them moments. Balak, Lillian and Hezra were all armed with weapons but they would be useless on their own. They raised them to a ready position and braced themselves for battle. Emma carried a knife but knew that she would be useless as her fear had rendered her helpless. They approached a door ahead of them and one of the Persuaders opened it. He never saw the attack coming.

One of the Possessed leapt out from the darkness and collided with the Persuader, knocking him off of his feet. The others quickly grabbed the Possessed and threw it against the wall. Balak wasted no time and stabbed him, killing him instantly. He watched as the Destroyer inside attempted to flee from the body but was no match for the ready Persuader.

The group continued down the spiral stairs and into the next room which was the dining hall. The large, open room left them at a disadvantage as there were entrances from all sides and nowhere to hide. They grabbed a heavy wooden table and pushed it against the door as they closed it behind them but they soon realized how futile that was as the Possessed pushed the door open and right back into them. All they could do now was run or fight. Balak quickly realized what the Persuaders meant by being outnumbered. Possessed stormed in from all angles. They poised for attack and the sight of it was unnerving. The Persuaders pushed the humans behind them and formed a tight wall. However, Balak refused to stay in his place and pushed his way to the front, sword at the ready. Then the attack came.

The scene was nothing but chaos: good versus evil. Lillian couldn't help but see how majestic the fight was. The Possessed used their strength and leapt through air but the Persuaders were equally ready. Sevron called out orders and the fighting began. The Persuaders hindered the attacks and Balak took to battle. They fought as strong and as quick as they could, taking down as many of the Possessed that they could.

Balak was enraged for the fight. He stayed close to the people and attacked what he could reach. Every swing of his sword was a release of the vengeance that he had held up inside of himself. At one point, he was attacked from behind and knocked forward, landing on his face. The Possessed man swung his fist into the center of Balak's back. He struggled to knock off his attacker but this position left him weak. He pushed up to no avail but, then, the Possessed collapsed on top him. He looked up to see King Hezra smiling down with his sword in his hand. Balak knocked the man off and rejoined the fight, but it seemed too late. The Persuaders had been pushed back. They needed a way out and fast.

From the other side of the room, the doors again burst open and a team of Bodainian soldiers came filing in and instantly joined the fight. Normally, the Possessed would be too strong but the strength and speed of the Persuaders easily evened out the match.

"It's the king!" one of them shouted. "Protect the king!"

The soldiers quickly pressed their way toward the king's position while the fight raged on. They shuffled them toward the kitchen and in to safety. As they were leaving the room, Lillian looked back at the chaos. She knew who had started this and she wanted him to pay, but they would have to survive this night first.

Hezra grabbed one of the soldiers and said, "We have to leave the palace and get to safety. We need to get to the library. There is an escape route hidden in the walls."

The captain in the room said, "My King, we just came in through the front and it is clear. All the attention was drawn to your position. We should go there and flee into the city; we can do our best to hide amongst the people. We already sent for reinforcements and hopefully they will meet us there soon."

Hezra gave his approval; however, the only way to the front was to go back through the dining hall. They huddled in close and opened the door. The scene was horrific as bodies were scattered around the floor. Lillian gasped at the sight and covered her mouth as she wept allowed. All of this was senseless. Michael promised freedom but really he just wanted to bring destruction and enslave. To make matters worse, he had deceived so many people along the way affecting not just their everyday lives but, more importantly, their eternities.

The soldiers pushed them along the wall. While they were in the kitchen, Destroyers entered the fight separate from the Possessed. The angelic battle was being waged not just on the ground but also in the air as they fought with their wings spread wide behind them. They darted in and out of their physical form as they fought. Many of them perished and their bodies dissolved into smoke and disappeared forever.

Emma breathed a sigh of relief as they exited the hall. The soldiers were correct. No one was following them. They kept a quick pace as they made their way to the front steps. The palace was dark and Emma wished she could tell what time it was but she knew it was late. Outside was not any better. A cold rain had begun to fall and lightning flashed in the sky; the thunder indicated that they were in the middle of the storm. The soldiers made their way down the front steps and formed positions to escort the king into the city. It took only a moment for Balak to realize that Emma was not with them. The group continued on while Balak stopped and turned around. Emma had collapsed at the top of the steps. Balak ran back to see that she was still awake but something was obviously wrong.

He crouched down in front of her and said, "Emma, we must go. We can't stay here any longer."

"Why are we running?" asked Emma. "Michael won't stop attacking just because we survived today. Where could we possibly go?"

"We have to leave the palace," said Balak. "It clearly isn't safe anymore."

"Obviously!" replied Emma. Tears rolled down her cheeks and mixed with the downpour of rain. "But so many people have died so that we could live. How many more have to die for us?"

Balak moved toward her and held her shoulders in his hands. "Believe me, those men died fighting for something they believed in. There is great honor in that and we will not give up so that their deaths can be in vain. We must get the king to safety."

"But who are we?" she asked. "What makes our lives better than theirs? I can't go on like this! I can't watch more people die so we can live!"

"There is no way to answer that," replied Balak. The soldiers continued to work out their escape plan but waited at the gate. "When I woke up in the palace and you tended to my wounds, you told me that everyone deserved a second chance. Before I met you, I wondered if I had missed my second chance. I was lost and empty; however, your belief in me and in my redemption, proved to me that there was still hope even amidst all this pain around us. I do not know what I – what we – can offer to the world but, for the moment, we are still here to accomplish whatever that may be. And we can do that together."

Emma stared deeply into his eyes as the rain continued to fall from the sky above.

"Emma, I know we have not known each other long, but, because of you, I am not the man I used to be. Will you, by the grace of the Amari, be my second chance? Help me be the man I used to be."

Emma wasn't sure but she thought she saw a tear roll down from Balak's eye. It was more than enough for her. She reached up and kissed Balak's lips. It seemed so crazy in the moment but, to her, it also seemed so right.

Emma pulled away and said, "I will gladly be your second, third, and fourth chance." Balak smiled back at her as she said, "After that, though, you are on your own,"

"Deal," he replied.

Balak helped her stand to her feet and took hold of her hand. From down below, Lillian found herself smiling at them. It was the first time in a long while that she genuinely had something to be excited about. They all rejoined the group and they continued the advance to the gate. Lillian wrapped her arm inside of the king's and stayed close to him. Through the rain, it looked like they could get away just fine, but it was Hezra who noticed something was wrong. There were no guards at their post along the wall. They were all missing.

He cautiously moved forward and Lillian sensed his tension and asked, "What is it? What is wrong?"

Hezra didn't have time to answer before the banging began.

"I don't think we are free quite yet," he responded. "The gate must have been locked for a reason but there is no one around."

The banging became louder and the soldiers raised their swords and formed their positions. Their eyes were glued to the gate as it began to rock back and forth. Something behind it really wanted to get inside.

"Brace the gate!" someone shouted.

The soldiers ran forward and placed their bodies against the back of the gate. Most of the soldiers had stayed behind to fight off the Possessed and there hadn't been much time for them to regroup yet, so there were less than ten soldiers protecting the king. The gate was reinforced with a large wooden beam that had been lowered into a brace. The beam crossed over where the two large wooden doors met. The banging on the gate stopped as they pressed against it. The soldiers relaxed for a moment as they wondered what had happened. They relaxed a little too much.

Whatever was on the other side began to push back. The soldiers braced themselves but it wasn't enough. The beam holding the doors together began to crack and splinter. The soldiers pushed back but their strength in numbers was beginning to fail. As the beam began to give way, the soldiers were called back into position as they realized they were no match for what was on the other side. Balak led Emma, Lillian and Hezra back to a secluded place away from the gate. He drew his sword and moved to go join the soldiers when Emma grabbed his hand. The look on her face told him not to go. He wanted to join the fight but he could see that he needed to be there with her right then. They huddled together and watched as the beam on the gate broke into two pieces.

The thunder clapped and the lightning seemed to grow fiercer as the gate slowly pushed open. Standing behind it was one man; at least, it looked like a man. They had no clue what to expect next- Shod had arrived.

27. HOPE SEEMS LOST

Inside the palace, Sevron helped take care of the last remaining Possessed. The battle was long and, by the look of it, the Bodainian soldiers did not fare very well, but they fought brilliantly. However, the loss of Persuader life also weighed heavy on him. He needed to make sure that they did not die in vain. He needed to regroup with the king's men.

He opened his wings and flew toward the ceiling. He disappeared out of his human body and took on spiritual form. He left the battlefield behind him and escaped into the sky. His escape did not come as quickly as he had hoped. Once out of the hall, he was blindsided by a Destroyer. The two tumbled through the air and landed on the roof. Sevron kicked him to the side and rolled onto his feet. He barely had enough time to draw his sword as he was attacked by another Destroyer. His sword absorbed the impact as the Destroyer's sword glanced off of his. The Destroyer had the upper hand and slammed his fist into the side of Sevron's head. Sevron recovered and swung his sword at the Destroyer. Their swords clanged together in a series of strikes when Sevron saw the first Destroyer moving in for an attack as well.

Sevron quickly exchanged his spiritual form and entered into human form to avoid the blow. He rolled to the side and regained his footing as the Destroyer's entered physical form as well. Their attacks came swiftly but Sevron was ready. He defended against their swords well, ducking and countering, delivering a few blows of his own. He hadn't noticed that he had been backed up to the edge of the roof. His foot slipped and he regained his footing. He had to think fast as being pinned down would leave him ultimately helpless. He defended himself and then leapt backward off the roof. He allowed himself to free-fall for a few seconds and then spread his wings, gliding to the next secure footing. It was time to end this.

Instead of waiting, Sevron took the attack back to the Destroyers. He moved with precision as they landed on the roof beside him. The first Destroyer swung his sword to attack and Sevron dodged it but managed to swing the Destroyer around by grabbing onto its wing. Before the Destroyer could react, the sword from the second Destroyer pierced his skin and he vanished. Sevron could easily handle one now. The Destroyer hissed at him but it was too late. Sevron's blade found its mark. The battle was over. He wanted to get back to protecting Lillian. He spread his wings and lifted off into the sky. As the lightning flashed, he could see something terrible. Destroyers were moving in and surrounding the kingdom; their silhouettes were illuminated with each flash. The Persuaders were outnumbered before but the situation just went from bad to worse. He moved on to find Lillian but stopped in his movement. The orders from the Amari had changed. This was a human fight now.

Shod walked through the gate and stared at the small army in front of him. He rolled his head, tightened all the muscles in his upper body and roared into the night. To the soldiers, he looked like just one man. They had no way of knowing that he was Ozgul's pet, a warrior who knew no surrender. Shod did not draw his sword with the jagged edges that he enjoyed so dearly. He waited for the soldiers to make their first move.

"Form up!" came the shouts of a captain. "We must secure the king's position! Deal with this man and then evacuate the king!"

The soldiers came at Shod with everything they had but it wasn't nearly enough. They quickly realized that Shod was more than just a man as he flung them around like sacks of grain, never drawing his sword once.

No one was supposed to know about Shod, but Balak did. He knew the soldiers wouldn't be fighting much longer. He had to help. He couldn't just sit by and let Ozgul destroy more lives. He looked at Emma and she knew that he must act. The look on her face was one of fear. She did not want him to go, but he did.

Shod was distracted and did not see Balak coming from behind. Balak moved fast but silent as he approached and, as soon as he was close enough, he swung his sword fast and hard. The blade came down on Shod's shoulder and pierced through his armor and into skin. Shod's knees buckled under the pain and he roared again into the night. He swung his other arm behind him and struck Balak with a powerful blow that knocked Balak backward. He lost his grip on his sword as it remained in Shod's armor but regained his footing. Shod reached up and grabbed the sharp blade with his opposite hand and lifted it up out of his shoulder. The blade cut his hand but he did not feel it.

Balak scanned the ground for another sword and saw one off to his right. He ran to pick it up and noticed a soldier attacking Shod. Balak studied his opponent and saw that he had done enough to cripple Shod's right arm. He hoped that it was Shod's good one. Nursing the wounded arm, Shod attacked the soldier, grabbed him by his armor and threw him at least fifteen feet away. Balak realized then that both of Shod's arms were probably his good one. He charged at Shod again.

Shod reached for his sword and drew it out as Balak neared. The swords met and clanged in the night; water sprayed from the impact in all directions. Balak's body felt weak with each blow but he gave it his all with each strike. Shod countered with his own attacks which were starting to wear Balak down. As he moved back defensively, he tripped over a soldier's body lying in the road. As Balak fell to the ground, Shod roared and brought his sword down toward Balak's body. Balak was able to roll out of the way before the blade made contact. The force of Shod's swing shattered the ground underneath it and became lodged. Balak took the opportunity to kick at Shod's knee. The impact made Shod stumble and he let go of his blade to catch his fall as his other arm was useless. Balak scrambled to his feet, laced his fingers together and brought his hands down as one large fist onto Shod's shoulder but the pain just angered Shod more.

Ignoring the sword, Shod swung his fist at Balak's side where his wound from before was still healing. Balak cringed from the pain and instinctively reached for the wound. Shod regained his balance, grabbed Balak's shoulders and threw him off to the left. Balak's body slid across the wet pavement and he rolled onto his stomach. Shod was quick and made his way over to Balak. He grabbed Balak by the back of his shirt and pulled him to his feet. Balak raised his hand to try and protect himself but Shod's punches were strong and menacing. He fell to his knees and looked up as Shod meant to deliver one final blow.

"*Stop!*"

Balak couldn't see through his swollen eyes but he recognized the voice. Shod waited and did not deliver the blow.

"We need him alive, Shod."

Michael walked into Balak's view and said, "Well, Balak, it seems like you finally got what you deserved. Now everyone you care about is in jeopardy because of you."

"Leave . . . them alone," said Balak.

"No," replied Michael, "I don't think I will."

Michael pushed Balak over, looked at Shod and said, "Well done. Bring Balak with us, but do not kill him. That honor will be taken by me."

Balak's eyes rolled into his head and he blacked out.

28. JUDGMENT DAY

Balak awoke to the sound of a large crowd around him. His eyes were closed and his head was throbbing, but at least he was alive; at least he thought he was. He moved his arm to hold his head and that was when he noticed that his hands were bound behind him. He slowly worked at opening his eyes as the daylight came streaming in. He could tell his right eye was swollen, but he managed to get it open. He found himself lying down on the ground and as his eyes adjusted he could see a large crowd of people before and below him and most of their eyes were fixed on him.

He rolled over onto his stomach and used his shoulders to push himself up. As he did, the uproar in the crowd began to rise. They were pointing and shouting at him and some in the crowd began to throw things in his direction. He sat there and looked around only flinching as things hit his face. From what he could tell, they were up on a wall attached to the king's palace. It looked like it was designed for the king to address a large crowd when necessary. The open space on the ground below left plenty of room to allow hundreds of people to hear. In the middle of the crowd, he saw a large pile of wood with a large beam coming out of the middle of the pile. Someone was getting burnt at the stake and Balak assumed that it had to be him. His head turned to the right as he heard a familiar voice beside him. The voice belonged to Michael.

Today was the seventh day of Michael's promise of something evil coming if the Phayladin was not turned over to Michael. The large crowd must have been summonsed by Michael to attend or they just came to see what was happening. Whatever the reason, Michael had their full attention now. Standing behind Michael was Senator Lorcene, dressed as a proper Senator.

However, Balak paid more attention to who was absent at the moment. He couldn't seem to find King Hezra, Emma, or the princess. He hoped they had gotten away in time.

Balak turned to see Michael's eyes meet his own. There was a look of victory in them that Balak didn't like. He tried to stand but the pain was too much. Balak was really tired of getting beat up all the time. He tried again and this time he was able to stagger to his feet. He wanted to show Michael that he was not completely done yet although, in reality, he did not have much fight left.

Michael approached him and said, "Just wait until you see what I have in store for you next." He turned to the crowd and continued. "People of Bodain! I trust that you have been pleased and satisfied with my presence in your kingdom. I have withheld nothing from you and have given you gifts beyond your wildest dreams. I have kept many of you from the brink of death and asked for almost nothing in return. I hope you see that the power I have has been kept from you, hidden by the Amari in order to watch you suffer. Unfortunately, your leaders have failed to turn the Phayladin over to me! In fact, your leaders have abandoned you. They fled from this kingdom like cowards because of their sin. You have taken my gifts and given me nothing, and I warned you that something evil was coming, something that I could not stop, but you didn't listen!"

Michael waved his hand in the air as if giving approval to something. All within the crowd, Possessed came to life. They hissed and growled at the crowd and the crowd cried back in fear. Michael was proving that his army was everywhere. The Possessed pushed their way to the outside of the crowd, locking them into their vicious circle. There was no way out. Michael called for attention again and the crowd was silent. They were now hanging on his every word.

"Don't you want to be *free*?" he shouted. "I cannot allow you to follow that criminal - that arrogant, criminal of a god. Don't you see? I have to save you from yourselves. However, I do want to be generous to you again and give you a few more minutes to fulfill your end."

Michael walked over to Balak and grabbed him by his shirt. He forcefully dragged Balak over to where Michael had been before and placed him front and center before the crowd.

"I wish to be a generous person once more!" Michael shouted. "As many of you have probably heard, this broken man standing before you has been hiding in fear within the walls of this great kingdom. This man is responsible for the perversion of Ozgul's great name all across Eret. This man is none other than General Balak!"

The crowd erupted at the revelation of who Balak was. He could feel the hate being thrown in his direction but he was beyond self-pity. He had made mistakes in his past but he had come to grips with it. Maybe it was Emma. Maybe it was his family. One thing he knew for sure, he was ready to accept whatever punishment the Amari had in store for him. Balak felt Michael's foot in his back as his body lurched forward. He tumbled down the stairs leading to the ground as pain shot through his whole body. Michael shouted something and Balak felt his body being lifted off of the ground and carried away from the steps. Hands passed him along the top of the crowd as Balak just stared up at the sky above. The trip was short and they dropped his body onto the wood pile. Someone grabbed his body and dragged him up to his feet. They stood him against the vertical beam and tied him up against it. Balak saw nothing but anger and hatred. He looked up as Michael began to speak again.

"In the absence of the king, or any member of the royal family, and in accordance with Bodainian laws, I now concede to Senator Lorcene to continue with the passing of judgment."

Senator Lorcene stepped in front of the crowd and said, "This man has been identified and charged with treason, murder and a litany of other charges. Before we can pass sentencing upon him, we must hear from the people. Is there anyone who will speak for the prisoner? Any witnesses that can confirm who this man is and what he has done?"

The crowd eagerly looked around for anyone to speak.

A soft but firm voice spoke and said, "I wish to speak on his behalf!"

The crowd looked in the direction of the voice to see an older man standing with his hat in his hand.

"My name is Jeremiah, and this man is my son."

Balak looked toward his father and could not believe what he was seeing. He wanted his father to run and get their family to safety.

Jeremiah looked at his son held up on the beam and said, "It's okay, son. Your mother and sister are safe. A young girl named, Emma, came to take us to safety, but I couldn't let you be here alone. Not like this."

Balak did his best to hold back his tears but he was too tired to fight them.

"I love you, son. All of you. I should have told you that before today."

"Father, leave here," said Balak. "You don't have to do this. You are in danger!"

"How sentimental!" shouted Lorcene. "However, we are in the middle of something here. Speak on behalf of the criminal or let us proceed."

Jeremiah cleared his throat and said, "Yes, very well. I cannot deny that my son has committed these crimes. I am just here today as a father begging you for any form of leniency. You see, Balak was taken from us long ago. It was my fault, I suppose."

Tears formed in Jeremiah's eyes as he spoke.

"As a father, I should have been there to protect him. I never even went looking for him, but, now that he is back, I've realized that he cannot be excused for his crimes."

Jeremiah looked at Balak as Balak wept.

"But neither can I. I ask you to sentence me to death in the place of my son for my failures. If I had done better, no one would have died by his hands. I pray that he can forgive me the way that I have forgiven him."

The crowd seemed to have some compassion left in their hearts as Jeremiah's pleas were heard. There was a long pause after Jeremiah's last words but that was soon interrupted by Michael.

"How touching!" he shouted. "Unfortunately, you have admitted that your son is a murderer. However, if you wish to join him, no one will stop you."

"Thank you for that, at least," said Jeremiah.

The crowd didn't move an inch except to let Jeremiah through. He walked up to the front of the woodpile standing in the gap between Balak and Michael. He climbed up and stood directly in front of Balak.

"Father, you don't have to do this," said Balak.

"Balak . . . son, there is nothing that matters more to me in the world right now then doing this. I don't want you to die alone, not like this. Just tell me one thing. Will you let the Amari give you his forgiveness and come home? I need to know that I will see you again."

Balak nodded his head and said, "I already have. I'm safe now. I'm safe."

Jeremiah smiled and said, "Good. Now let's enter into eternity to--"

His last words trailed off. Balak heard the sound come from behind his father and looked over his shoulder to see Michael holding a bow in his hands. He had just fired an arrow into Jeremiah's back. Jeremiah's body fell forward into Balak's and Balak pulled on his ropes to try and break his arms free. He just wanted to hold his dying father once more but the ropes held tightly.

Jeremiah's hands grasped Balak's shoulders and he looked at his son and said, "Trust the Amari. He will give you the strength you need to endure. I love you—"

Jeremiah collapsed into the wood pile below.

Balak looked at Michael with a fury. Balak blocked out all sound and kept his eyes locked on one thing- Michael. Whatever Michael was saying, Balak chose not to hear. The only words that he could hear were the dying words of his father as he replayed them in his head. *Trust the Amari . . . I Love You.*

Balak screamed into the air. The cry was one of intense agony but it turned into anger- a righteous anger. Balak could see a smug look on the faces of Michael and Lorcene as they looked over their victory. He struggled hard against the ropes and flexed every muscle in his body trying to free himself. It wasn't working. He relaxed his muscles and tried to calm himself, but the body of his father was lying at his feet. This was something he could not change. It was then that he noticed the knife in his father's belt. He wanted desperately to get it into his hands.

From the platform, Lorcene must have pronounced Balak guilty as three men with torches moved in to light the wood under

Balak's feet. There were no cheers for his death, only a look of shock on the faces of the people. Balak tried to calm himself as he hoped for a solution to his problem. He didn't want to die without seeing his father's murderer brought to justice. He turned to the only thing he could think to do. He began to pray.

There was nothing elegant about his prayer. No special words or phrases. He spoke from the heart to a god he believed was listening and asked for one thing. Justice.

As Balak prayed, a wind began to stir through the crowd and weaved its way in and out of the people, kicking up dirt and debris. The visible movement and the force of the wind caused people to look around as the wind grew more violent. It danced its way to the three men who were about to light the wood. It swirled around them and up to the torches, extinguishing the fire abruptly. In what seemed like an explosion, the wind violently pushed back the crowd leaving a straight path between Balak and Michael. Their faces no longer showed amusement. The guards looked at each other confused and that is when Balak received an answer.

Miraculously, the ropes binding him to the wooden beam fell off of his arms and into the wood below. Balak reacted quickly as he reached down and grabbed the knife from his father's waistband. He jumped off the pile and quickly ran toward Michael who was caught off guard. Michael waved for the Possessed to attack but they were unable to move. As he was a few feet in front of the steps, Michael decided to intervene.

He summoned up a dark power inside of him that was fueled by the Destroyer living in him and shot an unseen power toward Balak. Balak felt like he had run into a brick wall and he stumbled to the ground. Michael's power began to push Balak back but Balak was nowhere near done. He pushed his feet into the dirt below and dug them in deep; his fingers began to do the same. With a power unknown to him, he began to claw his way toward Michael. The pressure on Balak's body was intense and every step was difficult but he soon found himself making progress. His hands were digging up the earth around them leaving holes in the ground as he moved them forward. Michael could not understand what was happening and began shouting at Balak from above while everyone else evacuated the platform.

Step by step, he drew closer to Michael who tried to intensify his attack, but it wasn't working. By the time Balak reached the steps, his movements were fluid and swift. There was nothing holding him back. He pushed himself to within a few feet of Michael and stood to his feet. Michael began to back away and realized there was no stopping Balak. He lowered his hands and as he did, Balak surged forward, grabbed the knife from his belt, and stabbed it into Michael's stomach.

"By the power of the Amari," began Balak, "I find you guilty of killing my father. Your sentence . . . is death."

He pressed the knife in deeper and pushed Michael backward. He stumbled over himself and landed with his back against the wall. Balak enjoyed the look of defeat on Michael's face; however, the look did not last very long. Michael began to laugh as he died.

"Balak," he said through gasps of air. "Do you think that killing me makes . . . what you've done okay? I . . . may die here but my victory is not over."

In the crowd behind him, cries for help began to slowly move throughout the crowd. People watched in vain as the miracles that Michael had performed began to reverse themselves. Throughout the kingdom, anything that Michael had done for the people was being taken away from them. Wounds reappeared, diseases returned and deformities showed themselves again. People began to weep openly as they had been deceived.

"You see, Balak, you can't stop everything from . . . happening. In the end . . . you will die."

Balak crouched down in front of Michael and said, "At least I die with honor."

Michael laughed again but it was interrupted with a cry of pain.

"I warned you!" he yelled. "There is an evil coming that cannot be stopped! It is my final gift to you all! Today! Bodain will burn!"

Michael let out his final breath as a strange noise was heard in the skies above. Balak and the crowd looked to see what it was but the low hanging clouds concealed it. The noise appeared again and again; popping noises were heard all over the sky. That's when the whistling began and it was growing louder. The dark clouds were illuminated by something behind them. Spots of bright light appeared and then it happened. The clouds rolled out as a giant ball of fire came crashing through. It landed outside the kingdom but the explosion shook the ground beneath the people. It was not the only one though as they began to appear one at a time. Fire was falling from the heavens.

The crowd began to panic and run for their lives. Explosions rocked the area and then throughout the kingdom. No one was safe. The stone in the walls of the surrounding buildings began to crumble under the impact. Balak wanted to flee but he had nowhere to go. He ran out to his father's body. As fire rained down from above, Balak turned his father onto his back and draped his lifeless arms across his chest. He could not leave his father behind, but he needed to find safety like everyone else. He looked around and saw the Possessed ransacking everything, even getting caught in the explosions themselves. Balak knew that many lives would be lost. He picked up his father, jumped down from the woodpile and ran into the palace. He needed to find his family. He needed to find Emma. The search began as Bodain crumbled to the ground.

Morgan slowed his horse at the top of the hill. Something had caught his attention. To the west, in the direction of Bodain, he saw the dark clouds and could hear the explosions echoing through the valley. His kingdom was in trouble and he wasn't there to help them.

"Prince Morgan, we need to continue," commented a Persuader.

"Bodain is in trouble," he replied. "I need to be there. I am their king."

"There is nothing you can do for them. You must rely on hope. We have to get Ethan to safety."

Morgan looked down at Ethan who hadn't moved since they began the trip. In his heart, he believed that Ethan would tell him to go home.

"Can't you all just get Ethan to safety while I go help my kingdom?" asked Morgan,

"We can, but, if we do it, we cannot tell you exactly where we are going. The Phayladin will be lost to all of you unless you make the effort to hunt him down. We have to keep his location a secret while he heals. The world will need him at full strength for what he must endure ahead. Can you leave knowing this?"

Each explosion felt like an impact on his soul. Each explosion meant that someone else could be dying. Each explosion meant that the life of his family was in danger. He had to go home.

Morgan helped get Ethan down from the horse and into the arms of a Persuader. They wasted no time as the Persuader lifted Ethan up, spread his wings and flew away. Morgan kicked his horse toward Bodain and just prayed that everyone was okay. He would find Ethan again soon. That was a promise.

www.ingramcontent.com/pod-product-compliance
Lightning Source LLC
Chambersburg PA
CBHW060129130626
46556CB00006B/2284